"How do you kn〈…〉 take the painting 〈from you?"〉 he asked softly.

"Because I trust you, my lord," she said without hesitation. "You understood the merit of the picture the instant you saw it—not just its value, but its power. Which means that by trusting you I am either very brave, my lord, or very foolish."

He chuckled as he let his hands drop away from the painting. "Tell me which you are."

"I am sorry, my lord," she said, "but you must decide for yourself."

He cupped her jaw with his palm, turning her face up to his. "Then I should say you're brave, Mary." His mouth was just over her lips. "Very, very brave."

How many favors would she grant him? How adventurous did she really mean to be, here beneath the willows?

THE ADVENTUROUS BRIDE

Miranda Jarrett

MILLS & BOON™

Pure reading pleasure

First published in Great Britain 2008
Harlequin Mills & Boon Limited,
Eton House, 18-24 Paradise Road, Richmond, Surrey TW9 1SR

ISBN: 978 0 263 86253 9

Set in Times Roman 10½ on 12 pt.
04-0408-86650

Printed and bound in Spain
by Litografia Rosés S.A., Barcelona

Miranda Jarrett considers herself sublimely fortunate to have a career that combines history and happy endings—even if it's one that's also made her family far-too-regular patrons of the local pizzeria. Miranda is the author of over thirty historical romances, and her books are enjoyed by readers the world over. She has won numerous awards for her writing, including two Golden Leaf Awards and two *Romantic Times BOOKreviews* Reviewers' Choice Awards, and has three times been a Romance Writers of America RITA® Award finalist for best short historical romance.

Miranda is a graduate of Brown University, with a degree in art history. She loves to hear from readers at PO Box 1102, Paoli, PA 19301-1145, USA, or at MJarrett21@aol.com

Recent novels by the same author:

PRINCESS OF FORTUNE
THE SILVER LORD
THE GOLDEN LORD
RAKE'S WAGER*
THE LADY'S HAZARD*
THE DUKE'S GAMBLE*

*A *Penny House* novel

Author Note

I'm delighted to be launching a new trilogy of books with THE ADVENTUROUS BRIDE. Join Lady Mary Farren and her sister Lady Diana, daughters of the Duke of Aston, as they begin a rollicking journey with their governess Miss Wood across England, France and Italy—a trip filled with excitement, danger, laughter and, of course, with love.

In eighteenth-century England, aristocratic young gentlemen were expected to sow their wild oats on the Continent, and the wealthier and more blue-blooded the gentleman, the wilder and more far-flung the oats. But what of well-bred young ladies like Mary and Diana, with a similar desire for adventure and experience before their proper arranged marriages? What intrigues await them on the other side of the English Channel, travelling gloriously far from homes, consciences, and anxious mothers and fathers?

For the beautiful daughters of the Duke of Aston, the adventure is about to begin…

Chapter One

Aston Hall, Kent
June, 1784

With a little twitch of her gauzy muslin skirts, Lady Mary Farren took her place among the dancers in her father's ballroom. The evening was warm, the tall windows thrown up to catch any possible breeze from the gardens outside. Beneath the dozens of flickering candles in the chandeliers, the flushed gentlemen around her were trying their best to be handsome and gallant, the ladies striving to be beautiful and flirtatious, and all of them were confident they represented the very cream of their little county society.

This had been the only life Mary had known in her eighteen years—the only life she'd been permitted to know as the eldest daughter of the Duke of Aston. But in three days, that would finally, blissfully change forever, and Mary—ah, Mary couldn't wait.

Even as the musicians finished the last notes of the dance and her partner bowed across from her, Mary was eagerly ticking off the last details for the journey in her head: the bespoke traveling clothes packed in the new brass-studded trunks, the passages booked and the letters of introduction held safely in readiness, the maps and guides and—

"Lady Mary, if you please." Miss Wood, Mary's longtime governess and soon-to-be companion on her journey, stood beside her, her small, plump hands clasped across the front of her plain gray gown. "A word alone, my lady, if you please?"

At once Mary nodded, leading the way to one of the window alcoves where their conversation would be lost in the music and chatter around them. Though at twenty-eight Miss Wood was still a young woman herself, the governess was always the very soul of discretion and propriety, and only a genuine emergency would bring her into the ballroom, where she was as out of place as a mourning dove among gaudy parrots. But since the duchess's long illness and death four years before, Mary had capably assumed many of her mother's duties for her father, and it was quite appropriate for the governess to seek her out now.

But oh, please, let this be nothing that would delay her departure! God forgive her this once for being selfish, and wanting nothing to stop her first chance at a life beyond Aston Hall!

"What is it, Miss Wood?" Mary asked now, keeping her voice low. Possible disasters raced through her head: an accident among the staff, a mishap to a guest, grievous news from afar. Anything could be possible. "What has happened?"

"It's your sister, my lady," Miss Wood said. "Your father His Grace has asked for her to join him, and I cannot find her anywhere."

"Diana's gone?" Mary's anxiety took a sharp new twist. It wasn't that she feared some dire mishap had befallen her younger sister. Diana was always the cause of mischief, never the victim, beautiful and blithe and as irresistible to men as they were to her.

It simply didn't seem to be in Diana's blood to be otherwise. Where Mary was responsible and considerate, Diana was neither. How many times had Mary been left to soothe their father's wrath after Diana had been traipsing gaily about the countryside with yet another smitten young gentleman, always skipping just on the edge of real scandal and ruin without a thought for how it would affect her chances for a respectable marriage? How many promises had Diana made to reform, only to beg Mary to make things right again with Father when the next gallant appeared beneath her window?

"You have looked everywhere, Miss Wood?" Mary asked, praying that for once the governess might be mistaken. "I'm sure I saw Diana dancing not a half hour ago."

Miss Wood's round face lit with hope. "Do you recall her partner? Perhaps she's with him, my lady, and we—"

"She was dancing with Dr. Canning, as a favor to Father." Mary sighed. Dr. Canning was at least seventy, with thick spectacles and scattered wits, and little ability left for wooing any female. "He's a most kindly old gentleman, but I'd scarcely think Diana would vanish to the garden folly with him."

"I've already looked in the folly, my lady." Miss Wood glanced over her shoulder, to where Mary's father stood with several friends. Despite the gaiety swirling around him, he was not happy, that was clear enough. He had summoned Diana, and as both a duke and a father, he expected instant obedience. But Diana hadn't appeared, and now Father was glaring across the room at them with his arms folded—no, battened—over his silk-covered chest.

"I've checked her bedchamber, my lady," continued Miss

Wood more hurriedly, "as well as the schoolroom, the library, the withdrawing room, even the creamery."

"Do not even *mention* the creamery!" Mary sighed again, this time with exasperation. Whatever had occurred in the creamery last summer between Diana and a certain young tutor down from Oxford still made Diana giggle into her napkin whenever the butter was passed at table. Mary didn't want to know, truly she didn't. "Perhaps Diana's only gone to the privy."

Miss Wood shook her head. "The waiting-maid there hadn't seen her all evening, my lady, and—"

"The stables." To her dismay, Mary suddenly recalled Diana smiling down at the brawny new groom as he'd helped her mount her mare this morning. When he'd returned Diana's smile more warmly than was proper, Mary had thought it only because he was new to the staff, and hadn't yet realized his place. Now she thought otherwise.

And oh, what Father would say if he ever learned of it!

"The stables, my lady?" Miss Wood asked. "Do you believe that—"

"It's only a guess," Mary said quickly. "I'll hunt for Diana, while you tell Father that—"

"I am sorry, my lady, but I cannot permit that," Miss Wood answered firmly. "Not to the stables, not alone at night."

"But if I can find Diana before—"

"Your place is here at the ball, my lady," Miss Wood insisted. "You remain here with His Grace's guests, and I'll go look for Lady Diana."

"She's my sister," Mary said, looking over the governess's head to her irate father, "and I'll go find her myself."

Miss Wood frowned. "But His Grace—"

"Tell Father Diana will be there directly. He won't even realize I'm gone." Mary turned away to slip through the nearest door to the garden before Miss Wood could protest again.

She ran down the slate steps and along the path of crushed stones, bunching her skirts at her sides so she wouldn't trip. Here away from the heat of the candles, the evening was cooler, and Mary breathed deeply, steeling herself for whatever might lie ahead. There was no telling where or how or even if Mary was going to find Diana.

To be honest, she hoped she didn't. Just as she and Miss Wood were set to leave for the Continent, Diana and Father would be setting out this week for London, where Diana would be introduced at court and, with her beauty and a little luck, attract a suitable husband of a suitable rank and fortune. It was exactly what Diana claimed to want most from life, and why she would risk it now for the sake of a flirtation with a groom was beyond Mary's comprehension.

Purposefully she kept to the shadows, taking care not to be noticed. The yard before the stables was filled with the guests' carriages tonight, and the waiting drivers and footmen sat on the carriage-steps or on the lawn, talking and laughing and making bawdy-talk with the housemaids who'd somehow slipped free of the party inside. There was no sign of Diana, nor of the new groom, either, though likely by now they'd retreated to some more intimate place.

Confound her sister for putting her in this position again! Doubtless Diana had convinced herself that she wasn't breaking any promises to behave at all, that dallying with a servant somehow didn't count. Mary hated having to play watchdog again, almost as much as she'd hate having to face Father one more time.

It wasn't that she didn't love Diana, because she did, with all the love and devotion that two motherless sisters could have for one another. That would never change. But standing in Diana's beautiful, irresponsible shadow, always ready to catch her if she tumbled or protect her if she erred, had become an exhausting place to be. Wistfully, and guiltily, too, Mary longed to be known not as His Grace's daughter or Lady Diana's sister, but simply as herself. On the Continent, far from Aston Hall, she prayed she would.

Now she hurried around the curving brick wall and through the stable house's side door. Except for the snuffling and whinnying of the sleepy horses in their stalls, the stable seemed empty and dark.

"Diana?" she called. "Diana, are you here?"

No answer came, not that Mary really expected Diana to come popping out from the loft like they had when they'd been little girls playing in the hay. This was different—far, far different.

She cleared her throat and raised her voice. "Diana, Father's asking for you. If you're—if you're *hiding* in here, you must come back to the house and the dancing at once. Do you hear me?"

No answer again, but this time Mary was certain she heard a rustling that wasn't a horse, a muffled giggle from one of the farther box stalls. For Mary, that was more than enough. She seized one of the lanterns that hung by the door and marched back to the stall, holding the light high before her.

"I am serious, Diana," she announced crossly, the flickering light bouncing and bobbing over the planked walls. "Come now, or I'll flush you out like Father's hounds do with a fox, see if I don't."

At the last box, she shoved the gate open and raised the lantern over her head like a beacon.

. And gasped.

It was hard for Mary to tell which were her sister's body and arms and legs and which the groom's, they were that wrapped around one another. Diana's yellow gown was hiked high over her legs with shameless abandon, the man's tanned hand spread possessively over her pale thigh above her bright pink ribbon garter. She'd pulled his shirt free of his breeches, her own hands twisting along his broad bare back. Her blond hair was half-unpinned and loose, her cheeks flushed, every inch a wanton rather than a peer's daughter.

"Mary!" Diana squeaked, clinging more closely to the groom and slipping around him as if to hide. "Whatever are you doing here, *spying* on Will and me?"

"I'm not spying, Diana," Mary said, her own face hot with embarrassment. "Father wants to see you at once, and you know you must go. Can't you see that I'm trying to save you from yourself?"

"Ah, now, my lady, where's th' sport in that?" The groom twisted about to leer at her, keeping one arm curled around Diana's waist while he beckoned to Mary with the other. "Better t'spend than t'save, I say. Come along, sweetheart, there's plenty o' me t'share with both of you sisters."

Before Mary realized it, he'd reached out and taken her hand to pull her closer. Too shocked to speak, she struggled to jerk free, the lantern swinging wildly in her other hand.

"Stop, Will, don't!" Diana cried. "Mary, hush, it's not—oh, dear God in heaven, Father! Oh, no, *Father!*"

Her heart pounding with dread, Mary slowly turned. It wasn't a tease; it wasn't a jest. There by the gate stood Father, as furious and grim as she'd ever seen him, with Miss Wood and Robinson, the stable master, hovering behind him.

She gave a tiny, desperate dip of a curtsey, the best she could manage under the circumstances. If only Miss Wood had let her handle this herself, instead of bringing her father into it!

"Father, please," Diana began breathlessly. "This isn't what it must seem."

"No, Father," Mary agreed with desparate haste. "It's not, not at all."

The groom pulled free of Diana and touched his knuckle to his forehead. "Beg pardon, Your Grace, but her ladyship's speaking true. This don't be what it seems, not by—"

"Hold your tongue, you wretched fool!" Father's expression darkened, black thunderclouds by the lantern's light. "No excuses from any of you. I know what I see, and I know what this is."

"Don't fault Mary, Father, I beg you." Diana shoved down her skirts and tried to smooth her hair. "She was only—"

"I'll tell you the same as I told your sister, Diana," Father said sharply. "No more excuses from either of you."

"We're not making excuses, Father," Mary pleaded. "I was only—that is, we were—"

"No more." His hand sliced through the air, a sharp gesture to match the cutting edge of his voice. "Make yourselves decent, and come to me in the library. *Now.*"

He turned on his heel and left them, his back ramrod-straight with his anger, and Miss Wood scurrying after him into the dark. The stable master grabbed the groom by the shoulder and half-shoved, half-dragged him from the stall.

Mary looked at her sister. Diana bowed her head. It was too late for explanations now, too late for remorse or contrition.

All they could do was obey.

An hour later, Mary sat on the edge of the bench in the hall outside the library, her feet flat on the floor and her hands clasped in her lap. Diana had gone in first to Father, and though Mary could not make out their words through the closed door, she could hear enough to know that Father's anger hadn't cooled a bit, and that Diana's wailing tears and shrill protests had done nothing to help her cause.

Mary bent her head, closing her eyes and pressing her hands over her ears to try to shut out her quarrelling family. Soon enough she'd be called in to stand between them. She'd have to soothe Father's temper, and coax fresh promises of reformation from Diana. One more time, she'd make some manner of a shaky peace, the oil poured on the constantly roiling waters of Aston Hall.

From behind the closed door came the crash of hurled porcelain, and Mary hunched her shoulders like a turtle retreating into its shell. In three days, she'd sail for France, and be free of it all.

Only three more days….

The door flew open. "He is cruel, Mary, unspeakably cruel to me and to you—to us both!" Diana sank down on the floor before the bench, her wrinkled yellow skirts spreading out around her, and clutched Mary's hands in her own. "Oh, Mary, I am so vastly sorry!"

"Don't fuss over me, Di," Mary whispered urgently, knowing they'd little time before it was her turn. "What made him most cross? Quick, quick, tell me! What must I say to coax him back to good cheer?"

But Diana only shook her head, her face still flushed with weeping. "Oh, Mary, how can you forgive me? I only meant to amuse myself for a moment or two, and now *look* what has happened! For Father to make us both suffer so, when—"

"Mary, come," called Father sharply from inside the library. "I know you're waiting out there, for you always were the obedient one."

"Don't worry, Diana, I'll set things to rights." Mary smiled, and gave Diana's hands one final squeeze to reassure her. Then she smoothed her skirts, raised her head high, and joined Father in the library.

"Here you are at last, Mary." He was sitting in his leather-covered armchair, pushed back from his desk. Though a widower, Father was still in his prime, his belly flat beneath his Chinese-silk waistcoat and besotted ladies tittering about him wherever he went. Unlike most gentlemen of his generation, he'd chosen to follow the newer fashion, and had abandoned wigs in favor of his own dark hair cropped short and feathered with gray.

Yet as Mary came to stand before him, what she noticed first was how the large vein in his forehead pulsed, a bad sign that she recognized all too well. His temper seemed to simmer around him like a swarm of hornets, anger and disappointment and general irritation vibrating together in the warm night air.

"Your sister has shamed me again, Mary," he began, his voice an irate growl. "Not even you can defend her this time."

"I would not defend Diana, no," Mary countered with care, searching for the best way to soothe him. "Thus I ask not for forgiveness for her, but for mercy."

"Oh, mercy you." He snorted with disgust. "Come along, Mary, I'd expect more wit from you than that."

"Mercy doesn't require wit, Father."

"No, but I do." With his guests now departed, he'd shed his coat and rolled back the ruffled cuffs of his shirt to his elbows, his thick fingers drumming irritably on the carved mahogany arm of his chair. "Why do you defend Diana, anyway? She was acting like a common slattern with that rascal, as if her good name and mine weren't worth a brass farthing."

"She didn't mean to upset you, Father, I'm sure of it," Mary said. "I'll grant she was irresponsible—"

"Oh, aye, letting some base-born groom ruck up her

skirts," he growled, and struck his open palm on the arm of the chair with frustration. "I've no right to be upset about that?"

"Yes, Father," Mary said, knowing from experience that this was always the safest reply, and often the only acceptable one. "Of course you have."

"Then why does your sister keep shaming me like this?" Unable to sit still any longer, he shoved back his chair and rose, turning his back to Mary to stare out the window. "It's high time she weds. I'm too old for her willfulness. She needs a strong, young husband to thrash her into obedience, some young lion who'll break her spirit and fill her belly. That's what she needs—an honest husband and a brood of children. What better way to make a wild filly into a mare?"

"Yes, Father," Mary said again. "If Diana can only find a gentleman she can love with all her heart—"

"Don't speak to me of drivel like that, Mary," Father snapped. "Love! The last thing your sister needs is a dose of *that* foolishness."

"No, Father," Mary said softly. She remembered her parents as being devoted to one another, as much in love as any sweethearts. Since her mother's death, Father spoke of love with only bitterness and scorn, and no tenderness for Mama's memory, as if her last, wasting illness were some personal affront to him. "But if she is able to make a favorable match in London, one that pleases you, then—"

"No London." His hands were clasped so tightly behind his back that they looked more like clenched fists. "How can I possibly introduce Diana to Her Majesty after such scandalous behavior?"

"But none of the guests learned of it," Mary protested. "The only one who might talk would be that wretched groom, and I'm sure Mr. Robinson will speak to him so he won't—"

"That 'wretched groom' will have the next three years of his life to repent," Father said curtly. "I've ordered Robinson to give him over to the press gang, so that he might serve His Majesty's navy instead of my daughter."

"The press gang!" she exclaimed, appalled by so severe a punishment. "Oh, Father, you would not send Diana away, too!"

"If it were my choice, I'd lock her away in the darkest convent I could find," he said grimly. "But you've asked me to be merciful, Mary, and so I shall."

"Then you will forgive her?" Mary asked with fresh hope. "You'll take her to London, and to court?"

"I said I'd be merciful, not a fool." At last he swung around to face her. "I'm sending her abroad with you."

Chapter Two

Calais, France

With the small brass bell jangling overhead, Lord John Fitzgerald stepped into the musty shop that housed Dumont's Antiquities, and paused to let his eyes grow accustomed to the gray twilight. John had been here many times before; he knew what to expect, even the murkiness and mildew, and none of it fooled him. Though Dumont himself was French to his bent old bones, the signboard that hung outside the shop was painted in English, a beckoning convenience for Dumont's mostly British customers.

It was a credit to the Frenchman's shrewdness that he acknowledged the importance of those British visitors to his trade, just as he recognized how they'd reverently interpret every speck of ancient dust as proof of authenticity. Since the last peace had been signed between Britain and France and travel to the Continent had once again become fashionable, scores of English gentlemen and ladies trooped through Dumont's shop with their eyes wide and their purses open, ready to lap up whatever tales he told about his dubious wares, and to pay whatever he asked for the privilege.

John, however, knew otherwise. He'd a gift for discerning the false from the true, and he wasn't afraid to say so, either. In a shop that prospered from deceptions, his eye and his knowledge made him the least-welcome of Dumont's customers: an English gentleman too knowledgeable to be properly fleeced.

"Ah, *bonjour,* my lord." Dumont groaned sourly, and rolled his eyes toward the dusty heavens. "So you've returned to plague me again, eh?"

"And a good day to you, too, Dumont," John said, his gaze swiftly scanning the cluttered shop for anything new of value. Because Calais was so often either the first or the last stop on his journeys, he was a frequent visitor. "I've returned because I've heard you've new stock from Florence."

"Like a highwayman you are, my lord, come to steal from a poor old man." With a great effort, Dumont dislodged himself from the high-backed chair behind the counter. "Why won't you leave me in peace, eh?"

"Because once in a great while, Dumont, I find a treasure here in your rubbish heap," John said, unperturbed by the old man's comments. He had been away from London for over a year now, and was at last planning to return to London later this week. He needed a small gift to take to the opulent Duchess of Cumberland, a most loyal friend. His dalliance with Her Grace had begun last winter in Rome, and ended there, too, quite amicably for both parties. But still John believed a little token, something for her new house in Grosvenor Square, would make a pretty gesture. Her Grace had already promised him her support when he finally returned to London; God only knew that he'd need such powerful allies after last year's disastrous scandal on the beach at

Brighton. Besides, he liked to leave ladies sighing fondly after him; such thoughtfulness had always served him well.

"'My rubbish heap'. Oh, you're cruel, my lord, too cruel." With another groan, Dumont shuffled forward, his arms cocked at the elbows and his hands folded loosely over his leather apron like an elderly squirrel. "But I've serveral new pieces, yes. One collector's misfortune is another's bounty, my lord, and so it shall always be."

"I trust it's no gentleman of my acquaintance," he said, purposefully bland and disinterested. Paintings and other art were often the first things to be sold when a gentleman suffered a financial reversal. Depending on the circumstances, John might well be able to turn this to his own advantage, and resell the art in London for a profit.

He'd offer no excuses for it, either. Younger sons didn't have to, particularly youngest sons who'd had the misfortune to be born sixth in line to an Irish peerage with a bankrupt estate. Oh, he'd a miniscule income from a distant uncle and tolerable luck at the gaming tables, and by necessity and inclination he'd mastered the arts of friendship and favors from his wealthier fellows—and from ladies, too, on occasion. But if John's life had given him a rocky path to climb, so be it. He'd simply seen the rough diamonds scattered among the stones and gathered them up, and where, really, was the sin in that?

"I've many sources of supply, many sources," Dumont was saying vaguely. "You can scarce expect a man of my age to recall them all. Are you here today with a specific purchase in mind, my lord? Might I guide you to your selection?"

"I'll keep my own eyes open for what pleases me." John could be vague, too; it was another of his talents. He let his gaze wander the shelves crowded with bits of ornamental glass and porcelain, statues and carvings, paintings and sketches. The Duchess of Cumberland wasn't choosy about quality, but she did demand that her possessions—and her gifts—reflect the grandeur of both her person and her station. Anything gilded would do, or a Venus, or even a fat little Cupid might—

"*Here* you are, my lord." Dumont was proudly displaying a small bronze statue of Mercury. "From the very hands of that great master Benvenuto Cellini himself. You can tell by the delicacy of the work, the exuberance of the line, each the mark of true sixteenth-century genius!"

The shopkeeper handed the bronze to John, then pressed his plump, white palms together as if in prayer, his voice hushed with reverence as he hovered at John's side.

John carried the little statue to the shop's bow window and tipped it toward the weak sunlight. It was a respectable forgery, the patina nicely burnished to mimic age. But the Mercury's expression was simpering and cross-eyed, and if he ever straightened the leg that was bent in flight, one winged foot would likely dangle down a good two inches below its mate.

Dumont inched closer, misreading John's silence. "You are in awe, my lord, as is proper, yes? To be able to cradle such genius in your hands is a gift, a blessing, an honor, a—"

"A cheat," John said mildly. "You know as well as I that this sorry little rascal's lucky if he's three years old, let alone three hundred."

Dumont's eyes popped wide with wounded indignation, his white brows bristling upward. "No, my lord, no! I had it on the very best advice that this bronze is *authentique!* That you would accuse me of such delusion, such—"

"I'm not accusing you of anything, Dumont," John said. "Nor am I telling you anything that you don't already know."

"But my lord, I cannot see how—"

The brass bell over the door jingled. Instantly Dumont turned toward it, grateful for the interruption. John looked, too.

And smiled.

How could he not? The girl was young and lovely, her beauty radiant enough to glow with its own light in the dismal shop. She was undeniably English, and likely wealthy, too. There were good-sized pearls hanging from her ears, and gold beads around her throat and over the wrists of her kidskin gloves. Her petticoat and jacket were costly but outdated, printed with oversized tulips that would make a fashionable Parisian shudder, tulips that contrasted garishly with the girl's creamy English complexion and dark chestnut hair. No more than twenty: a small, neat waist, high, rounded breasts, trim ankles and a pretty foot.

He appraised her quickly, efficiently, as he had the bronze Mercury. But what made him smile was how briskly she snapped her beribboned parasol shut, how she sailed into the little shop with her back straight and her head high and a guardian footman trailing after in her wake, as ready to conquer this foreign place as any admiral.

Dumont coughed delicately, and patted the sides of his grizzled wig. "If you pray excuse me, my lord, I must greet the lady."

"Of course you must, you old rogue." John slipped the bronze Mercury more comfortably into the crook of his arm, content to watch this little scene unfold from the curving recess of the bow window. "Go on, go on. How could you resist such a pretty pigeon waiting to be plucked?"

But Dumont was already with the girl, bowing and scraping as if she were the queen.

"Good day, *mademoiselle,*" he said in English, as quick

as John had been to recognize her nationality. "Allow me to welcome you to my humble little shop. I place myself and my establishment at your complete disposal."

She nodded with her stern small chin, already looking away from Dumont to the crowded shelves and walls behind him. "I should like to see whatever quality paintings you have in your stock."

"Be assured that every painting I have is of quality, *mademoiselle*." Dumont puffed out his narrow chest with unfounded pride. "I would not have it otherwise."

"Show your respect," the footman ordered sternly. "Her ladyship's not one o' your common mam'selles. She's Lady Mary Farren, daughter of His Grace the Duke o' Aston."

The girl wrinkled her nose. "Oh, please, Winters, that's not necessary. The man doesn't care who I am."

But Dumont cared very much, and John could practically see the newly raised prices bobbing over the Frenchman's head. The daughter of an English duke was indeed a rare little pigeon to find in a grimy old port like Calais.

And though the daughter of a duke, the wife of no husband. Interesting, thought John idly. Why wasn't she in London, pursuing a suitable mate the way every other girl of her age and bloodlines would be? She was certainly fair enough, and there was undoubtedly money for a dower. Was there some sort of fascinating scandal that had washed her up on these shores?

Very interesting. Perhaps she could be persuaded to help amuse him until he sailed….

"Oh, my lady, forgive my ignorance of your great station!" the shopkeeper cried. "To be honored by your presence, your custom! How dare you believe I wouldn't care!"

"Well, yes, thank you," Lady Mary said, obviously unimpressed. "Now, if I might see your paintings."

John smiled again. He liked a direct woman, one who didn't need a lot of long-winded flattery.

"*Mais oui,* my lady." With another bow, Dumont ushered her along the wall, passing several grim-faced portraits to stop before a pastoral landscape with a pair of pipe-playing satyrs, prancing through the flowers on their goatish legs. "Now *this* is a picture of the first order, my lady. The school of Claude, if not by the master himself."

The girl didn't answer, bending down to study the painting's surface more closely, her brows drawn into a skeptical frown.

Undaunted, Dumont plunged ahead. "The brushwork is superb, is it not, my lady? I sold a picture much like this— though not half so fine—to an English gentleman last week, and delighted he was to procure it for his estate."

"I should not," she said, stepping back. "Be delighted to possess such a picture, that is. Who would wish to look at those dreadful satyrs every day over tea?"

"Ahh, so her ladyship has a certain taste," Dumont murmured, wincing. "A refined taste, that is."

"What I have a taste for is quality, sir," the girl said with thumping conviction. "It's not the satyrs themselves that I dislike, but how clumsily they're painted. You slander Claude, sir, by claiming this daub's by him."

"The school of Claude, my lady, the school," Dumont said hastily, moving to a morose still life painting of wilted flowers and rotting fruit. "Perhaps you would prefer a more edifying picture, my lady, a reminder of our own mortality and a caution against the consequences of a worldly life."

"A lady should have no need of such reminders, sir," she said. "But this picture here—this one I quite like."

Gracefully the girl stepped around Dumont and crouched down before a small painting propped against the wall. She tipped the heavy gold frame back with her gloved fingers and smiled with triumph.

Dumont frowned. "That one, my lady? Oh, I fear not, I fear not!"

John's curiosity rose. From his place by the window, he couldn't see the little painting behind the sweep of the girl's pale linen skirts. What kind of eye did the girl have? Was she taken by a simpering shepherdess or droop-eared puppy the way most young English ladies would be, or had she discovered something with true merit?

Still crouching with her hand on the frame, Lady Mary looked up at Dumont, her face full of disbelief. "However could you fear a painting such as this one? It's fine, most wonderfully fine, and not at all fearsome. Why didn't you show it to me first?"

To John's surprise, Dumont scowled, his wizened hands now folded defensively over his chest. "It's new to the shop, my lady, and since I believe in honesty with my customers, I must confess that I know nothing of its painter nor its history. Without that knowledge, I cannot in good faith sell such a picture to you."

"You cannot sell it to me, sir?" She narrowed her eyes, shrewdly calculating the challenge by tipping her head to one side so the pearl earring bobbed against her cheek. "Cannot, or will not?"

"Whichever pleases you to believe, my lady." Dumont grabbed the painting from Lady Mary, and shoved it behind the counter, out of her reach. "But I regret that I must remain firm. The picture is not for sale."

And that, at last, was enough for John.

"Dumont, Dumont, what's come over you?" he said, stepping forward from the window's curve. "You know better than to deny a lady's request like that. I assure you, my lady, his manners are generally more agreeable than that."

She straightened at once, clasping her hands tightly together around the handle of her parasol. "Forgive me, sir, but I do not believe I know you."

Dumont sighed, and made a testy wave of his hand. "My Lady Mary, my Lord John Fitzgerald."

"My lady, I am honored." With the Mercury still cradled in one arm like an unappealling infant, John made a graceful bow. "And I am at your service, willing to be your champion against this dragon."

Dumont the dragon snorted, with disgust, not fire.

Nor was Lady Mary amused.

"My lord." Her expression was frosty, with no smile to spare for John. "I do not recall asking for a champion."

"You didn't need to," he said as winningly as he could, doing his best to disarm her. He was unaccustomed to women rebuffing him like this. He knew he was a well-made man, only twenty-nine, and handsome enough to make most females smile back when he smiled first. He wasn't exactly vain about his appearance, but he had come to expect a certain response to his charm, and it felt odd now not to receive it from Lady Mary. Perhaps she was more trouble than she was worth, a challenge he'd be wiser to turn away from now.

But not quite yet. "Come, come, Dumont. Let me see this picture, and—"

"I'm perfectly capable of conducting this transaction myself, Lord John," she interrupted, her cheeks flushing. "I would not have ventured into this shop myself if I couldn't."

"It's hardly a question of incapability, my lady." John set the Mercury down on the counter beside him with a thump. "I only thought you might need a bit of assistance in your negotiations with Monsieur Dumont."

"I need nothing of the sort," she said tartly. "If I can

manage the affairs of my father's household and estates, then surely I have the ability to choose a picture to my liking."

How the devil had he ruffled her feathers so badly? He let his smile fade, and tried a different tactic. "Then it's no wonder your father has showed his confidence in you by letting you come to the shops by yourself."

She gave a small, restless twist to her shoulders. "My father trusts me so much that he has sent me abroad while he remains in England. He has no doubts about my capability."

"You are traveling alone?" John asked, so surprised he was almost stunned. Usually young English ladies on the Continent were so burdened with parents and chaperones and elderly maiden aunts that it was a marvel they managed to see any sights at all. "You are here by yourself in Calais?"

"Here now, m'lord, none o' those questions," the footman warned, moving between John and Lady Mary. He was formidable, a large country specimen, and John was disinclined to quarrel with him. "Her ladyship don't have to answer them."

But with an impatient quick sigh, the girl ducked around the footman to confront John once again.

"I am traveling with my sister and our companion, and several servants," she said, her dark eyes wide and earnest. "So you see that 'by alone' I meant without Father."

John knew otherwise. Without her father or any other male relative, she was as good—and as vulnerable—as travelling alone. The only difference lay in the words, and what she chose to believe, the pretty, parsing creature.

Perhaps she was not so great a challenge after all.

"And as you travel, you're collecting art," he said. "With your father's trust, of course. But do you consider yourself a *connoisseur*, Lady Mary, or merely a *dilettante?*"

Doubt flooded her face, exactly as he'd intended. "I'm not certain I'm either."

John smiled, his suspicions confirmed. Of course the foreign words would be unfamiliar to her; likely she was as willfully ignorant as every other English lady, and couldn't tell a *bonjour* from a *buongiorno*.

"Ah, well, no matter," he said expansively. "It was unfair of me to ask."

"I'm perfectly aware of my own ignorance, Lord Fitzgerald," she said, bristling at the condescension that he hadn't quite bothered to keep from his voice. "My father has always been afraid I'd become too educated and unattractive to gentlemen, so what I do know has been slipped to me on the sly by Miss Wood, like sweets stolen from the kitchen."

"Forgive me, Lady Mary," he began, thankful that she wouldn't realize how easy it was for his wicked old mind to jump from stolen sweets to lost innocence. "I didn't intend—"

"I rather think you did," she insisted. "Don't pretend otherwise."

"I'm not pretending," he protested, though even he knew he was. "I'm being perfectly honest."

"Oh, yes, as honest as Monsieur Dumont." She tapped her gloved fingers on the counter, a muted little thump of vindication. "So you see, Lord Fitzgerald, that while I do possess the interest to become a *dilettante,* I've too imperfect a store of knowledge to reinforce that interest, and as for being a *connoisseur*—why, until I've visited the galleries in Paris and Rome and seen the works of the great masters with my own eyes, I could scarce pretend to be a *connoisseur.*"

"No," admitted John. She'd just beaten him at his own game, but he liked her for it—liked her far more, in fact, than when she'd been merely another pretty young lady with skin like sweet country cream. "Not under the circumstances."

"Indeed not," she said, and at last she smiled. "All I am at present is a humble small collector, buying pictures that please me, rather than those of value or significance. Which is why I want this one so vastly much."

"You'll have it." He wanted to make her smile at him again. Her teeth were small and white, with the front two overlapping a fraction with intriguing imperfection. "Dumont, the picture."

But the Frenchman only shook his head as doggedly as before, his jowls trembling. "I regret to tell you the same, too, my lord. I cannot sell that painting, not to the lady nor to you."

"At least you can let me see what you're hiding." In one swift motion, John leaned over the counter and seized the painting by the frame.

"No, no, my lord, I beg you, please!" cried Dumont frantically as John held the picture high out of his reach. "It is not for you!"

"Mind you, my lord, I saw it first!" The girl hurried to John's side, hovering as if she feared he'd try to escape with the picture. "I'm willing to pay whatever he wants!"

"Of course you are." John turned the frame toward the window's light. For the first time he could see the painted image, and the sight was enough to make him whistle low with appreciation. This was no common forgery, no piece-work daub made up to sell to some ignoramus on his Grand Tour, nor was it the sentimental tripe John had expected the girl to choose.

The picture was undeniably old, at least three hundred years, and painted on a wood panel instead of framed canvas. Italian, most likely Florentine; no Northern artists painted like this. The angel was kneeling, the feathers of his multicolored wings fanned over his back and a sword of orange flames in his hands. His halo was thick with gold leaf, his rainment the particular brilliant blue that came only from ground lapis. But the angel's face was the real jewel, his expression fiercely intense—a militant guardian angel.

"Isn't it beautiful?" Lady Mary said, leaning closer to see the picture over John's arm. "It's been cut down quite shamefully from something bigger, of course, perhaps an altarpiece, and the frame may be newer."

John raised one brow with surprise. "Would you venture its provenance?"

She was too intent upon the painting itself to realize she was being tested. "Florentine for certain, from the 1400s. The paint's that odd eggy stuff, tempera, not oils—you can tell by how smooth it is, without any brushstrokes. Perhaps a Giotto, or a work from the studio of Fra Angelico, if not by the master's very brush."

"Most Englishmen would prefer the later work of Guido, or Titian. They'd find earlier paintings like this one too crude."

She raised her chin: determined, not stubborn. "Then most Englishmen are fools who cannot see the merits of what's set before them."

An admirable answer, thought John. "How do you know it's not a fake?"

Her gaze slid from the painting to John. "I don't," she admitted reluctantly. "It could have been made last week by some artful criminal, and I'd be none the wiser. All I know is what I've read, and the engravings I've seen in books, and a handful of old Italian paintings that a neighbor of ours had brought back from his Grand Tour. That's how I know the difference between tempera paints and oil."

"That's all?" he asked, surprised again. If that truly was the sum of her scholarship, then she'd guessed very well indeed. "Only what you've learned from books and your neighbor's souvenirs?"

She nodded, and smiled wistfully, a small smile that didn't show her teeth. "Likely you'll laugh at me for admitting this, but I know what the painting itself tells me, too. The colors, and the angel's expression, even the patterning along the hem of his raiment and across his wings—it all seemed so magical that I feel certain it's real. How could anyone make a forgery of that?"

John didn't laugh. How could he, when she looked up at him with such honesty and conviction from beneath those thick, sooty black lashes?

"So much for pleading beginner's ignorance, my lady," he said softly. "A painting only speaks to a *connoisseur*'s ear, and despite your inexperience, you already had the wisdom to listen."

"There now, my lord, you see why I cannot sell this picture!" Dumont made another futile grab at the painting, still well beyond his reach. "Even this young lady recognizes its value, its significance!"

"What this lady recognizes, sir, is that the picture is mine," she said with fresh determination. "Or it will be, as soon as we settle on a price."

"Name it, Dumont," John said. "I'll pay whatever you ask and make a gift of the picture to the lady."

She gasped, her eyes indignantly round. "I've no intention of accepting such a gift from you, Lord John! I mean to buy the picture myself, honorably and respectably!"

"We can quarrel over that once Dumont's set the price." Purposefully John frowned down at the Frenchman, hoping to intimidate him into compliance. He was sure that Dumont had mentally ticked the asking price higher and higher with each attribute that Lady Mary had described, and it was up to John to tick it back down again. "Be as honest as you claim, Dumont. You know you'd have the devil of a time selling this painting. Most of your customers will think it's ugly as sin."

"It's not ugly!" protested the girl. "It's—"

"It's unfashionable, Dumont, and you know it," John said firmly, ignoring the girl for now. "Her ladyship is simply being an enthusiastic amateur, and you know that, too. I'll give you ten *livres* for it."

Dumont scowled back. "Why won't you believe me, my lord? The picture's not for sale."

John sighed wearily, He was already offering more than the picture was worth, yet for some incomprehensible reason it had become very important to him to buy it for the girl. "Very well, then, Dumont. Eleven *livres,* and that's being deuced generous."

Still Dumont scowled. "I am very sorry, my lord, but I fear I cannot accept."

"You're a stubborn old wretch, Dumont." John glanced back down at the painting. The girl was right; the angel *was* magical. "I'll give you twelve *livres* and not a *sou* more."

Dumont groaned and bowed his head. "My lord, my lord, I regret it to the bottom of my heart, but I cannot—"

"I'll give you twenty *louis d'or* for the picture, *monsieur.*" The girl had already pulled a fat little purse from the pocket in her skirts and was beginning to count out the heavy gold coins in a row upon the counter. "That should be more than sufficient. Winters, take the picture from his lordship. We'll take it with us back to the inn to make sure it's safe."

The footman reached for the painting as he'd been ordered, but John pulled it away. "Here now, Dumont! What's become of all your reasons not to sell to me?"

"The lady's overcome my scruples, my lord," he said sadly, as if there'd ever been a doubt that his greed would triumph. He took the coins as fast as Lady Mary offered them, sliding them into the inside of his black serge waistcoat. "I'm honored and delighted to concede that the picture is now hers."

"If you please, m'lord." Lady Mary's footman reached out for the picture, and this time John had no choice but to relinquish it. The girl had already hidden the purse back in her pocket, while Dumont had produced a grubby old coverlet, which he and the footman began tying around the painting.

Soon she'd step outside that door and into the French bustle of Calais, and be gone to John forever, the way the women he met on his travels always were, leaving a pleasant memory and little else.

But this time, with this girl, John didn't want that to happen. He'd never liked mysteries; he'd always preferred answers, and the facts to give those answers meat and bones. He wanted to know why the daughter of an English duke was wandering about Calais without a train of attendants. He wanted to discover exactly how so young a lady had come to possess such expertise about painting from the little training she'd claimed to have. He wanted to know why this particular unfashionable little painting meant so much to her that she'd overpay for it by such an unconscionable sum.

And, most of all, he wanted to learn what he'd have to do to make her smile at him again.

Dover could wait. Now Calais seemed worthy of a longer visit—as long as was necessary.

He cocked his elbow and offered her his arm. "Let me accompany you back to your lodgings, Lady Mary," he said. "Calais can be a wickedly unwelcoming place for British travelers."

She looked at his arm as if it were a large and venomous

snake to be avoided at all costs. Needless to say, she did not take it.

"But you are British yourself, Lord John, aren't you?" she asked. "You are not French?"

He sighed, wishing he didn't have to answer so complicated a question this soon in their acquaintance. "I was born not far from Kerry, in Ireland. So yes, I suppose I am more British than French, or Spanish, or Italian. But I left that place so long ago that I scarce can consider it my home."

She tipped her head to one side. "Everyone has a home, some place that calls them back."

"Then call me a citizen of the world," he said, sweeping his arm grandly through the air, as if to encompass the whole scope of his life. "I'm a wanderer, Lady Mary. Wherever I find myself, then that is my home."

Most women found this a wildly romantic notion. Alas, Lady Mary was not one of them.

She frowned. "How can you claim to be at home nowhere, yet everywhere? That makes very little sense, Lord John, very little indeed."

"But it's true," he said confidently, willing to persist. "I can tell you the most hospitable taverns in the American states, or the least agreeable ones to avoid in the East Indies, and everywhere else in between. Calais here is like a nearby village to me, I've visited so many times."

"Then you surely you must know a score of different amusements for yourself in Calais that do not require my presence." She nodded to the footman, who tucked the swaddled painting beneath his arm to open the door for his mistress. "Good day, Lord John."

She unfurled her parasol and raised it over her head in a single graceful sweep, and without so much as a glance for John, she was gone.

"Forgive me, my lord," Dumont said behind him. "But you played *that* hand poorly enough."

"The game's hardly over, Dumont." John could see her still through the grimy window, her back straight and her step quick and purposeful, white skirts flicking back and forth around her legs. He'd find her again, of course. It wouldn't be difficult. Daughters of English dukes were rare enough in Calais that it would only take an inquiry or two in the right places to find where she was lodging. And then—well, *then* he'd decide what he'd do next.

But before he did that, he had a few questions to ask here, questions that, with the proper answers, could make Lady Mary wonderfully grateful to him. "In fact, I'd say the game's only begun."

"Not with that one, my lord." Dumont sniffed, wiping a gray cloth over the bronze Mercury that John had left on the counter earlier. "A beautiful English lady, yes, a lovely young lady, but also one who is accustomed to having what she wants, and nothing less."

The girl and the footman and the painting with them disappeared around the corner, and John turned away from the window. "Then the answer's a simple one, Dumont. All I must do is make sure I'm what she wants."

Dumont pursed his lips into a tight, skeptical oval.

"You doubt me, Dumont?"

The Frenchman shrugged, signifying everything and nothing.

"Please recall that I, too, am accustomed to getting what I wish." John rested his arms on the counter, lowering his face level with Dumont's. "And what I wish this moment, Dumont, is to know exactly what is wrong with that painting you just sold."

"Wrong, my lord?" Dumont drew back and sputtered with

too-nervous indignation. "What—whatever could be wrong with it? You heard the lady herself, vouching for its veracity, my lord, and I would never—"

"It's stolen, isn't it?" John asked. "Isn't that why you didn't want to sell it to her?"

"What you say, my lord! Such an accusation, a defamation, a—"

"Yes or no, Dumont," John said, more firmly this time. "The lady might know her antique painters, but at her age she can hardly be expected to recognize the signs of thievery. Was your first reluctance to sell the final kick of your moribund conscience, done in at last by greed?"

Fear replaced indignation in the old Frenchman's eyes. "My lord, I cannot say how —"

"Yes or no, Dumont," John said, convinced now that he'd guessed right. "It's one thing to offer new-minted kickshaws as the Caesar's own to some fat mercer's wife from Birmingham, but it's quite another to sell stolen goods to a peer's daughter. I'm quite certain those sharp-tempered fellows in the governor's offices down the road would agree."

"By all that's holy, my lord, I swear that I know nothing of thievery, nothing of stolen goods!" cried Dumont, his voice trembling. "If you report me, they'll close down my shop and take away my goods and I'll be left with nothing, my lord—nothing! Oh, have pity on an old man in the last years of his life!"

"I will if you tell me the truth," John said, too familiar with Dumont's histrionics to take them seriously. "How did you come by that painting of the angel?"

Dumont nodded eagerly. "It was brought to me last week, my lord, by a foreign man, perhaps a Dutchman. He told me it grieved him to be forced to sell so fine a picture, but a bank draft he'd been expecting had not come, and his affairs were desparate. It's a common story, my lord."

"I imagine it is," John said dryly. "How much did you give him?"

"Three *livres,*" he answered, so promptly that John was certain the unfortunate Dutchman had received only half that sum. "As you noted yourself, my lord, it is an unfashionable painting, and on most days would be difficult to sell."

"Then why in blazes did you refuse to sell it to me?" John asked. "The truth, now."

Contritely Dumont bowed his head. "The truth, my lord, is that I knew her ladyship would give me more for the painting than you would, and she did."

"The truth, the truth." John sighed, and stood upright. He'd no doubt that that *was* the truth, or at least as much as he'd get today from Dumont. He'd get no special gratitude from Lady Mary for that scrap of truth, either. But half a truth was better than none, and that single smile from Lady Mary—ah, that was worth all the truth in Calais.

Chapter Three

"Wherever have you been, Mary?" Wanly Diana pressed her hand against her temple, as if the effort of greeting her sister was simply too much. Their Channel crossing yesterday had been grim, rough and stormy and far longer than they'd been told. While Mary had proved a model sailor with a stomach of iron, her sister, Miss Wood and their lady's maid, Deborah, had suffered so severely from the effect of the waves that they'd had to be half carried from the boat to the dock last night. Then before they could retreat to their inn to rest or even change into dry clothes, they'd had to present their names to the governor, as was required by French law, and then they'd gone to the Customs House to wait while their belongings were searched, cataloged and taxed. The officials brazenly expected their garnish at every step, holding their hands out for the customary bribes before any of the English were permitted to pass into the town. After such an ordeal, it was really no wonder that the three women had required at least this entire day to recover.

Now Diana lay against the mounded pillows in the bed, the curtains of the room still drawn against the sun even though it was now late afternoon. A tray with a teapot and a few slices of cold toast, delicately nibbled on the corners, showed she'd tried to take sustenance, and failed.

Diana groaned, and flung her arm dramatically across the sheets. "Oh, Mary, how much I've missed you!"

"And I missed you, too, lamb." Mary leaned forward and kissed her sister's forehead. "At least your coloring's better. You must be on the mend."

"Thank you." Diana smiled, happy to have her back. "Though it hasn't been easy, you know. Miss Wood and Deborah have been ill, too, and the servants refuse to speak anything but wretched, wretched French!"

"Of course they speak French, Diana. This is France. If you'd paid more heed to our French lessons with Miss Wood, you would have had no difficulties now at all." Mary crossed the room to the window, and pulled the curtains open, letting the sunlight spill across the floor. "I've been away for only an hour at most, and when I left you were deep asleep."

"But then I woke, and you weren't here." Diana covered her eyes with her forearm against the window's light. "It seemed as if you were gone much longer than an hour."

"I wasn't." An hour, Mary marveled. Why had it seemed like so much more to her, too? Only an hour, the hands on her little gold watch moving neither faster nor slower than usual, and yet in that short time, so much had happened.

Diana pushed herself up higher on the pillows. "You weren't supposed to go out at all, not alone. You know what Father said."

"He meant that for you, not me," Mary said. "And besides, I wasn't alone. I took Winters with me."

"Oh, now *that* changes everything," Diana said. "Winters the half-daft footman, protector of our maidenly virtue!"

"He was quite sufficient for accompanying me," Mary said, thankful that the half-light of the room hid her blush.

All she'd intended was a short stroll to give herself a break from the sickroom. But then she'd seen the intriguing little shop, and had promised herself only a minute or two to explore inside. Before she'd realized it, she'd discovered and bought a beautiful old painting of an angel for a frighteningly high sum. She'd ignored all the cautions and warnings she'd been given before she'd sailed, and let herself be drawn into a conversation with a stranger. "I'm not you, you know."

"A pity for you that you aren't," Diana said sagely. "A little bit of me wouldn't hurt. You'd enjoy yourself more."

"I enjoyed myself well enough." Mary took the painting from the table where she'd left it, guiltily trying not to think of the stranger who'd bid against her in the shop. She could only imagine how gleeful Diana would be if she learned of him; Mary would never, ever hear the end of it. "I bought a picture of an angel."

Proudly Mary held the painting up for her sister to see. She should have known better.

"How ghastly," Diana said, wrinkling her nose. "Angels should be beatific, but that one looks as if he'd bite your leg off as soon as sing a psalm. What a pity Winters didn't stop you from spending Father's money on *that*."

Mary turned the painting back to her, balancing the heavy gold frame against her hip. If anything, the picture seemed even more special than when she'd first seen it. She liked the stern-faced angel, ready to defend his faith or whatever else had been cut away with the rest of the painting.

"You're only showing your own ignorance, Diana," she said, more to the painting than to her sister. "To anyone with an eye, this is a very rare and beautiful picture."

The stranger hadn't teased her when she'd babbled about the painting's mystical attraction to her. He'd even seemed to *understand,* which had been more than enough for her to like him instantly. He'd said his name was Lord John Fitzgerald, that he'd been born in Ireland, and that he was a citizen of the world, whatever that might mean. But there'd been no question that his eyes had been very blue and full of laughter, even when his mouth had been properly severe, and that his jaw was firm and manly and his black hair cropped and curling. From his speech and clothes, he'd seemed the gentleman he'd claimed to be, but then he'd tried to buy the painting for her as a gift, something no true gentleman would ever do.

But maybe this was only one more thing that was different between England and France. Maybe here it was perfectly proper for strange gentlemen to offer expensive gifts to ladies. Maybe in France such conversations and such generosity happened every day, without a breath of impropriety.

And maybe such an exchange, with such a charming gentleman, was exactly the reason she'd wanted to come abroad in the first place—except that she'd been too self-conscious to enjoy it, exactly as Diana had said. She'd meant to be cautious, reserved, her usual sensible self. Instead he'd doubtless considered her to be a hopeless prig, too timid to take a gentleman's arm. Not that she'd have another chance, either, not with Lord John. They would be leaving Calais for Paris as soon as it could be arranged, and because her life was never like a novel or play, her path would never again cross with his.

"Ahh, Mary, you've returned from your walk." Miss Wood joined them, as pale as Diana, but neatly dressed in her usual gray gown and jacket and white linen cap, as if to defy any mere seasickness to steal another day from her. "No doubt the fresh air off the water would have done Lady Diana and me some good as well."

Diana groaned at the suggestion, flopping back against her pillows. "She didn't just walk, Miss Wood. She went into a shop, and bought an ugly picture."

"It's not ugly, Diana," protested Mary. "It's simply not to your taste. Miss Wood shall be the judge."

She turned the painting toward the governess, but Miss Wood's startled expression told Mary more than Miss Wood would ever dare speak.

"What matters is that the picture pleases you, my lady," the governess said, ever tactful. "Each time you glimpse it, you'll remember this day, the first of our adventure abroad."

Mary looked back at the picture. It would, indeed, remind her of Calais, just as that fierce angel would forever remind her of Lord John. But of an adventure—no. Foolish, foolish she'd been, and far too cowardly to seize the adventure that had presented itself.

"Perhaps in the morning you can show us what you've discovered about this town, Lady Mary," Miss Wood was saying. "I should like to see the gate to the city properly before we leave. It's regarded as the centerpiece of Calais, you know, with a great deal of history behind it. We can even return to the shop where you bought this picture, if you wish."

"No, no!" Mary exclaimed, stunned by such a suggestion. What if Lord John were there again, and thought she'd come hunting for him? Or worse, a fear that was more selfish and unworthy: what if she did meet him again, but this time he saw only Diana, the way that always seemed to happen? "That is, since I already bought the choicest piece in the shop, there's no reason for returning to it."

Diana made a disparaging sniff. "If *that* picture was the choicest, then I've no wish at all to visit such a place. Surely there must be some public parade, or park where people of fashion gather. Why, I've heard Calais has more officers of every service than even Portsmouth."

"No officers for us, my lady, and no parade grounds," Miss Wood said, clasping her hands at the front of her waist. "I needn't remind you of the warning your father His Grace gave to you before we sailed. You are traveling to improve your mind and edify your soul, and to learn to modify your behavior regarding every classification and rank of men."

Diana clapped her hands to her breast as if she'd just sustained a mortal wound. "Ugly paintings and stupid old gates for months and months and *months*. How shall I ever survive?"

"With grace and dignity as befits your station, my lady." Miss Wood swung open the window, letting in a breeze redolent of the ocean, mingled with the tavern's stables on the other side of the yard. "Besides, I expect us to be leaving Calais the day after tomorrow. That's scarce time for any intriguing, no matter how determined."

"You are too cruel, Miss Wood!" cried Diana, hurling one of her pillows across the room at the governess. "Too, too cruel!"

"So you've often said, my lady." Unperturbed, Miss Wood plucked the pillow from the floor beside her, smoothed the linen with her palms, and returned it to the end of the bed. "But you'll have to tolerate my decisions, especially now. There was a letter waiting here at the inn for me from Monsieur Leclair, the gentleman His Grace your father engaged as our bearleader."

"'Bearleader,'" Mary repeated, unable to resist the silliness of the expression. "It sounds as if we're his pack of she-bears in some vagabond circus. Why aren't they just called guides?"

"Because they're not, my lady," Miss Wood said patiently.

"In any event, Monsieur Leclair's mother has been taken grievously ill, and he begs our understanding and forgiveness while he makes arrangements for her. Instead of attending us here in Calais, with our leave he shall join us in Paris instead."

"Of course he'll have our leave," Mary said. "Poor Madame Leclair! She should have her son with her. We can manage perfectly well on our own from here to Paris."

Diana smiled mischievously at Mary. "You are *so* independent, Mary."

"It's an admirable trait to possess, Diana," Mary said, praying that Diana would offer nothing more incriminating. "Especially whilst traveling."

Miss Wood nodded with approval. "That is true, my lady. We'll have our two days here in Calais, and then on to Paris. That was the itinerary approved by His Grace your father, and we shall follow it even without Monsieur Leclair to lead us."

Two days, thought Mary with regret, and one of those days was nearly done. Miss Wood and Father had been wise to leave no time at all for intriguing in Calais. Their only miscalculation had been which daughter had longed for the intrigue.

"Oh, *monsieur,* I do not believe I could allow that," said Madame Gris, the innkeeper's wife, guarding the doorway to the private dining room as conscientiously as any royal sentry. The *Coq d'Or* had its reputation to maintain as a respectable house, especially among the English gentry. "The young lady is dining alone, and wishes not to be disturbed. Her governess and her sister—the *mal-de-mer,* you see."

"Then all the more reason, madame, that the lady's in need of company and cheer." John glanced down at the bouquet he'd brought for Lady Mary, a confection of pinks and roses gathered in a paper frill and red ribbon, the way that the French did so well. Other times, he would have simply sent the flowers, but given this was bound to be a hasty flirtation at best, he'd decided to bring his offering himself.

But Madame Gris still shook her head, her plump chin shaking gently above her checkered kerchief. "This is no scandalous house of assignation, monsieur."

"Keep the door open, madame, and listen to every word that passes between us," John said, placing his hand over his heart. "I swear to you that not even a whisper of scandal will pass my lips."

The innkeeper's wife stared at him with disbelief. Then she tipped back her head and laughed aloud.

"You'd laugh at me, madame?" John asked, striving to sound wounded, yet unable to keep from joining her laughter. He never had been able to feign earnestness, and he hadn't succeeded this morning, either. "You'd laugh at my humble suit?"

"'Humble,' hah," she said, giving his arm a poke with her finger. "I'd wager you've never been humble about anything in your life, *monsieur,* a fox like you! Go, go, take your posey to the lady, and plead your heart to her. But mind you, the door stays open, and if I hear one peep from her—"

"No peeps, madame," John said, winking wickedly as he slipped past her. "Only the greatest gratitude for your kind understanding."

Madame Gris laughed and jabbed at John again, her good humor following him as he headed down the hallway to the small private parlor at the end. The inn had welcomed its respectable guests for the last two hundred years, and the wide old floorboards creaked beneath John's feet, and he had to duck his head beneath the age-blackened beams overhead. Yet the whitewashed room before him seemed to glow, the windows with their diamond-leaded frames open to the bright summer morning and sunlight falling over the girl.

Lady Mary was sitting in a spindled armchair with her back to the half-open door. Her hair was loosely pinned in a knot on top of her head, the sunshine turning the escaped tendrils dark red. She was dressed in a simply cut white linen gown with a wide green sash around her slender waist, the style that the French queen had first made so famous, yet now was associated almost entirely with English ladies. Lady Mary wore it well, the simplicity suiting her creamy skin and dark hair and the full, layered skirts, falling softly around her chair, made translucent by the sun.

Yet what caught John's attention first, and held it, was the delicate curve of her neck, the pearl earrings gently bobbing on either side of her throat. With her head slightly bent over her dish of tea, her nape was exquisite, the vulnerability of it almost heartbreaking.

His weight shifted, just enough for his foot to make the floorboard beneath it squeak. She twisted around in her chair and caught her breath, a slice of bread with jam forgotten in her fingers.

"You!" she cried, her cheeks flushing a furious pink. "How did you come here? How did you find me?"

"Calm yourself, Lady Mary, please, I beg you!" he exclaimed, holding one hand palm up to signal for quiet, and the other brandishing the flowers. He'd told Madame Gris that she could interrupt if she heard the girl object, and he had no doubt that the innkeeper's wife would enjoy doing exactly that. "I don't mean you the least bit of harm!"

"Oh, no, no, I didn't intend that." Hastily she rose to her feet in a swirl of white linen, the bread still in her hand. "That is, you have surprised me, but I—I am not upset. Not in the least, not when—oh, blast!"

A forgotten, glistening blot of red jam dropped from the bread in her hand and splattered on her arm, barely missing her white sleeve. She dropped the bread, grabbed the napkin from the table, and slapped it over the jam, pressing the cloth there as if she feared the errant jam would somehow escape to shame her again.

John smiled: not only because he knew he was the cause of her being so discomfited, but because that extra blush and fluster was a side of her he hadn't seen at Dumont's. There she'd been so much in control of herself that she'd been able to steal the painting away from him. But now—now she was as rattled as a cracked teacup, and all because of a blot of jam.

"I'll have you know I'm not like this, my lord," she confessed. "Not generally. Not at all."

"I'm not like this, either," he said. "Rising at this unholy hour, begging Madame Gris for entrance, startling ladies at their breakfast. Not like me at all."

"Of course it's not." She rubbed the napkin over her arm one last time to make sure the jam was gone, crushed the napkin into a lumpy knot, and stuffed it under the edge of her plate. "I wouldn't give you permission to walk with me yesterday, but if you ask to take breakfast with me now— even though it's a meager sort of French breakfast, without eggs or meats—why, I shall agree."

"You will?" No matter how confident he'd been before, he hadn't expected this invitation. Not that he meant to accept it. Because he half expected her sister or governess to join her at any moment, he'd rather coax her out-of-doors, away from the inn, where he'd be sure to keep her company to himself. He already had an image of the seasick sister: plain and peevish and nothing like Lady Mary, and as for the governess—well, she was a *governess*. "You'll walk with me after all?"

"I will." At last she smiled, only a moment. "It's not often one has the chance to set mistakes to rights. Those flowers are quite lovely. Are they for me?"

He handed the bouquet to her with the same bow that yesterday had earned him only disdain. Now she took the flowers with a happy little chuckle, cradling them in her arms.

"So you will accept flowers," he teased, bemused, "but not a picture."

She looked down at the flowers, then back at him. "I suppose that's a contradiction, isn't it?"

He shrugged. "Only a small one. Life is full of contradictions. None of them really signify."

"But this does," she insisted, once again the serious girl from yesterday. "That painting has already existed for hundreds of years, and with luck and care will exist for hundreds more. Yet these flowers, however lovely, will not last more than a day or two. Which makes them far more appropriate as a token from you to me."

"Lady Mary," he teased, striving to seem wounded. "Are you implying that my admiration for you will only last a day or two?"

"Admiration, fah," she scoffed. "You must know me to admire me, and you'll scarce have time for either one. Come to the window. Do you see those men in the yard with the blue carriage?"

He came to stand beside her, exactly as he'd been told, and exactly as he'd wished. The window was small, and to look through it with her as she'd ordered, he had to stand so close beside her that he could smell the scent of lavender soap on her skin.

"I see it," he said evenly, as if standing beside her without touching her wasn't a refined kind of torture.

"That's our coach," she said, "or rather, my father's coach, though how bitterly he complained over the French taxes he had to pay for the privilege of the convenience! It was sent in pieces on the boat from England, and once the men have put it back together, we'll be ready to leave for Paris. We've already sent a wagon ahead two weeks ago, filled with more trunks to the apartments we've let in Paris."

"He could have hired a cabriolet here for less than the taxes." John had heard of the richer and more cowardly English who'd import their own carriages to the Continent, but he'd never seen one for himself until now. "Your driver will have the devil of a time maneuvering that great beast on French roads. Monsieur Dessin has tidy cabriolets for a *louis* a week."

She sighed. "Father didn't trust hired carriages. He won't even use a post chaise. He says they're unsafe, and that the cushions harbor fleas and bedbugs."

"So instead he would rather import a carriage just for you," John said, almost—almost—feeling sympathy for her insulated plight. "What better way to spare you from having any actual contact with the people, let alone their bedbugs, whose country you are crossing?"

"That was Father's decision," she said, and John liked the way she made it clear she didn't agree with her father. "You cannot imagine how difficult it was to persuade him to allow me to leave Kent, let alone come to France."

He smiled, thinking of how different it was for well-bred boys and girls, especially when the difference was widened by wealth, or the lack of it. "My father was so eager for me to leave home that he shipped me off to Calcutta when I was fourteen, with the sum of my belongings in a single trunk."

"Calcutta!" she said, her dark eyes widening with wonder. "Oh, what adventures you must have had there!"

"Oh, by the score," he said lightly, for most of his adventures in the service of the East Indian Company were not the sort he'd wish to share with her. "Likely more than you'll find if you stay locked in Papa's coach."

"But I've already had two adventures, my lord." Her chin rose with the same challenge that she'd shown the day before, and he could see the swift rise and fall of her pulse at the side of her throat. "I cannot believe you haven't guessed them."

"Only because you haven't asked me to."

She laughed, her eyes sparkling with her secret. "I bought my first painting yesterday."

"Ahh, the picture." He needed to talk to her about that painting, and his suspicions about it, and about Dumont— all of which would certainly qualify as an adventure by anyone's lights. That had been the main reason he'd permitted himself to come call on her here in the first place. But now that he was here, with her telling secrets, he didn't want to be…distracted by the painting. Not yet. "I suppose in Kent, that would be considered an adventure. Though I'm almost afraid to ask after the second."

"You shouldn't," she said, her voice once again dropping to a breathless whisper. "My second adventure was meeting you."

"You flatter me, my lady." He chuckled, delighted with her answer. For whatever reason, she'd clearly thought better of running away from him yesterday. Now it seemed as if she were practically willing to leap into his arms—yet still, somehow, on her own terms. He took the flowers from her arms and tossed them back onto the table, his gaze never leaving hers. "I wouldn't say we've had an adventure, not yet."

"Miss Wood believes we'll be leaving tomorrow." Wistfully she glanced back at the men assembling the coach in the yard. "That's not much time for—for a true adventure, is it?"

Idly John brushed a loose lock of her hair back from her forehead, letting his fingertips stray down along her temple to her cheek. "That depends, my dear lady, upon how adventurous you are."

"I *will* be adventurous, my lord," she said fervently. "If you ask me again to walk with you. I told you that before. I *will* go, and I will enjoy myself, and your company."

A walk: a *walk*. So that was her idea of adventure. How did the English aristocracy manage to reproduce itself if it continued to keep its women so idiotically innocent?

"Be adventurous, pet," he said softly, his finger gently caressing the soft skin beneath her chin. "Come with me, and I can guarantee that you will enjoy—what in blazes is *that?*"

With a startled gasp, Lady Mary jerked away from him and rushed back toward the window. Dogs were barking, men were shouting and women shrieking, horses were snorting and pawing the dirt, and she heard the groaning, creaking rumble of an enormous wagon or carriage laboring to stop before the inn.

"I can't see!" cried Lady Mary with frustration, her head already leaning through the open casement. "What do you think it is, my lord? What can it be?"

"The *diligence* from Paris," Jack said, frustrated as well. "It's a kind of oversized public coach made of wicker, usually packed with at least a dozen travelers from every station of French life."

"Oh, I must see that!" She pulled her head back in from the window. "If I'm to be adventurous, I must go out front to the road!"

Eager to see the arrival of the *diligence,* she grabbed his arm and pulled him along down the hall with her, out the front door and to the road. A servant from the inn stood on a stubby stool beside the door, solemnly ringing a large brass bell by way of announcement, as if the rest of the racket weren't announcement enough. A small crowd had already gathered, some with small trunks and bundles of belongings who were waiting to climb on board, others there to welcome disembarking passengers, and still more in tattered rags, waiting with hands outstretched to beg. Surrounded by clouds of dust from the road, the lumbering *diligence* finally ground to a stop before the inn, the four weary horses in the harness flecked with foam and coated with dirt, and the men riding postilion on their backs, not much better, their whips drooping listlessly from their hands.

"What a curious coach!" exclaimed Mary, standing beside John. "I never would have seen such a thing if I'd stayed in Kent!"

It was, she decided, as good as any play. With its thick wooden wheels and double-horse team, the *diligence* did resemble its English cousins. But the body of the coach was long and flat, and made not of panels, but of tightly woven splints, with a small, covered compartment with an arched roof in the front to protect the driver. The passengers packed inside and on top looked like so many eggs gathered in a basket for market.

And a diverse assortment of passengers it was, too. There were the usual half-drunk sailors with long queues down their backs and soldiers in ragged uniforms to be found on any English coach. But there were also two fat monks in brown robes, their tonsured heads gleaming in the sun, a grumpy-faced woman dressed in a red-striped jacket who carried a cage full of chirping canaries, an old man with an extravagantly tall white wig and a rabbit-fur muff so large it hung to his knees, and a pair of young women with gowns cut low enough to display their rosy nipples through their neckerchiefs, much to the delight of the sailors and soldiers. Around her bubbled a rush of French words and exclamations and likely curses, too, all in dialects that bore scant resemblance to what she'd learned in the schoolroom.

"So does the Paris *diligence* qualify as another adventure, my lady?" John asked. He was smiling so indulgently at her that she felt foolish, more like a child hopping up and down before a shop window full of sweets than the touring lady of the world she was trying to be.

Purposefully she drew herself up straighter. "It would be an adventure if I took my passage to Paris in it. Hah, imagine what Father would say to *that!*"

His smile widened, daring her. "Then do it. The driver and postilions will change the horses, turn about, and leave for Paris again. I'll come with you for—for companionship. You'll have a score of chaperones to keep your honor intact, you'll improve your French mightily, and I'll give my word that you'll have a true adventure."

She stared up at him, more tempted than she'd wish to admit. "But we've no provisions, no food, no—"

"Dinner and supper are included in the fare," he said. "And I guarantee that those meals, too, won't be like anything you find in Kent."

"None of this is like Kent," she said, but she was laughing, pushing her breeze-tossed hair back from her face. She'd never even considered doing anything as scandalous as riding in a public coach for days and nights at a time with a man she scarcely knew, and yet somehow now it seemed less scandalous than, well, *adventurous.*

"Then come with me," he said, cocking his head toward

the unwieldy *diligence*. "Be brave. This is Calais, not your blessed Kent. No one knows you here, nor cares what you do. When else will you have such an opportunity?"

She shook her head, laughing still. What was it about him that made the most ridiculous proposal she'd ever received seem so wickedly intriguing? If it had been Diana with one of her swains, she would have been horrified.

"Do you like strawberries, my lady?" he asked, out of the blue. He raised his dark brows, and held out his hands, slightly curved, as if offering the largest imaginary strawberry for her edification. "Juicy and sweet upon the tongue, fresh as the morning dew in the mouth?"

"Excuse me?" she said, and laughed again. She'd never met another gentleman who could make her laugh so often, or so richly. She'd always prided herself on being practical, responsible, capable. Who would have known that she'd have such a store of laughter inside her, as well? "Why ever ask me of strawberries now?"

He shifted behind her, resting his palms on her shoulders, and gently turned her toward the *diligence*. "Because there, climbing down from the top, is a sturdy French farmwife with a basket in each hand, the sort of deep, narrow basket that is used only for strawberries in this region."

He'd kept his hands on her shoulders after the reason for having them there was done, and his palms were warm, the weight of them oddly pleasant, as if in some strange way they *belonged* there.

She twisted her head around to face him. "I do like strawberries, Lord John," she said, delighted by how his eyes were the same blue as the June sky overhead. "In fact I am monstrously fond of them."

"Then I shall fetch some for you directly," he said. "Perhaps they'll persuade you to make an adventurous journey with me."

He winked—*winked!*—and gave her shoulders a fond, familiar pat before he went striding toward the farmer's wife with the berries. The tails of his coat swung with a jaunty rhythm, his square shoulders broad and easy, his dark hair tossing in the light breeze.

If he'd tried to kiss her, she would have kissed him back. It was a staggering realization for her to make. He might still kiss her once he'd returned with the berries, and she knew she'd kiss him them, too, and that was more staggering still.

"Lady Mary!"

She frowned and glanced around her, not knowing who was calling her name. Hadn't Lord John just reminded her that in Calais she was a stranger?

"Lady Mary, here!" The shopkeeper Dumont was standing in the shadow of an alley beside the inn, half-hidden by a pyramid of stacked barrels. He wore an old slouch hat pulled low over his face, a grimy scarf wrapped many times around his throat, and the same leather apron she remembered from his shop. Agitated, he looked from side to side to make certain he'd not been noticed, then beckoned to her.

"If you please, my lady, if you please!" he called in a anxious quaver. "I must speak to you at once!"

"On what subject, *monsieur?*" She hesitated, unwilling to be drawn so far from the bustle of the inn's front door, even on this sunny day. "Why do you wish to speak to me?"

"The picture, my lady!" His claw of a hand beckoned again. "The angel! Do you have it still?"

She took one reluctant step closer, and no more. She glanced swiftly over her shoulder, wishing now that Lord John had returned. "Of course I've kept the picture. I only bought it from you yesterday."

"Has anyone asked you for it, my lady?" he asked urgently. "Does anyone know it's in your possession?"

"Only those in my traveling party," she said, her heart racing with fear of what she didn't understand. "*Monsieur,* I do not believe that any of this is your—"

"You must tell no one, my lady," Dumont interrupted, his voice shaking with emotion. "Tell no one that the picture is your property now, or that you bought it from me, or even that you have seen it!"

"You can't threaten me like that!" she exclaimed, trying to be brave. "I paid you dearly for that painting, and if it's your game to try to intimidate me into selling it back to you, why, I've no intention of doing so!"

The old man shook his head. "I would not take it back, my lady," he said vehemently. "It is yours now, and the peril with it, and I—"

"Lady Mary!"

That voice Mary recognized at once.

"Miss Wood!" Quickly she turned to her governess, glad for an excuse to leave Dumont and his unsettling questions. "Oh, Miss Wood, how glad I am to see you feeling better!"

"What I am feeling, my lady, is inestimable relief at finding you unharmed." She bustled forward and took Mary firmly by the upper arm. "But look at you, my lady! Out in the street by yourself, without a hat or parasol or gloves to keep you safe from the sun! Now come inside and gather yourself, my lady, so that we can go."

"Go?" Mary asked, confused. Her governess was dressed not for walking, but for traveling, in her quilted skirt and jacket. "Where are we going, Miss Wood? Do you wish to visit the Calais gate?"

"We're leaving Calais directly, my lady," Miss Wood said. "I have had enough of this wretched inn and the insufferable people that own it. I'm told our coach is ready, and now that we don't have to wait for Monsieur Leclair to join us, we'll depart as soon as you are dressed properly. Hurry now, please, we need to make as much progress as we can before dark."

"Now?" Mary said faintly, looking past Miss Wood to scan the street for Lord John. The *diligence* was empty, with only a few people still gathered around it. But where was the farmer's wife with the basket of strawberries, and where was Lord John?

"What is it, Lady Mary?" asked the governess, concern in her voice. "Are you unwell? You look as if you've taken too much of the sun, out here without your hat. Your cheeks are pink."

"I was expecting a—a friend, Miss Wood," she said. Perhaps he'd had to follow the woman for the strawberries. Perhaps she wouldn't sell them to him at all, and he'd gone elsewhere. He wouldn't abandon her the first time she turned away, not after offering to take her clear to Paris. "A friend."

"A friend, my lady?" Miss Wood frowned. "Forgive me, my lady, but what friend could you possibly have here in Calais?"

What friend, indeed? Mary shook her head, unwilling to believe the empty proof of her own eyes. Perhaps it was for the best that Lord John had disappeared like this. She could hardly have introduced him to Miss Wood, or worse, to her sister. This way she'd still had an adventure, only just a smaller one than he'd proposed. She would dutifully leave Calais now with the rest of her party, and disappear, and treat him the same as he'd treated her. Her reputation was spared a journey with him in a crowded *diligence*. There'd be no farewell, no regrets for what had never happened. Only the slight sting of disappointment, and she already knew how to cope with that.

Her smile was wistful, her feelings bittersweet. No more

laughter, and no promised strawberries, sweet and juicy on the tongue. No more adventures today.

She glanced back to the end of the wall, where Monsieur Dumont had warned her about her painting. Now he, too, had vanished. She couldn't have imagined all of it, could she?

"Come, Lady Mary," said Miss Wood, leading her back into the inn. "Deborah will have your trunk packed by now, and Lady Diana should be ready, too."

But as she began up the stairs with Miss Wood, Madame Gris hurried toward her, the beautiful ruffled bouquet of roses and pinks in her arms.

"My lady, a moment, please!" she called. "You forgot these in the parlor, my lady. The flowers the gentleman brought for you, my lady, and such pretty ones they are, too."

Miss Wood looked sharply at Mary, her expression full of silent questions.

"I am sorry, Madame," Mary said slowly, "but I'm afraid you're mistaken. Those flowers weren't for me."

Madame Gris's brows rose with surprise. "But my lady, I am sure that—"

"No, Madame," Mary said. "The bouquet was not meant for me, and neither was the gentleman."

Chapter Four

John stood in the street with the basket of strawberries in one hand and a tiny tin pail of cream, covered with a checkered cloth, in the other. He did not quite feel like a fool—it would take more than this to do that—but he wasn't happy, either.

Where in blazes had Lady Mary gone, anyway?

He looked back once again to the *Coq d'Or,* hoping to find her standing where he'd left her. This time Madame Gris herself was standing in the open front door, ordering a servant with a trunk to carry it to the back of the inn. Madame's manner was brusque, the blunt side that her guests seldom saw. But taking the edge from this particular order were the incongruous pink-and-white flowers in her arms—the same bouquet that John had brought earlier to Lady Mary.

"Madame Gris!" He hurried forward, the basket of strawberries swinging from his hand. "Have you seen Lady Mary?"

Madame's expression seemed faintly pitying, not a good omen. "I've see her, yes, my lord," she said. "I've seen her, and she said she didn't want the flowers, and she didn't want you, either."

He couldn't believe that, not after she'd so obviously been enjoying herself, and his company. She couldn't have feigned that. She was too young, and too inexperienced for such dissembling; it was much of her charm for him. But what could have changed her mind so fast?

"Are you certain, madame?" he asked. "She left no message for me?"

"No, my lord." Madame shifted the flowers from one plump arm to another. "But she was with her chaperone, the small, plain woman. She could have ordered her ladyship to come away. They're to leave at once, in that grand private coach of theirs."

"Oh, yes, the coach." She'd go to Paris as her father had intended, sealed up tight in a lacquered cocoon of English money and privilege. "Of course."

Madame Gris nodded sagely. "A high-born English lady like that—she has no choice, does she? She must marry where her father says, yes?"

Now the strawberries in his hand did feel foolish, and so did the cream. The girl might laugh with him, and rhapsodize about old pictures, and pretend she was considering running off to Paris with him in a public conveyance, and smile so softly that he'd let himself believe she'd never smiled that way at any other man—she might do all that, but in the end, she'd go back to where she knew she belonged.

And not dawdle with the rootless sixth son of an impoverished, obscure Irish marquess.

"Forgive me for asking, my lord, but what should I do with these flowers?"

"Whatever pleases you, madame, for they didn't please her." He dropped the strawberry basket and the pail of cream on the bench beside the door. "Do the same with that rubbish as well. If she didn't want me, odds are she'll have no use for that blasted fruit, either."

And without another word, he turned away, determined to leave behind her memory as surely as she'd forgotten him.

With an ivory-bladed fan in her hand, Mary sat in one corner of the coach and Diana sat in the other, with Miss Wood riding backward on the seat across from them. The leather squabs had been newly plumped with fresh sheep's wool for the journey, and the heavy leather straps beneath them that served as the springs to cushion their way had been refurbished as well. The coach's glass windows were folded down, letting in the fresh, tangy breezes from the sea on one side, and the summer-sweet scent of the fields of low grain on the other.

The post road from Calais to Paris was an easy one, along the coast to Boulogne-sur-Mer and past the lime-washed houses of the hilltop town of Montreuil. The road turned inland at Abbeville, to Amiens and Chantilly and finally Paris. Mary had marked the names on the map she'd brought with her to trace their journey, and the road was scattered with inns and post stops well equipped to cater to foreign travelers.

At the last stop, they'd opened the hamper filled with cold chicken, wedges of ripe cheese, and biscuits that Miss Wood had had prepared, and Diana still sipped lemon-water from the crystal glass that had been carefully packed for them, too. They'd every comfort imaginable for their journey, and yet as Mary stared out the window, she was far from happy.

The *diligence* would have been hot, crowded and uncomfortable, but it would have been different, and it would have been exciting, too. Lord John would have made it that way, and she would have relished every noisy, dusty minute on the road.

But this coach could very well have been carrying her from Aston Hall to church, it felt so much like home. Safe and comfortable and secure and very, very boring.

With a sigh that soon lapsed into gentle, wheezing snoring, Miss Wood's head tipped to one side, her small-brimmed gray bonnet slipping over her closed eyes.

Diana chuckled, swirling the lemon-water in her glass. "So, sister dear," she said softly. "Tell me *all.*"

Mary glanced pointedly at their governess. "Hush, Diana, you'll wake Miss Wood."

"You won't wriggle free that easily, Mary," Diana whispered, her blue eyes wide with anticipation. "The servants were all atwitter about it at the *Coq d'Or.* Who was the handsome gentleman you met for breakfast?"

One by one, Mary clicked the blades of her fan together, then patted it lightly into the palm of her hand. The sooner she told Diana the truth, the sooner it could be forgotten, and besides, it had never been in her nature to keep secrets.

"I don't truly know who he was," she confessed ruefully. "It was all in passing, you know. He said he was an Irish lord, but I never learned much else of him beyond that."

"A lord is a good thing," Diana said eagerly. "A very good thing. Unless he was lying, of course. Gentlemen lie about titles all the time, just to impress ladies."

"He could have been, and I wouldn't know." Mary sighed, feeling foolish for having been so trusting. Her habit was to believe what people told her of themselves, which was, apparently, not the best advice when dealing with strange gentlemen. "He wouldn't even admit to having a home. He claimed he was a citizen of the world, at ease everywhere he traveled."

"Everywhere there's not a magistrate out to find him," Diana said wryly. "But now I'm being unfair, aren't I? Was he handsome? Young? Virile to a fault? Full of charm and honey-words?"

"Oh, yes," Mary said, remembering how his eyes danced and sparkled when he teased her. "And he made me laugh."

Diana raised her glass of lemon-water toward Mary. "Proving you have most excellent taste. Being my sister, I always thought you must. Oh, Mary, I'm so *excited* for you!"

Pointedly Mary glanced at the sleeping governess. "Miss Wood knew nothing of this."

"Likely Miss Wood already does. She knows *everything*," Diana whispered fiercely. "There's never keeping any secrets from her. She's a very hawk for secrets. Why else do you think we were rushed so from Calais?"

Mary frowned. She thought she'd been most circumspect regarding Lord John, but the haste with which Miss Wood had forced them to leave Calais argued otherwise. Maybe, for once, Diana was right.

Diana leaned closer. "So tell me, Mary, tell me! How did you find this paragon-lord at breakfast? Did he bring you shirred eggs and bacon, or beckon you with a pot of fresh tea?"

"He found me yesterday." Mary smiled, remembering. "He tried to buy the painting of the angel for me, but I wouldn't let him, and outbid him instead."

Diana wrinkled her nose. "You bought that awful picture because of him? Oh, Mary, that's more blame than any man can bear!"

"Wait, Diana, I must speak to you about that painting," Mary said, leaning closer. "I think there might be something—something peculiar about it."

"Oh, yes, rare ugliness such as that is—"

"Be quiet for once, and mark what I say," Mary said, lowering her voice further. "This morning, before we left Calais, the old Frenchman who sold me the picture came to the inn, and warned me about telling anyone I'd bought it. He begged me to keep everything about it a secret."

"Why?" Excitedly Diana bent forward, the coral beads of her earrings swaying against her cheeks with the carriage's motion. "What could be dangerous about a painting, especially a painting as ugly as that?"

Mary shook her head. "I don't know. I've hidden it away in my baggage, just to be sure. But all I can guess is that it's a forgery, and Monsieur Dumont wished me to help preserve his reputation by keeping it a secret."

"Then I'll gladly keep the old rascal's secret, for it's of no account to me," Diana said. "I'll swear I've never laid eyes upon the wretched thing. And I'll keep your secret, too, Mary."

"That I bought the picture?"

Diana winked slyly. "No, silly, about your gentleman."

Mary's smile tightened. "There's scarce anything to keep secret, Diana. Besides, you're traveling with Miss Wood and me to become more seemly in your behavior, not to corrupt mine."

But Diana only smiled wickedly, and uncorked the decanter that held the sweetened lemon-water. "I think we'd both fare better on this journey, Mary, if we reached a sort of compromise between us. I'll vow to behave with more decorum, and you must promise to strive for less."

"I'll do no such thing, you ninny!" exclaimed Mary indignantly. She'd already pledged to herself to be more adventurous. She didn't need to do the same with her sister, or even share her resolution. "Why should I make a ridiculous promise such as that?"

"Because mine would be equally ridiculous for me." Diana took Mary's glass from the hook built for the purpose into the coach's side. She refilled it, pressed it into Mary's hand, and then tapped her own glass to the rim of Mary's. "To forgetting whatever needs to be forgotten."

Mary pulled back her glass. "I won't drink such a preposterous toast. 'Tis far better to learn from past mistakes, than simply to forget them."

"Hush your squawking, Mary, else *you'll* wake Miss Wood." Diana glanced one more time at the sleeping governess. "Would you rather come all this way from home only to perish of tedium, smothered by the dust of old pictures and places?"

Mary thought again of the resolution she'd made. Even though she'd never see Lord John Fitzgerald again, he had immeasurably brightened her first days abroad. Shouldn't her adventures with him be a beginning for her, and not the end?

Diana touched her glass gently against Mary's. "Very well, then," she whispered. "We'll drink to the future. To Paris, Florence and Rome."

"To Paris, Florence and Rome," Mary repeated, then grinned. "And to—to adventure!"

It was nearly midnight by the time that John decided to return to his lodgings at Dessin's. He had done his best to put the day behind him. He'd drunk more than he should have, and he'd wagered more than he should have over cards. Yet the wine hadn't made him drunk enough, and the other gamesters had proved less skilled, depriving him of the punishment of losing. Nothing, it seemed, was going the way he'd wanted today, and there wasn't a damned thing he could do to change his luck.

He decided to walk rather than hire a chaise, his hat pulled

low and his hands in the pockets of his coat. Calais was not
Paris, and at this hour there were few others on the street with
him, the sound of the waves on the nearby shore clear
throughout the city. Only a girl as sheltered as Lady Mary
Farren could find Calais a city full of excitement and diversion, and despite his resolve not to think of her again, he
couldn't help smiling as he remembered how she'd practically hopped up and down with delight at the sight of the
basket weave *diligence*.

He'd known from the beginning that she'd never be more
than a diverting amusement for a day or two, an idle flirtation not meant to last. So why, then, did he feel so sorry for
himself that it had ended before it had truly begun?

His life was his own, to arrange as he pleased. He had women
enough in it, beautiful, clever, willing women, with rank and
money of their own. He didn't need to bend to the demands of
some high-nosed duke for the privilege of courting his daughter.

And yet, there'd been something about the girl, something
as indefinable as the painting of the angel, that made his
regret over her loss sting. He kicked at a stone in the street,
muttering halfhearted curses at his life and fate in general,
and turned down the last street.

He smelled the smoke before he saw the flames, heard the
shouts of the men running to the burning store with fire-
buckets heavy with sloshing water. Then John was running,
too, joining the growing crowd before the burning shop.
Blown by the breeze from the water, the bright orange flames
licked through the curving bow window, the panes of glass
shattering with the heat within. Like customers trapped
within, statues stood silhouetted against the fire, their somber
expressions lit one final time by the bright light. The flames
themselves shifted colors, burning blue, green, orange, with
each different treasure they consumed.

Another quarter hour, and Dumont's Antiquities would be gone.

"I'd wager the old miser set it himself," one man in the crowd said to no one in particular. "They say the magistrates were sniffing about him as it was, for selling forgeries."

"Burn the evidence, eh?" another man said, his face almost jovial by the firelight. "Save the gold first, then burn the lot!"

John pushed his way to the front of the crowd, squinting against the flames and smoke. "Has anyone seen Dumont?" he demanded. "He lived behind the store. He could still be inside."

"Eh, let Dumont go to the devil," someone called. "That's where he belongs!"

Drunk with excitement, the crowd laughed raucously and whooped like savages before the flames, doing nothing to help the few men with the fire-buckets.

But John refused to stand by and do nothing. Swiftly he tore off his coat, tied his handkerchief around his nose and mouth, and ran down the narrow alley to the back door of the shop. The heat gathered between the brick buildings felt as hot as the flames themselves, pushing against John like an invisible hand. Yet still he kept going, his eyes stinging from the smoke, squinting as he tried to make out the back door. To his surprise, it was half open, and with his shoe he kicked at it, and pushed his way inside the billowing smoke.

"Dumont!" he called, bending low to try to stay below the worst of the smoke. "Dumont, here!"

No answer came, nor did he expect one, not now. If the old man were still within, the flames would surely have caught him, if the smoke hadn't. Coughing himself, John turned, crouching along the floor, and felt something soft and heavy, clad in rough wool. A leg, Dumont's leg, and without pausing John grabbed it and began to pull, dragging the old man from the fire and into the yard behind the shop.

Clear of the fire, John dropped to his knees, coughing and wiping at his eyes with his sleeve. His lungs burned as if they were full of fire, too, and he gasped for breath, tears streaming down his cheeks. He felt a hand on his shoulder, but he was struggling too hard to breathe to be able to turn.

"Are you harmed, *monsieur? Monsieur?*"

At last John forced himself to look through his tears to the man beside him: an officer of the local police, in the blue and white uniform of the garrison near the water. In case of a fire such as this, the police would naturally take the place of a brigade, protecting the town and its people however was necessary.

He sat back on his heels, still struggling to breathe. Behind him he could feel the heat and the crackling of the flames, but at least now with the soldiers here, the fire would soon be controlled.

"I—I am fine," he croaked. "Dumont—where—"

"I am sorry, *monsieur,* but Monsieur Dumont is dead," the officer said. "He was already dead when you pulled him from the door. So much risk to you for nothing, eh?"

"The—smoke?" John asked. "Or the—the fire?" His eyes still smarting, he wearily turned toward the old man's body, stretched out on the dirt beside him. He wiped his eyes again, trying to make sense of what he saw.

Dumont's face was smudged with soot, his coat singed and his white hair on one side scorched high against his blistered temple. His hands were bound with a cord behind his back, a rag tied tight around his head to gag him into silence. The front of his shirt was black with soot, and crimson with a garish blossom of blood from the gunshot wound on his chest, soaking through his coat and the waist of his breeches, even splattered across his once-white thread stockings.

"Murder, *monsieur,*" the officer said, giving the body a disrespectful poke with the toe of his boot. "Murder, and nothing less."

With a muttered oath against ineptitude, the Comte de Archambault read the letter one last time, crumpled it in his weakened fist, then tossed it into the flames in the fireplace before him. The task he'd ordered had seemed simple enough, yet once again the men he'd hired had not been able to rise to the challenge.

Of course the old man in Calais would claim no knowledge of the painted angel. If this Dumont had possessed any sense of his trade, he would have recognized the value of the picture at once, perhaps even its significance. He must also have suspected it was stolen, from the nameless thief's nervousness as well as his willingness to sell it for so little.

Surely Dumont would then have held the painting for a favored customer, or at least one willing to pay mightily for it. He wouldn't have offered it to the pair of bullies who'd broken into his shop and threatened him. No wonder the old man had suffered an apoplexy before he could give any real information, leaving those impotent, incompetent hired fools to shoot an already dead man and set fire to his shop in their moronic frustration.

Archambault groaned, and tapped his cane against the grate with frustration of his own. Did those fools really believe he'd accept their pitiful explanations? Did they truly think he'd excuse their failure as he'd excused no other?

With another groan, he slid the red porcelain parrot an infinitesimal fraction to the left along the marble mantelpiece. There, now it was centered again, symmetrical as all life should be. It was beyond understanding why the maidservants could not dust his belongings without disordering them this way.

He grimaced, and rubbed his hand across his silk-covered belly, hoping to ease the pain twisting within. One more servant to be dismissed for incompetence with a feather duster, two more agents to give over anonymously to the authorities in Calais for the old man's murder. He would not have their guilt taint his conscience, not so soon before his soul must stand in judgment. Others would soon appear to fill their spots, anyway, and take his money. Obedience and loyalty should be so simple. Why was it this difficult for him to find?

He turned away from the fire, and smiled as his gaze lit upon the painting of the Blessed Mother that hung beside his bed. The painting had been left to him by his grandmother, and the legends of their family with it.

Serenity, he thought. *Serenity.* The Blessed Virgin stood with her blue cloak outstretched like wings to shelter the miserable world gathered around her skirts, mendicants of every kind finally receiving respite and succor from Her, the Mother of the world.

Why couldn't he find peace, too, he wondered bleakly? Why was there no comfort for him?

The pain in his stomach was worsening each day, the disease eating away at him from within. None of the surgeons' bleeding, or purges, or fasts, or enemas, or noxious potions had helped. He was going to die, likely before his fortieth birthday this winter. Some nights when he lay alone in his bed, the sheets soaked with sweat and his body wracked with agony, he would pray for the sweet release of death, even if it came at the peril of his mortal soul.

As slow and bent as a crab, he made his way across the

room to the painting. He had no wife, no children. He'd always thought there'd be time before him to marry and sire an heir. Now there wasn't. He'd squandered the life he'd been given, and ruined so many others for the sake of—of what? For pleasure, amusement, a demonstration of power, or simply to stave off boredom?

He gazed up at the painting. *This* was what he had left, for the days he had left. This was all that mattered now, and his only hope for redemption. The picture's power was not in its size—it was small enough to fit into the bottom of a traveling trunk—but in the perfection of every tiny brush-stroke, dedicated to the Blessed Virgin.

He could not look enough at the perfect oval face, full of compassion and understanding. He wanted that serenity. He wanted that peace, that grace, yet he knew he'd never have it until he fulfilled his promise. Two centuries of war and the cruel hand of man's greed had separated the pieces of the triptych, but Archambault had vowed to make the Blessed Mother's altar whole again before he died, for Her glory and his salvation.

Last spring his agents had found the panel that had originally hung to Her right, with Archambault's own ancestors kneeling in worship beneath a chorus of cherubim. The panels had been cleaned, the gilded gesso frames restored.

Yet still the left panel remained lost, a lopsided disgrace to the Blessed Mother's perfection. He'd dared to believe it had been discovered in Calais this week. He'd believed, and been disappointed again. All his money, all his power and connections, yet once again he'd been left empty-handed.

"Forgive me, my lady," he murmured hoarsely, bowing as low as he could over his cane. "By my honor, I will find it. I will not give up the quest. If you will only grant me the time, my lady, then it will be done."

* * *

With her head against Diana's shoulder, Mary drowsed in the coach. While yesterday they'd made effortless progress, stopping for dinner and then at a tolerable inn for the night, this day had been one tedious delay after another. One of the four post horses slated for their team had turned up lame before he'd even been put in the traces, and they'd been forced to wait until another could be brought.

Lord John had predicted that the large English coach would be too unwieldy on more narrow roads, and he'd unfortunately proved an accurate prophet. Over and over again they'd come up behind a farmer's wagon, and it had taken considerable quarreling between their driver and the farmer, and then even more considerable wrangling of the wagon with the coach before they could pass. There'd even been one time where they'd been stopped for a herd of cattle to be driven from one pasture to the next.

The day had been very warm, too, the sun hot on the coach's lacquered roof, and the leather cushions had soon grown sticky to the touch. The sweat had collected beneath Mary's hat and down her neck, sliding down to dampen her shift and stays, and trickled down the back of her legs above her garters, until all she could think of was reaching the next inn and shedding every stitch of her hot, confining clothing, no matter how indecorous or untoward.

Now with their lanterns lit, the driver was striving to make up the lost time with his weary team, driving them as fast as he dared through the dark so they could reach their inn for supper, and the night.

The coach bumped over a rut in the road, waking Mary enough that she pushed herself upright and stretched her arms before her. As sleepy as she was, she sensed that something was different with the coach. She could hear the a new tension in the driver's voice as he shouted to the postilions, and the way the men riding on top of the coach were moving around, talking sharply to one another. Shaking off her sleep, she slid along the seat to the window, pushing aside the curtain to peer out into the night.

A dark horse was racing up beside them, his rider dressed in black with a scarf over his face. The only part of him that showed in the faint light of the new moon was the long barrel of the pistol in his hand.

"Halt your team, driver, or I'll shoot you dead!" the rider shouted. "Damn your eyes and beg for your life, and test me if you dare!"

Now Mary could see there were two other mounted men with the first, all with their faces hidden and drawn pistols in their hands. As much as she wished to flee, to escape as fast as they could, she knew it wasn't possible, and so did their driver. Already the coach was slowing. There wouldn't be much time to plan what might happen next.

"Diana, Miss Wood!" she whispered, unable to hide her desperation as she shook them awake. "You must wake at once—at once! We're being stopped by highwaymen!"

"Highwaymen!" Diana jerked awake, and grabbed Mary's hand. "Oh, what shall we do? What shall we do?"

"We must remember that we are English ladies," Miss Wood said, though the tremor in her voice betrayed her fear. "We must not let them intimidate us, and we must put our trust in God."

But Mary was already spreading her handkerchief open on her knee.

"Give me your earrings, Diana," she demanded, unhooking the fat pearls—left to her by their mother, and far too dear to give up to a thief—from her own ears. She took Diana's coral drops and laid them on the handkerchief beside her pearls. She rolled the handkerchief tightly, tied it into a knot, and stuffed it deep into the recess in the paneling behind the lemon-water decanter. "I'll give them my silver bracelet if they demand it, and you can give them that ring. Miss Wood, is there a small purse of coins we can let them have—reluctantly, of course, to make a show of it?"

Miss Wood drew out her purse, her fingers shaking. "They told me there were no highwaymen in France, not on the Paris road. They told me we'd be safe, wherever we went. We should have waited for Monsieur Leclair after all! Oh, my ladies, what will I tell His Grace your father?"

"You'll tell him we were as brave as can be," Mary said, seizing Diana's hand. "Oh, heavens deliver us, there they are!"

The door to the carriage was jerked open by a man still on his horse. "Out with you," the man ordered. "Now, you damned sluts!"

Miss Wood gasped. "We are not sluts! We are English ladies, and we—"

"Shut your trap, and get down," the man ordered, waving his pistol as his horse danced around the coach. "It's not your sorry asses we want anyway."

Diana hopped down first. "I thought highwaymen were supposed to be the gentlemen of the road," she said with a disdainful twitch of her skirts. "I thought you were supposed to be *gallant.*"

"Hush, Diana, don't." Mary circled her arm around her sister's waist, as much to restrain her as to comfort her. The driver, the postilions, and their other servants were already standing on the grass with their hands raised. Poor Deborah was weeping softly, the tears running unchecked down her face, exactly the way Mary felt like doing. "For once in your life be quiet!"

But though the first man kept his pistol trained on them, the second and third had gone to the back of the coach and were pulling at their trunks and boxes, striking at the locks with the butts of their guns. It made no sense to Mary; though she'd no firsthand experience with highwaymen, all the ones she'd read or heard about had taken the passengers' belongings and money from their persons, and then fled. It was odd that these men would prefer to ransack their luggage instead, though perhaps French highwaymen were different from English.

But they'd spoken to them in English, hadn't they? She'd been too frightened at first to notice. Yet from the very beginning when they'd shouted at the driver, they'd used English. Here in France, Mary had already learned that most Frenchmen stubbornly stuck to their own tongue, even if they did know English. Could it be that they'd come after them specifically, that they'd hunted them down like special prey?

More frightened than before, she pulled closer to Diana. She ordered herself to think clearly, to pay heed that all that was happening to be able later to tell the magistrate. She must be brave; she must not be a wilting, weeping coward. She and Diana had pledged themselves to adventure, hadn't they? Was there anything more adventuresome than being robbed at gunpoint by a masked highwayman?

And it was then she heard the other horses, faintly in the distance. Was it reinforcements for these men, or saviors for them?

Diana heard it, too. "Mary, listen!" she whispered. "I think I—"

"I know," Mary whispered back. "I *know!*"

But the first highwayman now heard it, too. He wheeled his horse around toward the noise, and shouted to the others, this time in French.

"Look, Mary, *look!*" Diana cried, pointing down the road. Lumpy dark shapes in the distance must be the riders, growing closer with every second. There was a sudden flash among the shapes, and the pop of a gunshot. The first highwayman shouted again, waving frantically at the others, and though Mary didn't know the French words, she was quite sure he was swearing.

Mary grabbed Diana's arm. "Come with me! Hurry, hurry!"

While the riders drew closer and the highwaymen shouted among themselves, Mary and Diana ducked around the open door and darted around to the far side of the coach. On the other side of the road stood a small copse of overhanging trees and bushes, and Mary pulled Diana toward it.

"Get down behind the leaves, Diana," she whispered urgently. "A blind man could see these white gowns in the dark!"

"Why are we hiding, anyway?" Diana whispered back. "Look, those evil men are riding away, and they didn't get a single thing of ours, either!"

"You don't know that." Trunks and boxes lay scattered in the road with the contents tossed around, ghostly bits of stockings and shifts and open books with fluttering pages. "They could have tried to take us as hostages, you know. Father would have paid whatever they asked."

"If they'd taken us hostage, they would have ravished us," Diana said, without quite the horror such a statement deserved. "It's the same with pirates."

"Diana, don't speculate," Mary said. "We don't even know what those men were searching for."

Diana pushed the leaves aside. "Jewels and money, like every other thief. Or our virtue. Look, here come those other men we saw before!"

Mary grabbed Diana's skirts and pulled her back down behind the bush. "You ninny! You've no notion of who those men are, either, yet you're running off to greet them like conquering heroes! For all *you* know, they're even more evil and wicked than the ones that stopped the coach in the first place!"

"And *you* don't trust anyone, Mary," Diana said, but she stayed low.

"Lady Mary!" called Miss Wood faintly on the other side of the carriage. "Lady Diana! Oh, where in heavens have you gone!"

But before they called back, the group of other horsemen came thundering past them. They paid no heed to the coach, or to the bushes where Mary and Diana were hiding, but raced past to chase the highwaymen. Only one rider stopped, drawing his horse up short before the ring of frightened servants on the grass.

"Maybe he's going to take Miss Wood hostage," Diana said, peeping over the top. "Except that Father wouldn't pay any ransom above two shillings for her."

"Hush, Diana." She couldn't see the newcomer, hidden with his horse by the coach between them, but she could just make out his voice, calming the frightened servants.

It couldn't be, could it? Could he really have followed her here? Could he truly have come when she needed him most?

"Lady Mary!" he called. "If you can hear me, it's safe for you to come back!"

"It *is* him!" She stumbled from the bushes, ignoring how her skirts were snagging on the branches. She had to go to him now, *now*.

"Where are you going, Mary?" Diana demanded, miffed. "I thought we had to stay here, or be carried off for ransom?"

"No ransom," Mary called back over her shoulder. "We're safe now!"

Lord John Fitzgerald was standing in the middle of the servants, holding the reins of his horse in one gloved hand and his cocked hat in the other. As a lord, he'd every right to keep that hat on his head before those who were obviously his inferiors. But tonight as he stood before a group of people who'd been badly frightened, he'd obviously judged it more important to reassure those same people by showing his face in the light of the lanterns hanging from the coach than to reinforce his rank.

"I heard talk at the last inn of a dirty-looking bunch of rascals, asking after an English coach," he was saying. "I recognized the coach as yours, and told the keep. Apparently there's been a rash of robberies on this part of the road, enough that there's been a reward posted. Others near the tap heard us, and volunteered to come with me to try to catch the villains."

"A good thing it was you did, sir," the coach's driver said. "Those bastards were bent on wickedness, no mistake."

"Which is to say we all thank you, my lord," Mary said, stepping into the lantern's light. "You saved us, and we're each of us in your debt."

Miss Wood gasped, and ran to her, grabbing Mary's hand. "Oh, my lady, I'm so glad to see you're unharmed! Is Lady Diana—"

"She's safe, as well," Mary said. Lord John had turned to her, and the pleasure she saw in his face made her forget the rest of the night's fear, and forgive her doubts and uncertainties. He smiled, and she smiled in return.

It was as easy, and as complicated as that.

"Did you bring my strawberries, my lord?" she asked, forgetting, too, the half-dozen bewildered witnesses.

He shook his head, his gaze still locked with hers. "Alas, my lady, I fear I've failed you on that particular errand. But how glad I am to find you!"

"Forgive me, my lady," Miss Wood said, clearing her throat with a polite small cough, "but it would seem that you are, ah, acquainted with our savior?"

Lord John answered before Mary had to. "I met Lady Mary yesterday, when we both admired the same picture in a shop. She outbid me for it, too."

"I see." And clearly Miss Wood did, her round face turning thoughtful as she looked from him to Mary and back.

Beneath her scrutiny, Mary blushed, and remembered Diana's warning that it was next to impossible to keep such secrets from their governess.

"It was the picture of the angel," she said hastily. "The one no one else likes. But his lordship did. His lordship likes it as much as I do."

"'His lordship'?" Miss Wood's eyes widened with interest. "Forgive me, my lord, for not recognizing you."

"Lord John Fitzgerald, your servant, ma'am," he said, but his expression was somber as he looked to Mary. "You do still have that picture of the angel, my lady, don't you? It's still in your possession, isn't it?"

"Oh, yes, my lord," Mary said quickly, wondering at the change in his mood. "It's hidden away where no highwayman would ever think to look. I took special care with it after—after, that is, I bought it."

Had Monsieur Dumont included Lord John in his warning about the painting? She couldn't imagine a reason why, but in front of the servants, she'd decided to be careful, and keep the old man's secret for him. For now the painting was wrapped again in the old cloth, and tucked deep in the bottom of the wicker hamper that carried their extra food for traveling.

Miss Wood nodded with approval. "It's wise to look after one's belongings, my lady, though I must say I doubt that any highwaymen would be interested in such a picture."

"The painting may not appeal to modern tastes, ma'am, but I can assure you it is of great value." Though he spoke to Miss Wood, to Mary it seemed as if his smile were meant only for her. "I've always believed in taking care of whatever I hold dearest to me."

Overwhelmed, Mary ducked her chin. She who was seldom at a loss for words suddenly couldn't begin to find a single one to express what she felt. He'd as much as said he'd followed her here, and rescued her in the process, like a hero in a play or novel. She'd been brave herself, and now in a way she was being rewarded. How could she ever have wished for a better adventure than this?

"How perfectly grand to be considered so dear to you, kind sir!" Diana said behind her. "And how shall I ever, ever be able to thank you enough for what you've done for us?"

Diana's voice was velvety soft, the voice she always used with gentlemen, and Mary didn't have to turn to know her sister must be using all her usual tactics: standing languidly with her weight on one leg, one arm folded across her ribs and beneath her breasts to push them up even higher than her stays, her other hand toying with the long curled lock of golden-blond hair falling over one shoulder. It was always the same with Diana, and it always had the same efficient effect on the gentlemen. What choice did they have, really?

Including, to Mary's sorrow but not her surprise, Lord John. He drew back his shoulders and widened his smile, his gaze now so intent upon Diana that Mary might have ceased to exist.

"Your smile is thanks enough, miss," he said. "No gentleman would expect more."

"Expectations have nothing to do with what a gentleman deserves," Diana said, her words husky with promise. "Who says there are no gallants left in England today?"

"So long as there are ladies in peril, miss," he said, so blessedly *noble* that Mary felt her stomach lurch, "there will be gallants to defend their honor."

"How fortunate for me," Diana said. "An introduction to this hero, Mary, if you please."

Mary sighed, but dutifully did as she was asked, the way she had all her life. "Diana, Lord John Fitzgerald," she said softly. "Lord John, my sister Lady Diana Farren."

Chapter Five

It was one of the longest dinners that John could ever recall having to endure.

Not that it should have been that way. Because of his well-timed arrival on the road, frightening off the highwaymen, he'd been lauded as a hero, and invited to share the meal. The *fricassee du poulet* was better than he'd any reason to expect from a country inn along the Paris road, with wines that were far more palatable than those served at most tables in Grosvenor Square, the light champagne the prize of a nearby vineyard. The private dining room was pleasant enough, with a set of double doors and the windows thrown open to let in the warm summer night.

Few would fault the company, either. Oh, the governess was much like governesses everywhere, a round little wren of a woman given overmuch to pursing her thin lips and offering judgmental pronouncements as conversation.

But the other two ladies, the ones the governess was supposedly guarding, were a different matter entirely. Lady Diana was one of the most seductive creatures he'd ever met, with golden hair and enormous blue eyes, and the kind of lush figure that painters chose for Aphrodite. Yet as beautiful as Diana was, what John noticed—and likely every other sensible man under heaven—was her manner. The flattery, the innuendo, the warmest of welcoming all seemed a second nature to her when addressing a man, and while such effortless seduction might be entertaining in a mistress, it was disconcerting in the supposedly respectable daughter of an English peer.

The longer she cooed and preened across the table from him, the less at ease he became. She greeted every word he said with openmouthed astonishment, praising him as a hero, a genius, the most clever and handsome man ever born, and coupled it with the heady habit of leaning forward so he could more easily look down the front of her gown.

Now he was a man, and because he wasn't a saint, he did look. How could he help himself? But he didn't like himself for looking, and the view, once glimpsed, wasn't really anything he hadn't seen before. But what made him most uncomfortable about Lady Diana Farren was how thoroughly—and, he thought, rather ruthlessly—she overshadowed her sister.

Instead of the quick, vibrant girl he'd remembered from Calais, and earlier this evening beside the coach, the Lady Mary sitting on the other side of the table seemed quiet and withdrawn. Beside her golden sister, she seemed muted and subdued and almost sad. Whenever he tried to engage her, she answered as briefly as was politely possible, and then looked back down at her plate. He saw far more of her dark lashes shadowing her cheeks than the bright, intelligent eyes beneath them, and not once in the course of the meal did she smile. He knew; he watched for it, and was disappointed.

The case clock in the front room of the inn was chiming half-past eleven by the time the cloth was finally drawn from the table and the last dishes removed, and he'd yet to speak to Lady Mary. Lord only knew he was obligated to. There was so much he needed to say to her: about the fire, and Dumont's death, and his concerns that her painting of the angel was somehow related.

But he also wanted to tell her a few things that weren't so grim, things like how he'd been disappointed that she'd left Calais without saying goodbye and how often he'd thought of her since. Small, foolish things that he doubted he'd ever tell her now, anyway.

Especially not if he couldn't see her alone.

His frustration growing, he was the first to leave the table. "You must forgive me, ladies," he said, "but this had been a long day for me, and if I don't retire to my bed now, I fear I'll topple over snoring onto the table."

"Oh, you wouldn't snore, my lord," Diana said, rising in a single sinuous motion. "Not a fine gentleman like yourself!"

Miss Wood stood, too, her hands neatly folded at her waist. "I am sorry if we've kept you awake, my lord. It's likely past time for us to seek ours as well. Ladies?"

Quickly Lady Mary pushed back her chair, clearly ready to beat as hasty a retreat as she could. "Good night, my lord."

"One moment, Lady Mary," he said before she could dart past him. "I'd like to see the picture again, if Miss Wood permits it."

"Of course she may, my lord!" Miss Wood nodded her encouragement to Mary. "We could scarce refuse you any such small favor. If you tell me where the picture is in your things, my lady, I can fetch it down."

"I'll get it myself, Miss Wood," she said quickly, glad for the excuse to leave. "It's still hidden."

"Oh, Mary, no one's going to steal your wretched

picture," Diana scoffed. "Lord John's only asking to see it to be polite, anyway."

John smiled, barely hiding his irritation with Lady Diana. "I'm sorry, my lady, but I am quite interested in the picture, and in your sister's interpretation. Since it so offends your sensibilities, you're excused. Lady Mary and I will study it ourselves."

Lady Mary sputtered in protest. "No, no, not alone, my lord, not when—"

"There's no harm in a moment or two, my lady, not for the study and appreciation of the painting in such a public room," Miss Wood said. "His lordship has earned our confidence. Go now, my lady, find the picture. Lady Diana, you and I shall make our good-nights."

John couldn't tell which sister was more distraught as they left him, hardly a gratifying reaction. He half expected Lady Mary to disappear again, or at least send some excuse through a servant. But before he'd realized it, Lady Mary had returned, brandishing the picture in both hands before her like an Amazon with her shield—albeit a shield framed in heavy gold leaf.

"Here it is, my lord," she said, still refusing to meet his eye. "You can see it's still in perfect condition. I haven't harmed it in the least. Now if you'll please excuse me—"

"I won't excuse you at all, my lady," he said firmly. "We must talk."

Her eyes flew open with the old fire he remembered. "You cannot force me to stay if I don't wish it! You don't have—"

"Dumont is dead." There it was, as undeniable as if he'd tossed a burning beam from the old man's store on the dining table before them.

She caught her breath, pressing her hand over her mouth

for a quick moment. "That cannot be! I saw him yesterday, before we left Calais!"

"He was murdered last night."

"Murdered!" she cried, horrified. "You are certain?"

"I saw the body and the evidence for myself," he said heavily. "He'd been shot in the chest, and then his store set ablaze, to make it look an accident."

Her face was so full of disbelief that he shoved back the sleeves of his jacket and shirt and held his arm out for her to see, no, to *witness*. The hair had been singed away, the skin red and puffy from burns. It hurt like hell, too, but at least he was alive. He'd witnessed more than his share of gruesome sights—India in particular had been full of them— but he still couldn't shake the memory of Dumont's face, half of it seared and red and burned, and the other still clinging to the final shocked expression with which he'd greeted his murder.

"I was there," he said grimly. "I saw it. I pulled Dumont's body from the flames."

"Oh, my lord, what great risk to you!" she cried, her voice squeaking upwards. "What if you'd been killed, too, if they'd murdered you, and—"

He glanced back at the door to the hall, the chattering voices of other patrons not far away. This was not a conversation he wished anyone to overhear.

"Come, let's go outside," he said, taking her gently by the arm. "You don't know who may be listening."

She nodded, understanding that much. He held his hand out to carry the painting for her, but instead she hugged it close to her chest.

"If I hadn't bought the picture when I did," she said, her voice trembling, "it would have been destroyed. Three hundred years, and then gone."

"Bring it with you. For God's sake, don't leave it behind." He guided her through the open doors, through the small yard and down the bank that led to a nearby stream. There they'd be hidden from the inn by the trailing willow branches and their words masked by the brook's running water.

She turned to him, her eyes enormous by the light of the new moon. "What did the magistrates tell you in Calais? Have they any suspects in this hideous murder and arson?"

"This is France, my lady, not England," he said, not hiding his bitterness. "Dumont was an old man without family or important friends, unloved and unlamented. Such men are not mourned in this land, nor do they receive justice. What can be salvaged from his store will be sold at auction, with all profits recognized belonging to the French king."

"That is hardly fair!"

"No, my lady, that is not England," he said. "You'll be well-advised not to die here, either, or your property will be likewise confiscated, and I swear that's the truth."

"Then tell me another truth, my lord." Accepting Dumont's death, her face seemed more resolute, more determined. "Tell me why you followed me here, and how I am linked in your thoughts to this fire. You did come after me, didn't you? It was not pure coincidence, as you let Miss Wood believe?"

"Not coincidence, no," he admitted. "But I couldn't speak freely without knowing which of your servants are to be trusted."

"All of them," she said loyally. "My father wouldn't keep them otherwise."

"As you please," he said, cocking a single skeptical brow. "The truth. I hired those men in Calais, meaning to offer them as an escort to you if you wished. I'd never guessed they'd be needed so soon."

"That was most thoughtful of you," she said quietly. "When we left, we'd no notion we'd need of such a guard. If our bearleader had been with us, I suppose he might have warned us, but—"

"He should have warned you, indeed," he said, angry with the man for not protecting them better. He'd had to pay a good deal more for the guards' services than he could really afford, and he'd expected a better effort in return. As it was, he'd had to leave his lodgings in Calais with purposeful haste, before the innkeeper had had time to realize John had shorted him on the reckoning—only temporarily, of course—so he'd the hard money to pay these worthless guards. "Where the devil was the rascal?"

"In Paris," she said, as if this were explanation enough. "Because his mother was ill, he begged our understanding for not coming to us in Calais. He's to join us now in Paris instead."

"He should never join you at all," he said bluntly. "A sick mother! I cannot believe you'd all believe such a preposterous excuse!"

"What I believe in is good faith and trust!"

"What you should believe in, my lady, is your own welfare," he said. "Do not forget that England and France have been at war more often in your lifetime than not. Consider how little regard a traveling Frenchman receives in London, and reverse that low regard upon yourself. In France it doesn't matter that your father's a peer, or that he's richer than Croesus. You're *English,* and few Frenchmen will see past that."

She gave her head an impatient shake. "I refuse to see how—"

"No, my lady, you must hear this," he said firmly. "There's no good faith and trust here for you. All the French will see is another English lady to part from her money, and nothing more. Likely this bearleader of yours has another pack of wealthy tourists dawdling on his string in Paris, and he's loath to part with them until he's thoroughly emptied their purses."

"That's barbarously unkind of you!"

"It's likely barbarously true, too," he said, "as you know."

She scowled, proof enough that she did in fact share that bit of unpalatable knowledge. "Did your men catch the thieves?"

"No." *Touché,* he thought. The men he'd hired had returned empty-handed, chagrined that the others had escaped. "But to be sure of your safety, I'll order them to accompany you to Paris."

"I thank you," she said, "but now that the thieves are gone, I'm not sure such a guard is necessary."

"I believe it is, my lady." He thought her thanks felt grudging, under the circumstances. "Otherwise I wouldn't offer."

"Will you be accompanying us, too?"

He wished he knew if she wanted him to come along or not. "I'd planned to leave for England this week. I've business in London."

"Of course." She looked down at the painting. "I thought he'd be my guardian angel, but it rather seems as if I'm the one keeping him safe. You, too. You're making a splendid case for the role."

He wasn't sure how to answer that. He wasn't even sure if she were serious. He longed for her favor, unlike her sister's false praise. Yet because it *was* Mary, and after that chilly dinner, he perversely rebuffed this compliment now, not letting himself trust it, and instead let the comment pass as if she'd never spoken at all.

"When you returned to Dumont's shop yesterday," he said, "did you see anything out of the ordinary, anything different from when you'd been there before?"

She frowned. "But I didn't return to the shop. I hadn't time before we left, and besides, I'd spent so dearly there the day before, I was loath to return."

"Yet you said you saw Dumont?"

"He came to find me at the inn," she said. "While you went to buy the strawberries, Monsieur Dumont called to me from the side of the inn. He was upset, my lord, so distraught that his manner made me—made me uneasy."

John nodded. He didn't want to make her uneasy himself, but this was more complicated—and more dangerous—than he'd first thought.

"What did Dumont say to make you upset?" he asked gently. "Did he try to buy the painting back from you?"

"Oh, no," she said. "He never mentioned that. Instead he wanted me not to tell anyone I had the painting, or tell that I'd bought it from him. He practically ordered me to keep everything a secret."

"Did he give you the reason for such secrecy?"

"He was in too much hurry for that," she said, "or perhaps he simply had no wish to tell me. I guessed it might be just as you'd said, that the picture was a forgery, and Monsieur Dumont feared for his reputation if others learned that he'd sold a false picture as genuine. Not that I cared. I'd still like the painting, no matter who painted it, or when."

"I wish it were as simple as that," he said, "but it's not. Dumont's been selling forgeries for years, mostly to English gentry on their continental tour who, like you, don't give a fig whether they've been taken for a fool or not."

She wrinkled her nose. "How nice of you to lump me in with that lot, even if it's true."

"I told you, no one cared, any more than you do," he said, refusing to let himself be distracted by that charmingly wrinkled small nose. "But Dumont's warning worried you enough that you hid the painting as you traveled?"

She smiled sheepishly. "It sounds superstitious, I know, but if he'd gone to such lengths to warn me, I felt I should do my best to protect the picture."

"Your hiding place may have saved it from the thieves tonight." He paused, trying to decide how much to tell her. He didn't want to frighten her for no reason, but it would be criminal not to warn her of what he feared was a genuine danger. "They showed no interest in your jewels or money, did they?"

Her eyes widened with surprise. "How did you guess? I'd hidden my mother's jewels because they couldn't be replaced, but the man that stopped us never even asked."

He saw that her ears were bare, without the heavy pearl drops he'd come to associate with her. "Yet they rummaged like gypsies through your trunks, and took nothing."

He reached out and turned the painting toward him. "I still don't know why, my lady, but I'd wager they wanted this, just as I'd wager that, with a last twinge of conscience, poor old Dumont regretted putting you in their path."

"Meaning he was murdered because of me?" she asked miserably.

"No, because of him." He took the painting from her and propped it in the wide crook of the nearest willow. The halo and wings gleamed dully in the moonlight, the angel's face turning ghostly pale. "The real question is why. What is it about this painting that makes people willing to kill—and to die—for it?"

She reached out and lightly traced the frame with her fore-finger, each of the four sides in turn. "After you said it might be a forgery, I took it back to my room, and studied it, truly studied it, for anything wrongful that I might spy. And there was nothing, my lord. No patches of new paint, or misplaced gold leaf, or brushstrokes that seemed an afterthought. Nothing."

He trusted her eye and her instinct. He wasn't sure why, given her lack of experience, but he did. Hadn't he learned long ago that there were plenty of things in life that could only be felt, not taught?

"Did you check the frame as well?" he asked. "That's newer, you know."

"Oh, I *know*," she said, showing all the confidence she'd so lacked at dinner. "Gold leaf over gesso, most likely only twenty or thirty years old. And it's been cut down from a larger picture, too: the border doesn't match in these corners."

He hadn't noticed that before, but now he did. The frame's border of curling oak leaves and acorns was mitered awkwardly, so the branches didn't match the way they did on the other two corners. He'd been right to trust that eye of hers— or rather, both of them, and lovely, clever eyes they were as they gazed up at him now.

"So of course you checked the inside of the frame, as well?"

"What, to make certain it hadn't been hollowed out, and pirates' doubloons stuffed inside?" She was trying to jest, but both of them realized this was too serious for that.

She sighed, and rested her palm on the frame, almost as if to comfort it. "No, the frame is fine. It's fine. All that caught my eye was a faded black scribble of crayon across the back, old enough to have been the mark of whomever sold the panel to the painter."

"Not enough for murder."

"Hardly." She folded her arms, as if bracing herself for more unfortunate news. "So if my angel is more of a magnet for trouble than a guardian for me, what should I do with him?"

"The wisest course would be to sell him," he answered. He'd considered this long and hard on the ride from Calais, and if he were honest, selling really was the only answer. "In Paris, as publicly as you can, so that whoever is trying to get it so badly can't avoid hearing of it. For your peace and safety, you've no real choice."

She glanced again at the painting, and didn't consider more than a moment. "And what if I don't wish to sell the picture? What if I refuse to take the wisest course?"

"Then you are either very foolish," he said softly, "or very brave."

The long willow branches rippled behind her and before her, the narrow leaves like feathers in the breeze. He took a step closer to her, brushing aside one of the branches that had blown between them. She held her ground and did not move, but he saw how her fingers tightened on her folded arms.

"Once you tried to buy the picture for yourself, my lord, and failed," she countered. "How do I know your advice is true? How can I be sure that it's not merely your way to get the painting away from me?"

"Because if that were true, all I'd have to do now is take it," he said, reaching out to hold his hands close to the sides of the frame without actually touching it. "You couldn't stop me, nor would you begin to know where to find me."

She narrowed her eyes, judging him. "You wouldn't do that, my lord."

"No?" He looked down at her, keeping his hands beside the painting as if ready to steal it away. "How do you know I won't?"

"Because I trust you, my lord," she said without hesitation.

He hadn't expected *that*. "Why?" he asked, amused. "Most ladies in your situation wouldn't, and I haven't given you any reason to do so."

"But you have," she said evenly. "You understood the merit of that picture the instant you saw it—not just its value, but its power. You couldn't feign that. Which means that by trusting you I am either very brave, my lord, or very foolish."

He chuckled and let his hands drop away from the painting. "Tell me which you are."

She tipped her head, and smiled with such supreme confidence he nearly laughed aloud.

"I am sorry, my lord," she said, "but you must decide for yourself."

"First you must stop this lordly nonsense," he said, "and call me by my given name alone."

"Very well." Her smile twisted wryly to one side. "Very well, *John*."

He cupped her jaw with his palm, turning her face up to his. "Then I should say you're brave, Mary," he said, his mouth just over her lips. "Very, very brave."

That was reason enough to kiss her then, to take her into his arms and coax her lips to part. She tasted at once sweet with innocence and spiced with eagerness, and not a glimmer of well-bred, maidenly reluctance. He'd sensed from the first that she was different from all the other young ladies in London, and he'd been right. She was brave, and no more afraid to return his kiss than she'd been to show her intelligence. He'd always liked a clever woman, and he liked one who could kiss with such abandon even better. His arms tightened around her, drawing her close against him, and she arched into him, resting her hands lightly on his shoulders.

He could feel the soft swell of her breasts pressing against his chest, above the stiffened bones of her stays.

How many favors would she grant him, he wondered? How adventurous did she really mean to be, here beneath the willows?

Hungrily he deepened the kiss, and she took him, her breathy sigh lost between their joined mouths.

From the open window of the inn's kitchen came a rattling crash of a dropped pan or kettle, followed by the outraged cook's screech and the poor scullery maid's wail. Startled by the noise, Mary broke away to look away from him and back to the inn.

"It's nothing, pet," he whispered, turning her face back toward him. "We're in France, you know. Here everyone shouts and breaks the crockery."

She smiled, brushing aside a stray lock of hair that the breeze had blown across her forehead. "I suppose I'm not so brave after all."

"Oh, but you are," he said. "You held fast, and wouldn't let me buy the painting ahead of you."

Her smile widened with pleasure that he instantly felt in return.

"What I paid was far too dear," she admitted, "but I kept it from you."

He laughed softly. "Yes, you did. And you actually considered running off with me to Paris in the *diligence.* Oh, I know in the end you didn't, but you considered it, which must have taken a goodly share of courage."

She laughed, too, a rich, warm little laugh that delighted him. "You told me to be more adventurous with my life."

"You are, and you will be," he continued. "Why, you were adventurous enough to keep the painting from falling into the hands of the highwaymen!"

She sighed. "That wasn't adventure. That was caution. I'm already an expert at that."

"But taking advantage of the confusion around your coach to flee with your sister, and keep the two of you from falling into their hands—that was thoroughly adventurous." He nodded sagely. "I can't think of another woman I've known who would have acted with such assurance."

She didn't believe him, or didn't want to believe him; it amounted to much the same. "Truly?"

"Truly," he said, sliding his hand along her arm, bare below her sleeve. Her skin was impossibly soft, and seductively cool beneath his own fire-roughened hands. "The only time I've seen your bravery waver was at dinner tonight with your sister."

At once she stiffened beneath his touch. "Why should my sister make me less brave?"

"I haven't a clue," he said, running the backs of his fingers over her cheek. "But you were different at dinner. Quieter. More somber. Willing to let your sister steal your thunder."

She brushed his hand away from her face. "Of course when I'm with my sister I'll be different than when I'm with you, John."

He laughed. "I should hope so!"

"That's not what I meant," she said, her voice decidedly tart. "I meant that despite what you may believe, there is a sympathy, an understanding, between my sister and me that I could never have with anyone else."

"Then she had a pretty way of showing it, Mary," he said, incredulous. "The velvet sighs and fluttered eyelashes were particularly—"

"You flatter yourself, *my lord*," she said sharply, with pointed emphasis on his title. "My sister has a warm-hearted manner with gentlemen, true, but it is a general manner, and not specific to you."

"But considering how she—"

"*Especially* not to you, my lord."

Too late he now realized he'd erred. The devil take him for a fool for mentioning another woman to the one in his arms—even if they were sisters.

"I'm sorry if I misspoke, my lady." He was willing to apologize if that could return them to where they'd been only a few moments earlier. "I meant no insult to you, or your sister."

"I'm sorry, too," she said, slipping free of him to stand just out of his reach. "I've scarcely known you for three days, my lord. I've known my sister since I was born, and I won't hear you speak ill of her now."

He folded his arms over his chest and frowned, as much at having his words misinterpreted as from seeing her willingness evaporate. He'd rescued her, praised both her person and her acuity, coaxed her, petted her, kissed her. What else could the woman possibly want?

Standing apart from him as she was, her lovely face was criss-crossed by the shadows of the willow branches and the moonlight, her expression completely unreadable to him. If this was how it was going to be with her, then he should leave now. There was no question of him going as far as Paris with them, anyway. He could be back in Calais in time to catch the packet to Dover at the end of the week. He'd cut his losses and put her from his mind, and look instead to whatever amusing new lady the future might place in his path.

He would leave *now*.

"If I ever speak ill of your sister, you will know it," he said irritably. "You'll know that—"

"I know what I know, my lord," she said, matching his irritation. "And what I *know,* my lord, is that I've no further wish to know you. Good night, my lord, and goodbye."

She darted forward and snatched the painting from the crook of the tree, and before he could stop her, she was marching up the hill away from him and back toward the inn, or marching as well as she could with her skirts hobbling her through the dew-soaked grass.

But he'd be damned if he'd let that wretched goodbye of hers stand as their last.

"Time to rise, my ladies!" Miss Wood entered their room with the maidservant carrying their breakfast tray. She drew the curtains on the bed with what Mary thought was an unnecessary flourish, the metal rings scraping and screeching along the rods and the sunlight bright enough to make both Mary and Diana wince and pull the coverlet over their faces.

Miss Wood was unmoved. "No dawdling now, sleepy-heads," she said with her usual cheerfulness. "We must keep to our schedule if we're to reach Amiens. Lady Mary, I'd think you'd be particularly eager, given your interest in the Romish cathedral there."

But while the ancient cathedral at Amiens was in fact one of the sights Mary wished to see on the Continent, the first thing she thought of this particular morning had nothing to do with rose windows or carved stone buttresses. Instead she thought of last night, and all that she and Lord John Fitzgerald had said and done, and how, at the last, she'd made an intemperate, righteous fool of herself.

Ignoring Miss Wood, she groaned at the memory of last night, and turned to bury her face in her pillow. Whatever spark of an adventure she'd had with Lord John was gone now, snuffed away by with her heavy-handed outrage. And over what, really? She'd defended Diana the same way she always did whenever others made sly remarks about her sister and her behavior. He'd no more right to slander Diana than any other man.

And yet his criticism had been different. True, he'd spoken lightly of Diana, the way other gentlemen had, but afterwards, when Mary had considered his words, she realized that in an odd way he'd meant to defend *her*. She guessed he'd intended it as some sort of peculiar compliment, speaking lightly of her sister to raise Mary up higher in his estimation, but if so, then he'd overlooked the loyalty she and her sister felt for one another. Was it any wonder that, in her confusion, she'd reacted as she had? Or was it any wonder, either, that he'd likely accept her farewell as the final words between them?

"*You* were late coming in last night," whispered Diana beside her, her voice still groggy with sleep. "I was long asleep before you returned. You and that Lord John must have found a great deal in that silly painting to discuss."

"You were asleep, *and* snoring." Mary slid to the edge of the bed and reached up under the frame. Blindly she groped about until she found the flat, familiar bundle of the painting, tied into the rope bedsprings where she'd hidden it last night.

"What are you doing?" Diana asked, propping her head up on one bent arm. "Looking for lovers hiding under the bed?"

"Only the ones you've hidden there." Mary sat upright and swung her bare legs over the edge of the bed. The bedstead was very high in the style the French seemed to prefer, so high that her dangling feet didn't touch the floor as she stretched her arms over her head. "What time is it, Miss Wood?"

"Half-past seven, my lady." The governess took the breakfast tray from the table and set it squarely in the middle of the bed. Behind her their maid had opened their trunks and was packing away the gowns and stockings and ribbons they'd worn yesterday in preparation for leaving. "High time you two ate and dressed, so we can be on our way."

"I'm not that hungry." Mary poured herself a dish of sugared cream with a splash of tea and slipped from the bed. "I'll dress in a moment."

With the tea-dish in hand, she padded barefoot to the window. Another fair day, with fat bumblebees buzzing lazily around the red trumpet flowers on the vines curling up the inn's timbered wall. She leaned a little farther out the window, looking toward the yard. The grooms were tending to their coach, wiping the splattered dirt and dust of the road away from the dark blue lacquered sides, and giving extra care to her father's ducal coat of arms, picked out in gold leaf on the door.

She'd never given much thought to what that coat of arms symbolized. It had simply always been there, ready to ease her family's way and protect them with privilege wherever they chose to ride behind it. Could that coat of arms really be as powerless here in France as Lord John had told her last night? Were she and her sister really so vulnerable here abroad, so ripe for the taking by every thief and sharpster, and even their own bearleader?

"Come away from that window at once, Lady Mary," Miss Wood scolded. "It's hardly proper for you to display yourself in your shift like that."

"Maybe Mary wishes to display herself." Diana smiled wickedly with her mouth bristling with crumbs from the roll in her hand. "Maybe she's hoping that Lord John Fitzgerald will be below, and gaze up at her in rapture, just like Romeo and Juliet."

Mary gasped with indignation, and guilt, too, but Miss Wood came instantly to her defense.

"That is neither kind, nor true, Lady Diana," she said severely. "Your sister has always behaved with impeccable decorum with gentlemen. You would do better to learn from her example rather than teasing her about his lordship."

Diana shrugged, unrepentant, her lace-trimmed night rail slithering down her bare shoulder and her golden braid unraveling into sinuous waves.

"Perhaps Mary would do better learning from my example where his lordship is concerned," she said, delicately pulling apart the flaky layers of the crescent-shaped roll in her hand. "Perhaps she already has."

"Oh, yes, as if I'd take lessons from you, Diana," Mary said, even as her cheeks flushed with private misery. Whatever other sins Diana might commit, she wouldn't have kissed a man and then harangued him like a vengeful harpy. "I shouldn't wish to think of what *you* would teach!"

"Exactly what you need to learn," Diana said, biting the roll. "That's why Father sent me with you, you know. So did Lord John kiss you last night in the moonlight, Mary, or did you kiss him?"

"As if I'd tell you any such thing, Diana." Mary dropped her tea-dish back onto the tray with an indignant clatter. Indignation was the only defense she could muster against Diana, and even she'd admit it didn't hold much water.

But it was still enough for Miss Wood. "It's too early in the morning for such foolishness, my lady," she said sternly. "Now come along, rise and dress yourself, and stop dithering on and agitating your sister."

"Besides, Diana, whatever implications you make don't matter a whit to me," Mary said. There was no way under heaven she'd discuss that kiss with Diana. It had been something passionate, something rare, something Diana, with more kisses than she could ever recall, would never understand. "His lordship is already returning directly to Calais, and then to London, so most likely we'll never see him again."

"Forgive me, my lady," Miss Wood said. "But that is no longer true. I spoke with his lordship earlier, while you were sleeping, and he has decided to change his plans. He is such a thoughtful gentleman! I understand, my lady, that you told him last night of poor Monsieur Leclair's delay, and his lordship was so sympathetic, and so concerned for our welfare without a bearleader to guide us, that he offered to assume the role himself, and accompany us to Paris."

"He *has?*" Mary cried with more alarm than joy. She had resigned herself to never seeing John again. Now if he were to travel with them, she'd be faced with all kinds of difficult questions. What would she say? How was she to behave? However would she face him after last night? "He *hasn't!*"

Diana laughed gleefully. "So you must have kissed him well enough after all, Mary, for him to wish to linger for more!"

But Mary had hurried back to the window, craning her neck to see their coach once again. He couldn't possibly be traveling with them all the way to Paris, not after last night. Yet there he was already waiting in the yard, exactly as she'd feared he would be, chatting and laughing with the grooms and stable boys and the footmen. John looked as merry as could be on this sunny morning, as if he'd not spent last evening speaking to her of murder and arson and thievery, of why her picture held such a great secret that others would kill to possess it, of her sister's velvet sighs and fluttering lashes.

As if he'd not kissed her with a hunger and urgency she'd never forget, a kiss that had left her vulnerable and confused.

"His lordship will make quite a splendid addition to our

little party for now, I think," Miss Wood was saying with satisfaction beside her. "And he spoke so highly and with such admiration of you, my lady, that I was sure you'd be pleased in return."

"Oh, yes," murmured Mary unhappily. "Most pleased indeed."

Chapter Six

"So tell us, friar," John asked, pausing to study the vast tiled floor of the Amiens Cathédrale Notre-Dame, stretching through the nave before them. "Is it true that the Romish worshipers would crawl on their knees along this very floor, clear to the altar?"

The old monk that was their guide nodded solemnly, his tonsured head gleaming faintly in the half-light that filtered down from the clerestory. "It is true, my lord. You see the pattern in which the tiles are laid, a labyrinth twisting like a snail's shell. The most faithful pilgrims would pray and follow every turn upon their knees, and offer up their pain as an unworthy gift to God."

"Gracious," murmured Miss Wood, her little gloved hand holding tight to the crook of John's arm. "What a painful way to affirm one's faith!"

"There are many paths to true righteousness, miss, and none are easy," droned the monk, not bothering to hide his weariness. Beyond him a half dozen elderly women swept the tiles with brooms as gnarled as themselves. "That is what the labyrinth signifies. Though the tiles are worn and cracked now, it is said that when this floor was new, so many pilgrims came here to pledge their faith that the white stone was stained crimson with the blood from their penitent knees."

"A righteous mess, if you ask me," whispered Diana behind her fan. "How you can find these gruesome old tales interesting is beyond me, Mary."

"Hush, Diana!" Mary ordered back in a fierce whisper. She doubted the old monk could hear Diana, as she and her sister walked some paces back from him, John and Miss Wood, but she was in no humor for Diana's flippancy today. "Even if you do not agree with another's faith, you can still respect it."

"Lah, Mary, there's a pulpit," Diana said. "Why don't you go climb its ladder, so you can preach more properly?"

"Stop it, Diana," Mary snapped. "Even you must be able to find beauty somewhere around you. That carved panel, or the stonework, or the colors of the window-glass."

"Or his lordship our substitute bearleader." Diana narrowed her eyes, appraising John as if seeing him for the first time. "He's a handsome sight, isn't he?"

Mary sighed with frustration. He *was* a handsome sight; there was little use in arguing that. Beneath his dark cocked hat, he wore buff-colored breeches and a cream linen coat without a waistcoat on account of the warmth, his shirt carelessly open at the throat with a loose knotted scarf beneath the collar instead of a neckcloth. Yet everything was still tailored to perfection, the nonchalance of his dress only serving to emphasize the breadth of his shoulders and the leanness of his body, and, most of all, the easy confidence that he wore like another suit of clothes.

Ever since he'd taken on the role of their guide at the inn near Abbeville, he'd been a model of decorum and efficient charm. He'd addressed her once again as Lady Mary, as if the kiss they'd shared had never happened. He'd been polite and respectful, but nothing more. He'd ridden on horseback alongside the coach and not far from the mounted escort he'd provided, and neatly avoided any inappropriate conversation. He'd been as informative as any hired bearleader, too, full of amusing stories about the countryside through which they journeyed. Miss Wood could not sing his praises loudly enough, and considering how he'd attended her more closely than either Mary or Diana, the governess had every right to be pleased.

"Do you think he's taken with Miss Wood?" Diana asked idly. "Perhaps he fancies governesses. They say some gentlemen like that, you know, being scolded and whipped like little babies. Miss Wood could certainly oblige. She's had enough experience ordering us about."

"How should I know what he fancies, Diana?" Mary asked, more plaintively than she could have wished. "It's not as if he's telling me."

Diana glanced at her with curiosity. "In Abbeville, I'd thought he rather fancied *you*, and you him. But since then the two of you scarce speak, which is hardly the way to fancy anyone."

They were passing a cluster of black-clad Frenchwomen, deep in their devotions, giving Mary another few moments to think before she answered.

"I do not know what Lord John's feelings are toward me," she said carefully. "I did enjoy his company in Calais. I won't deny it. We spoke of art."

"Art, hah," scoffed Diana. "That's not why men speak to women."

"With him it was," Mary insisted, even though she now doubted it herself. "What I cannot fathom is why he has attached himself to our party, and insisted on hiring those guards for us, too."

Diana nodded. "I've wondered that myself. It must be for your sake. I can conceive of no other reason."

Mary thought once again of the painting. John had not mentioned it again, nor had she, but still she'd taken care to hide it in different places among her belongings and in their lodgings. Her only question was who exactly she was hiding it from.

"Then it must be Miss Wood," Mary said glumly. "She's not nearly so opinionated as I. She'll agree with whatever he's telling her, just like she does with Father."

"You know more about pictures than she ever will," Diana said with gratifying loyalty. "A hundred times more. If that's what he wants to natter on about, then he should be doing it with you. At least you'll natter with assurance."

"He'll do what he pleases," Mary said with resignation. "Gentlemen always do. Now it's up to me to do the same."

"Not quite yet." Critically she smoothed Mary's hair beneath the frame of her hat, twisting a few loose curls into shape around her face. Then Diana folded her fan, and before Mary could stop her, she'd rejoined John, Miss Wood, and their guide.

"Tell me, Miss Wood," she began. "How much longer must we traipse through this gloomy old church?"

Miss Wood frowned. "We've only begun to see the cathedral, my lady. Why, Father Simon was just explaining how the cathedral was built to house the severed head of St. John the Baptist, brought back from the Holy Wars by the Crusaders. You do recall the Crusaders from our lessons, don't you, my lady?"

"St. John's head?" asked Diana with horrified fascination. "His *head* is here?"

"Yes, my lady, the French Catholics consider it to be among the holiest of relics, and believe that it can bring about miracles," Miss Wood said with uncharacteristic relish. "Father Simon says it's in a wonderful state of preservation inside its special reliquary."

"Is that so." Diana drew her handkerchief from her sleeve, fluttered her eyes shut, and dabbed delicately at her temple. "Miss Wood, I should like to sit. I—I do not feel quite myself."

At once Mary took her sister's arm. "You go ahead, Miss Wood, and I'll sit with her."

Surreptitiously Diana dug her thumb into Mary's hand to signify that this was not what she wished, even as she swayed against Mary for support.

"I should like you to stay with me, Miss Wood," she said faintly. "You are my—my comfort, and I know Mary would like to see the—the preserved saint's head."

"Whatever you wish, my lady," Miss Wood said, bustling forward to slip her arm around Diana's waist and ease her weight from Mary. "You should have told me before that you were feeling ill."

The old monk watched, his expression unchanged. "The cathedral keeps a withdrawing room for ladies, with light refreshments," he said. "Would it please her ladyship to retire there?"

"That would be most kind," Miss Wood said. "If you would but show us the way."

The monk bowed silently, and held out his open palm. John sighed with resignation, and pressed the necessary coin into the monk's hand. He bowed again, and turned to lead them. Mary began to follow Miss Wood, but Diana waved her away.

"You stay with his lordship, Mary," she urged wanly. "I would not wish to spoil your—your appreciation of the handsome sights."

Finally Mary realized what Diana was doing for her; that

last comment about the "handsome sights" left little doubt. She should be grateful, for Diana had meant it well, as a favor. But if things with John went as disastrously as she feared they might, then Mary would have nothing good to say later about her sister's interfering.

"Perhaps we should all return to the inn together, if Lady Diana isn't well," John said, looking solemn and responsible. "The cathedral has been here for five hundred years. I'd wager it will be here for us tomorrow, as well."

"No, no, my lord, that's not necessary," Miss Wood insisted. "I know Lady Mary wished most specifically to view Notre-Dame, and I trust her to your care. You can return to the inn when you please, and Lady Diana and I will do the same."

With that she turned away with Diana, following Father Simon into the shadowy passages.

And leaving her alone with John.

Self-consciously Mary cleared her throat. Surely the best course would be to act as if nothing had happened between them, either good or bad.

"Well, now, my lord," she said brightly—too brightly. "Here we are. What would you care to see next?"

His smile was genial but wary at the same time. "Do you truly wish to see the reliquary?"

"With the ancient but well-preserved head?" She shuddered. "No. Nor, I should think, would you, for all that the head belongs to your patron saint."

His smile relaxed a fraction. "Fortunately patron saints have fewer responsibilities in England. I'd hate to trust my fortunes to the poor fellow who lost his head at the request of a dancing-girl."

"Hush, you shouldn't make such jests here," she whispered, but she'd relaxed, too. "I've read that the carvings along the choir stalls are most impressive."

"Then let us go be duly impressed," he said. He'd stepped into the path of sunlight through a stained-glass window, half of his light-colored coat turned into a harlequin dapple of red, green and blue. "We can find them well enough without our guide. Can you believe that even a holy man in France expects his garnish?"

"You warned me it was so."

His smile faded. "I've warned you of many things," he said softly, and offered her his arm.

They walked slowly down the long nave of the cathedral, their footsteps echoing against the stone walls. At this hour of the morning, the morning mass was done, and there were only a few worshippers and pilgrims scattered throughout the vast space, with Mary and John clearly the only English. On either side, slender stone pillars rose impossibly high, arching far over their heads like delicate forest trees, so tall that Mary had to hold her broad-brimmed hat with her hand as she tipped her head back to see the elaborate tracery of the ceiling. Standing below so much magnificence, she felt small and humbly insignificant, exactly as those long-ago builders must have planned.

"How do you think they created such a place?" she marveled in a hushed whisper. "Five hundred years ago, without any modern devices or conveniences!"

"Father Simon would tell you they had the power of their faith," he said as he also gazed upwards. "That's the purpose of all this, you know—to make even the most confirmed heathen feel this same awe. Your angel has it, too."

She slid her gaze from the ceiling to his face, still holding the crown of her hat with her palm. "He would be at home here, I think."

"He might," he said evenly, then frowned, his glance

sweeping down her person. "You didn't bring the picture with you, did you?"

"Here?" she asked, incredulous. "Where would I be hiding it? Tucked inside my reticule? Under my hat? Perhaps if I were in court dress, I could hide it in my hoops, but not dressed like this."

His frown turned rueful. "You're right. Of course you left it at the inn."

She nodded, hesitant to confess her latest hiding spot at the inn. "It's in a safe place, yes."

"Then let it stay there," he said, "while we find those choir stalls."

The carving on the stalls was every bit as wonderful as Mary had heard, with every inch of the golden oak panels fashioned into scenes both from the Bible, and from what must have once been everyday life in Amiens. But even as she and John moved among the stalls, drawing one another's attention to the exquisite expression of this saint, or the entertaining posture of that donkey, she remained acutely, almost painfully, aware of the man beside her.

He praised her observations about the cathedral, and she marveled at how he was the first gentleman who'd even listened to her. He laughed, and she wondered at how precisely they found the same things amusing. His sleeve brushed against her arm, and it was enough to send shivers of sensation rippling through her. He smiled at her, and she remembered how it had been to be kissed by those same lips.

"Remember how the drapery falls around the figures," he was saying, bending over to run his fingers lightly over the gown of a tiny carved Madonna. "When you visit the grand churches of Italy, you'll see how differently the woodworkers there treated the same designs. The edges will be more defined, more—"

"Why are you here?" she blurted out, unable to keep quiet any longer.

He stood upright, his face full of surprise. "Why, to see the cathedral, of course. It's been years since I last was here, and—"

"That's not what I meant," she said softly. Now that she'd begun, she'd have to see this through. "I want to know why you've stayed with us, assuming this preposterous role as our guide."

He raised one brow. "Am I doing such a poor job of it?"

"No," she said, "and that's not what I meant, either. You've no responsibility to us. You told me yourself that you'd business that would take you to London, yet here you are, admiring carved drapery, as if you'd rather be nowhere else."

He smiled easily—perhaps too easily, she thought—and held his hand out to her with gallant nonchalance. "That's because it's true. I can't conceive of another place under heaven where I'd rather be than here beside you."

"That's rubbish," she said, and swatted his gallantly offered hand away. "I bid you goodbye the night beneath the willows—"

"You didn't bid me anything," he said. "You dismissed me."

"I bid you goodbye," she repeated, preferring to pretend he hadn't interrupted her, "yet you persist in lingering as if nothing—nothing—happened."

He frowned, as if trying to remember. "Not much *did* happen, by my recollection."

"Then your recollection, my lord, is faulty." Why was he so wretchedly determined to make this difficult for her? "You—you kissed me, my lord."

"That I did," he said, "and you kissed me in return. Rather well, too. But I'd no notion it was such a rare occurrence in your life that it merited such clamor and fanfare now."

She flushed with embarrassment. To admit that, yes, their kiss was in fact a rare and wonderful occurrence made her sound at best a pitiful spinster, or at worst a prude. Either one would likely make him laugh. And what if he chose to remind her of her vow to be more adventurous?

"Pray forget I spoke," she said, looking down at the worn tiled floor. "If it didn't signify to you, then it doesn't to me, either."

She turned away from him, but this time he caught her arm, keeping her there.

"Then tell me what other course I was to take, Mary?" he demanded. "You were silent and wounded when I took notice of your sister, yet when I chose your side instead of hers, you berated me for my cruelty."

"And so you talked to Miss Wood instead?" She was beginning to feel like the greatest possible fool. "For the sake of—of peace?"

For an instant he looked past her, before his gaze fixed once again on her face.

"Your Miss Wood is an agreeable enough little woman," he said, more gently this time. "Plain as can be, but still vastly preferable to coming between you and your sister. In fact she—"

He broke off suddenly, again looking past her face.

She twisted around to follow his gaze. "What is it?" she asked curiously. "What do you see that—"

"Mark that man in a dark green coat near the rood screen," he said, his voice lowered to a whisper. "I'd swear I've seen him before, near the stables of our inn."

She found the man at once, standing close to the rood screen as if inspecting it, his back to them. There was nothing really remarkable about him—he was of medium height, medium build, and his worn clothes were the same as a thousand other Frenchmen—and yet Mary agreed with John. The man *was* familiar, not a beggar, but an idler, the sort who loitered about inns and taverns in hopes of earning a few coins for carrying trunks or watering horses.

"Now look back to me," John ordered, "and then let's consider this panel before us as if it were the most fascinating sight you've ever seen in your life."

Mary obeyed, leaning forward toward the choir stall. "I've seen him before," she said, barely containing her excitement. "At least I believe I have. I remember remarking the big hole he has in the back of one of his stockings, where his hairy leg is poking out. He's one of those men who stands about in the stable yard, trying to look as if he belongs there, but most likely doesn't."

"I'd say that's what he's trying to do here, as well." He crouched down beside her. "No, don't look back again."

"Do you know who he is?"

"Not the faintest idea," he said, "except that he's followed us here, and is following us still. Do you carry a looking-glass in your reticule?"

She nodded eagerly, resting the little knitted bag on her knee to open it. Strange how the awkwardness that had plagued them earlier melted away now that they had a shared purpose. She handed him the pocket mirror: a round of enameled pink flowers on one side, and brightly polished steel on the other.

John took it, and grinned. "Always prepared, aren't you?"

"There's no fault to being practical." She watched as he cupped the mirror in his palm and carefully tipped it. Reflected in the shiny surface they both could see the man in the green coat, now flagrantly craning his neck to stare at them. There was a mean, desperate look to his face: a villain's face, thought Mary, and one she'd rather not see any more closely.

"Bold as new brass," John said, "and in the pay of someone else. He's not clever or discreet enough to be his own man."

"I'm sure I recognize him now from the inn," she whispered. "Not his name, but the face."

"No doubt of it," John said, hiding the mirror in his palm. "Let's test him to be sure we're his game."

John rose, making such a grand show of guiding Mary from one stall to the next that she almost giggled. Almost: until the next furtive peek in the pocket mirror showed the man had not only followed, but drawn closer.

"He wouldn't harm us here, not in the cathedral," she said, her uneasiness growing. "And you can't blame my angel picture this time."

"It would be easier to understand if I could." He looked to the end of the choir stalls. "How fast can you walk?"

"I can run, if I must." She lifted the hem of her skirts just high enough so he could see her shoes, more sturdy than fashionable, and purchased specifically for all the walking she'd planned on their tour. "I told you I was a practical country girl."

"Good," he said. "I want to leave this rascal behind before he tries any mischief."

He tucked her hand in his arm, and began sauntering past the stalls. "When we reach the end of the aisle, we'll duck to the left, around the back of the benches. There's a staircase beyond that which leads beneath the nave, and eventually back to the street. Ask your questions now, if you have them, for there won't be time once we start."

She shook her head, her heart racing with anticipation. She didn't feel to be in any real danger, not from that ragamuffin man in the green coat, but this—*this* was adventure!

"Then off we go."

Arm in arm, they turned past the last stall and down a narrow passage, with the stalls rising up higher on either side to shield them. As soon as they turned, John grabbed her hand, and together they began to run, through a row of stone arches and past a small shrine with rows of flickering votives and beneath the glowering stone stare of four tall apostles. The door was to the right of the statues, a short oak door with black iron hinges and a curved top that reminded Mary of all the cursed doors in nursery stories, the kind of castle doors that led to witches and dragons and other nefarious goblins.

John drew the bolt and shoved the door open, holding it for her as he looked past her for the green-coated man. "Hurry, lass, hurry!"

She hesitated for only a second. If witches and dragons were part of the adventure, then she'd have to take it, too. She grabbed her skirts in a bunch to one side, and plunged into the murky half-light with John close on her heels.

The stone steps were narrow with the treads hollowed in the center from centuries of use, the staircase itself a winding corkscrew. Mary felt her way along the chill stone walls, hurrying downward as fast as she dared. She could see neither where she was heading, nor where she'd come, only the next few steps before her.

"Almost to the bottom, Mary," John said. "We'll claim that lantern for ourselves."

She'd smelled the lantern with its smoky tallow candle before she'd seen its wavering light, hanging from an iron ring in the wall at the bottom of the stairs. She smelled other things, too: damp, and mould, and dust, and ancient smells she couldn't quite name, nor was she sure she wished to.

And as irrational as it was, she caught herself thinking of that severed head of St. John the Baptist, and where exactly it was kept between working miracles.

"Where are we?" she asked uncertainly as John—her John, the unmartyred one—plucked the lantern from the wall. "Is this the cathedral's cellar?"

"After a fashion," he said, taking her hand again to lead her. "Hurry now, we can't stop."

She followed, not really wanting to, but with no desire to be left behind, either. The lantern in his hand did little to pierce the darkness around them, and all she could see were more stone arches and huge stone pillars and more of the same low doors they'd already come through, though these were barred with heavy iron padlocks. Cobwebs brushed and caught against her arms and face, and she was sure she could hear the scurry of rats fleeing the lantern's sweep.

"How do you know where to go?" she asked, breathless from keeping pace with him. "You said you hadn't been here in years."

"I haven't," he admitted. "But I remember this way very clearly."

She brushed another cobweb from her hat. "I cannot believe one of the monks brought you down here."

"Oh, no," he said, his grin ghostly by the lantern's wavering light. "This isn't anything they'd care to show to visitors. No, I was with a friend, and we discovered this way on our own. We were in rather a hurry to leave, much as you and I are now."

"But through here?"

"I never like to take the obvious choice," he said blithely. "A notion you might learn to embrace, as well, my ever-practical lady."

She wasn't reassured. Wandering about beneath an ancient French cathedral wasn't a common pastime for English visitors. Even if it had been years ago, why had this unnamed friend and John been in such haste to escape? What manner of mischief had they been causing themselves?

She didn't know. And the less she knew, the more she wondered why she'd been so trusting to come down here with him now. Really, she scarcely knew anything about him beyond his name, and that wasn't reassuring, either.

"Are you certain this is the way to the street?" she ventured. "If it's been so many years since you've last been here, why, then—"

"One way down, one way up," he said, giving her hand a quick squeeze. "At least that's what I recall, and I—did you hear that?"

She did. The footsteps had an eerie echo, coming closer and closer. It had to be the green-coated man. No one else would have known they were here.

"Here." John grabbed Mary by the arm and pulled her with him behind one of the broadest pillars. He set the lantern on the floor next to the wall, whipped his hat from his head, and tipped it over the lantern's door to mask the light. At once the shadowy darkness turned inky-black, thick and impenetrable around them.

"Be brave, Mary." She felt John's whisper on her ear as much as heard it, the words warm and sure as a caress and his body close against hers. "Stand as still as you can, and leave the rest to me."

Swallowed into the darkness with them, the other footsteps stopped as their owner strained and strived to see. When the steps began again, they were slow and dragging, as the man slid each shoe cautiously along the stone floor to avoid tripping or falling. His breathing was openmouthed and ragged, from nervousness or exertion, and amplified by the dark. Mary opened her mouth to whisper to John, yet somehow he sensed it before she spoke, placing one finger gently over her lips to silence her.

Though she couldn't be certain, she guessed that John

must be counting on the man passing by without noticing them. Then they could slip away into the dark themselves, and finally return to the world outside.

She'd never dreamed she'd long for the sun as badly as this.

The man was coming closer, closer still. Now she could hear his breathing, a ragged pull of air ending in a wheeze, and the shifting that his coarse-woven coat made as it rubbed across his shirt. There was another sound, too, something muted and metallic that she couldn't quite place. She could smell him, too, both his clothes and his body stale and unwashed, with onions or garlic in the mix. He swore a mumbled oath in French, so close now that if Mary stretched out her hand, she'd touch him.

But she didn't. John did, and he didn't use his hand, either.

She felt him jump away from their hiding place. She heard a scuffle, a thump, the other man exhale sharply as if the wind had been knocked from his lungs, then a soft thump like a heavy cushion thrown to the floor.

And then, once again, silence.

Unable to keep still any longer, Mary bent to grab the hat from the lantern. The candle flared bright at the sudden burst of fresh air, the light shining over the green-coated man lying still on the floor, and John standing over him with a pistol in his hand.

"What have you done?" she cried. "Oh, dear God, if you have killed him—"

"Damnation, Mary, I haven't killed him, because he's not dead," John said sharply. "All I did was tap him on the head with the butt of the pistol, before he did the same to us."

He crouched down and retrieved a second gun from the floor where the man had dropped it, holding it out for Mary to see. "Do you believe me now?"

"It was never a question of *believing*." She was still shocked by what had happened, shocked by the too-quiet man on the floor in front of her, shocked most by the quickness of John's reaction and the pistol she'd had no notion he'd been carrying. "I didn't know you were carrying a—a weapon."

"You didn't ask," he said, without looking up from the other man's pistol in his hand. "It signifies nothing, Mary. Most gentlemen are armed while traveling, or at least they are if they value their safety and person. Likely your own father does, and you simply are unaware of it."

She wasn't certain her father did—*Father?*—but because she wasn't sure, she let it pass.

"But why would this man have followed us with—with a gun? Why would anyone wish to harm us?"

John didn't answer. He rolled the man onto his back and began searching through his clothes.

"Whatever are you doing?" Mary asked, shocked again. "We should be finding assistance for this poor man, not picking his pockets!"

John looked up at her, his features harsh in the lantern's light. "Why the devil would we help him? Mary, the man was hunting *us*."

"He had no reason—"

"Of course he did. We just don't know it yet, and there's not a scrap on him to tell us." Deftly he uncocked the other man's pistol, tapped the ball out into his palm, and then slid the gun skidding off into the darkness. He'd teased her about being practical, but she'd never seen another gentleman act with such ruthless efficiency as this. Where had he learned it, she wondered. What in his life could have prepared him for this?

He stood and tucked his own pistol inside his coat, reaching for the lantern. "Now come, we should be gone when he wakes."

"You would leave him here, alone in the dark?"

"I would," John said, reaching for her hand, "and I assure you, he meant to do the same to us."

Reluctantly she gave him her hand, hoping he wouldn't notice how it shook. She tried to tell herself that the danger was over, that John had saved her, yet she was more frightened now than when the man had been following them.

But she *would* be brave. If this must be the other side of being more adventurous, then she wasn't going to falter now.

She looked away from the man at her feet, took a deep breath, and forced herself to smile at John. "You can be practical, too. You did what was—was necessary."

"For you," he said solemnly, making the sudden flash of his smile seem all the more startling. "Come along, my brave country girl."

They hurried the rest of the way, finding the next set of stairs that took them back to the cathedral's nave. The sunlight still streamed through the colored-glass windows, the black-clad widows knelt at their devotions, the old women swept the tiles: nothing had changed in this world, and yet for Mary it felt instead as if nothing would ever be the same.

"You're pale, Mary," John said with concern as at last they stood on the cathedral's steps. "Let me take you back to the inn."

He raised his hand and stopped a hired chaise, helping her inside. The chaise was smaller than the ones in London, and smelled incongruously of chickens. She settled in the corner, smoothing her skirts over her knees before she folded her hands in her lap, setting her person to rights if not her thoughts. She *felt* pale, even if she weren't. How could she not, after such a morning?

"We must go to the magistrate first, John," she said as soon as he'd climbed in beside her. "We must tell him what has happened."

He reached out and rested his hand over hers. "Mary, Mary," he said softly. "I've told you before. This is France, and things are handled differently than in England. Because we are English, the French officials would refuse to believe us."

"But if we explained exactly what happened—"

"They'd claim that no such infamy ever happens in their town," he countered. "They'd say that we exaggerated, that we seek to defame their honor with false claims. Remember, this is a country where, if an Englishman dies, every last belonging he has in his traveling trunk is confiscated by King Louis's officers, simply for the inconvenience the corpse has caused to the French government."

Troubled, she looked back out the window toward the cathedral, as if half expecting to see the green-coated man reappear at the door behind them.

"I don't know what to do, John," she said uncertainly. "Considering how first our coach was followed and attacked by men who may or may not have been highwaymen, and now to have this other villain follow us through the cathedral—it's hard to ignore such things."

"How could you?" He raised their linked fingers to his lips, kissing the back of her hand, and then sighed heavily. "Though it grieves me to say so, Mary, I must give you the best advice I know. Leave France now. Go back to England as soon as you can arrange passage. Return to your father's house, and the protection his title and money can give you."

Mary pulled her hand away from his. "I'll do nothing of the sort. I've wanted this tour as long as I can remember, and I'll not turn tail and scamper away like a frightened rabbit now."

Leaning back against the cushions, he pulled off his hat, turning it upside down on his knee. He didn't seem ruthless now, only worn by the same weariness that she felt herself. The ribbon that banded the inside of the hat's crown had been singed earlier by the lantern when he'd used the hat to hide the candle's flame, the yellow silk scorched brown: a silent reminder to Mary of how he'd tried to protect her.

And the answer to every doubt and misgiving.

"I'd guess that if your father knew of what had happened," he said, studying the hat on his knee, "he'd come fetch you and your sister home himself, wouldn't he?"

"Oh, you've no notion." She smiled wryly at the thought of exactly how fast Father would appear in France if he heard even a hint of what had happened. If there was much that she didn't know of John, then there were an equally great many things that he had yet to learn of her and her family. "Father would come storming across the Channel to rescue us if he thought we'd been so much as shorted on our breakfast bill."

"Your father would do that for you?" he asked with an incredulity that made her realize that perhaps not everyone's father would be so protective or accommodating.

"Oh, yes," she said. "But so long as Miss Wood writes him that all is well, he'll stay content with his horses and dogs at Aston Hall."

He looked up at her without raising his chin, his blue eyes dark and unreadable. "And you, Mary? Wouldn't you agree that you'd be safer back with the horses and dogs as well?"

"Safer, perhaps," she said slowly. "There's no doubt of that. But there are still far too many other cathedrals and ruins left for me to see, and too many pictures waiting for me to buy to run home just yet."

He leaned across the seat and kissed her then: hard and fast, almost as if he seemed afraid she'd melt away before he'd finished. He ran his fingers lightly over her cheek, his expression unfathomable.

"Country girl," he said softly. "Don't ever ask me again why I stay with you."

Chapter Seven

With the late afternoon sun warm on his back, John rode alongside the Duke of Aston's coach on the road to Paris. After Lingueville, the vineyards and the orchards that had flanked the road gave way to the cultivated plantations belonging to the Duke of Bourbon. They'd be in Chantilly by nightfall, and stop there for the next three nights at the Montmorency, an inn named after one of the old noble families of the region.

From his horse, John could just glimpse Mary inside the coach, her head bent over her book. He liked her profile, her round cheeks and her straight inquisitive nose and the way tiny dark curls always seemed to work free of her hat to dance around her face. Every so often, she'd look up from her book and smile at him and blush, her expression charmingly startled, almost as if she'd expected him to have ridden away and was delighted to see that he hadn't.

He couldn't blame her. He, too, had expected that by now he'd have been long gone, rather then lingering with this party of high-bred English females.

Yet here he was. By being attentive, he'd won the complete

confidence of the little governess, who struck him as being completely over her head on this journey. She might be a genius in the schoolroom, but here abroad she was far too trusting, almost gullible. Lady Diana had been the opposite, pursuing him so openly that he'd been the one to step back, until she'd turned her attention to one of the guardsmen he'd hired.

But her sister Mary—ah, that had been different. The minute she'd found the picture of the angel in Dumont's shop, he'd been bound to her in a fashion he still didn't understand. What was it that had suddenly made him so deuced chivalrous? He found her lovely, amusing, and most desirable, but he hadn't seduced her. He hadn't even claimed any further favor than a kiss, which was so thoroughly uncharacteristic that it almost shamed him to consider. How could he expect to gain a share of her fortune behaving like this? At least he was glad that fate had tossed her into his path first, before she'd been scooped up by some unscrupulous rascal.

Well, no, he should be more honest, and rephrase that, even if only in his head: another rascal more unscrupulous than he was. Though he'd never worried about such things before, with her he'd caught himself wondering what her reaction might be if she ever learned of the more unsavory incidents in his past. Not that any of it could be changed now, by action or apology; the best he could do was to look ahead. At least he'd do his best to make sure no further harm would come to them before they reached Paris.

He caught Mary smiling at him again, her face dappled with the sunlight that filtered through the woven brim of her hat. She truly was the country girl she claimed, even if there'd been a coronet over her head since her birth. A pretty creature, with a surprising backbone. He liked that; he liked *her.* He smiled in return, unable not to, even if he'd wished otherwise.

But no matter how prettily she smiled or blushed, it always came back to the painting. It had to. The painting was the real reason he hadn't yet returned to England, and the reason he'd worked so hard to gain the trust of this little party of women.

If he'd believed in curses, then surely the picture of the angel was cursed as black as any scrap of paint and panel ever could be, with a string of countless other deaths besides old Dumont's to its credit over the last few hundred years. Likely the only sure cure would be to toss the thing in the fire, and burn it to oblivion.

But though John didn't believe in curses, he did believe in mysteries. Mysteries were amusing, perhaps profitable, and this one was a rare challenge. As beautiful as the old painting might be, beauty alone wasn't enough to kill for. There must be some painted clue or code that the uninformed wouldn't see or wouldn't know to look for. He wished she'd let him see it again, instead of hiding it away like an anxious squirrel with his acorn. Somewhere on or in that picture lay the secret that made that panel infinitely more valuable, valuable enough that Dumont had died for it. If John hadn't been as watchful two days ago in the cathedral, he and Mary might have been next.

But it was a puzzle that John meant to solve. He'd let fair Lady Mary keep her angel painting, just as he'd likely let her keep her maidenhead for whatever dull little peer would eventually be her husband. She'd never have to learn any of the unpleasant details of his past, or ask difficult questions he'd rather not answer. All John wanted was the prize for deciphering the riddle, whatever it might be.

"My lord John!" She leaned from the coach's window, an apple in her hand. "Are you hungry, my lord?"

Before he could answer one way or the other, she laughed, and tossed it to him. He caught it, and bit through the skin and into the flesh with such noisy relish that she laughed merrily.

"Like Eve, you are," he called to her. "Leading poor Adam to sin."

She laughed again. "I'll fear no temptation from you, my lord! I'm safe from any sin so long as I have my guardian angel!"

She ducked back inside the window, laughing still, but his smile was gone. Better to let her believe her painted angel was her guardian.

For now it would be up to him to make sure it never became an angel of death.

After the last dishes had been cleared away at dinner that night in the inn, Mary drew the letter from her pocket, and smiled as she carefully unfolded the thick cream sheet. Her announcement would be a surprise for John, and she wanted to make the most of the moment.

"You know tomorrow we are planning to visit the gardens of the Prince de Condé," she said. "But thanks to an old acquaintance of Father's, we've also been invited as special guests to tour the galleries within His Highness's palace."

She handed John the formal letter of invitation that would grant them entrance.

Diana leaned toward John, reading the letter over his shoulder without much real interest. "Fancy being so vastly important and regal that you make people present admission letters before you'll permit them to call upon you and gawk at your belongings. It's rather like tickets to the theater. I'll wager he won't even give us tea for our trouble."

"It's no trouble, Lady Mary," Miss Wood said sternly.

"It's a great honor, from a very great nobleman. You should be thankful that His Grace your father was able to use his influence to obtain such an invitation for us. Here in France, the Prince de Condé is second only to King Louis, and his palace here at Chantilly is said to rival Versailles itself."

Unmoved, John handed the letter back to Mary. "It's a château, Miss Wood, not a palace," he said. "The French are acutely aware of the difference."

"Whatever it's called, my lord, I'm sure it's very grand," Miss Wood said. "And very full of pictures. We'll be relying upon you to explain them to us, you know."

"I'm sorry, Miss Wood, but I'm afraid I won't be joining you." He rose, and pushed his chair back into place with both hands. "You'll have to rely upon His Highness or his staff to enlighten you about the pictures."

"Oh, please, my lord, you must come!" cried Mary, both disappointed and surprised. She rose, too, the letter clutched in her hand. "The invitation includes you, and besides, we've already written to accept!"

"The invitation is to the daughters of His Grace the Duke of Aston," he said with a forced lightness that didn't fool her. "I don't see how that can possibly include me, too."

"But it does," she insisted. "Though it doesn't spell it out precisely, it includes our entire party. That's just how such things are done. You should understand that. Miss Wood's not mentioned by name, either, but she's welcome to come."

"How flattering to learn that in your eyes I have the same social standing as Miss Wood," he said dryly. "But I can assure you, His Highness would welcome your governess into his château long before he would welcome me. Now if you'll excuse me, ladies, I'll wish you good-night."

Before any of them could stop him, he'd turned and left, with Mary still standing beside her chair, the letter in her hand.

"Oh, please, Lady Mary, go after his lordship!" Miss Wood exclaimed, fluttering her hands with distress. "Why would his lordship suddenly become so—so *wounded* because he'd not been named in the letter? It's hardly an intentional slight. How could His Highness have known his lordship would even be traveling with us?"

Diana sighed mightily, turning her wrist back and forth before the candlesticks to make the garnets in her bracelet sparkle. "Perhaps Lord John lost at cards or hazard to the Prince de Condé, and owes him some unspeakable debt. That's why most gentlemen quarrel, isn't it? Over gaming, and women?"

"Oh, hush, Diana." Mary frowned, looking out the door through which he'd gone. The notion of chasing after him to soothe his pride wasn't very appealing to her, but then walking through the château's famous galleries without him would be a disappointment, too. "I don't believe Lord John is guilty of either sin."

"No ladies?" Diana shrugged. "What a pity for you, Mary."

"You know perfectly well that's not what I meant." Mary shoved the letter back into her pocket and marched after him. She refused to beg him to join them tomorrow, but she did believe he owed her an explanation of why he wouldn't come. She wouldn't accept a bad case of wounded pride as a reasonable excuse, either.

He'd disappeared from the hall, and she hurried to the top of the stairs. The Montmorency's front room below was already filling with noisy men, determined on a hard night of drinking and smoking and telling lies, for in this Frenchmen seemed no different from Englishmen. If John had joined them, then she couldn't follow, and would have to give up the chase. But as she leaned over the railing on the staircase's landing, she saw the top of his dark head and the un-mistakable stride of his long legs.

"Lord John, stop!" she called after him, hoping she sounded imperious, as a duke's daughter should, and not at all like the fishmonger that she feared. "Stop at once!"

She bunched up her skirts to one side so she wouldn't trip, and swept down the stairs after him. Intent on John, she ignored the startled looks from other guests, and impatiently hopped down the last step.

"My lord, *if* you please," she called.

She turned, and there he was. At least he'd stopped when she'd ordered, a small grace.

"My lord," she said, and cleared her throat with a small *harrumph*. "My lord, I must speak to you."

"My lady," he said with a halfhearted flourish of his hand. "You are doing exactly that."

A man behind her guffawed, and she felt her cheeks grow hot. She'd never done well before audiences, and because she'd been so impulsive, an audience—a *growing* audience—was precisely what she had.

"Alone, my lord," she said, striving to compose herself. "I must speak to you alone."

All he did to earn a resounding chorus of hoots and howls was raise a single skeptical brow—a brow that represented every wicked woman who wished to consort with a man alone in an inn.

It was more than Mary could bear. Whatever she said now, he'd twist against her for the amusement of these cackling *fools* around them. Instead she grabbed his arm, and pulled him toward the back door of the inn, and into the yard.

At this inn, the stables and other outbuildings were to the side, and the small yard where they now stood was given over to a low henhouse full of clucking chickens, and a tiny kitchen garden kept by the innkeeper's wife, all enclosed by a stone and stuccoed wall. The wall kept out any chance of a breeze, and the lingering warmth of the summer day combined with the heat from the cooking fires to make the yard still and close, the air weighted with the scent of garlic and onions. Instead of the drifting willows and moonlight on the running brook behind the inn at Abbeville, here there were only cabbages and clucking chickens.

She dropped her hand from his arm, and took two steps back, away from him. She wanted distance for this, a proper distance, so he couldn't distract her with his smile, or his eyes, or any other part of him.

He tried, though. He was watching her so closely that she could almost feel his gaze on her skin, and when he tossed his hair back from his forehead and a tiny rivulet of sweat trickled down his temple, why, she was very nearly undone.

"So, my lady," he said softly. "We're alone. Speak."

"Don't give me orders," she snapped, surprised he'd dare.

He nodded, and shrugged. "Very well, my lady. Good night."

"No, stay, please!" She made an unladylike gulp of her next breath. "That is, stay. Stay until we've spoken."

He turned back toward her, his head cocked a fraction to one side. "So you may give orders to me, my lady, but I'm forbidden from returning the favor to you?"

"If you're a gentleman you will."

"And if you're a lady?"

"I *am* a lady," she said, at least on safe ground there. "Which is why I'm here, to ask for a civil explanation."

"Yes, my lady," he said dryly. "Whatever you wish, my lady."

The way he said it wasn't civil at all. "I thought I'd surprise you with the invitation to view His Highness's collection at his château. I thought you'd wish to see his paintings, particularly those by the Italian painters. I thought together we might be able to study other paintings, and determine the painter of my angel picture. I thought you'd be *pleased* to come."

"And you are angry because I'm not."

"Not angry, no," she said, though of course she was. "But I am disappointed by your lack of interest. Yes, that's it. I'm disappointed."

"You're disappointed because I didn't bow down at your slippers in my gratitude," he said. "You like to plan and order things, Mary, especially other people's lives. I wonder that Diana hasn't throttled you for how much you order her about."

"That's not true!" Mary cried indignantly, then realized perhaps it might be so. "That is, where Diana is concerned, there are times I must step in. I have no choice."

"Oh, none at all," he said, his sarcasm too thick to ignore. "I suppose that's why you've come after me now. You have no choice."

"And you are prideful!" she exclaimed. "Don't say that you're not, because if it weren't so, you'd be coming with us tomorrow. You cannot bear the thought of not having your own invitation from His Highness that—"

"Is that what you believe?" he asked, incredulous. "That I'm offended because I didn't have a wretched *letter?*"

She swept her hand through the air, irritated by his denial. "What other reason could it possibly be? Diana said that you must have lost money to the prince at cards, or have quarreled with him over a woman, but I'm certain it's your pride, pure and simple."

He shook his head with disgust. "Everything is pure and simple with you, isn't it? No wonder your sister knows more of men than you ever will."

That stung. "Do you owe money to His Highness? Is that it? Or have you disagreed over a mistress?"

"I assure you it's neither."

"Then shall you tell me?" She could feel the sweat trickling down the hollow of her back and between her breasts to soak into her shift and stays, as much from agitation as from the heat. "Or do you intend to force me to guess?"

He stepped forward, closing the careful distance between them. He was angry now, too, so furious with her that she could feel it like another wave of heat.

"I don't force women to do anything against their wills," he said. "Not even ladies."

She resisted backing away, and giving him that satisfaction. "Then stop being so willfully stubborn, and *tell* me!"

"I'll oblige you, my lady," he said, clipping off each word, "though God knows why I do. I will not go with you to the château not from pride, but because I wished to spare you the shame of my presence. I refused for your sake, my lady, not for my own."

"For *me?*" She shook her head, still too angry to find any logic to his explanation. "How can you place this upon me? You make no sense, my lord, no sense at all. How could I be shamed by your presence?"

"You'll have to answer that for yourself, my lady," he said, and turned away.

"Wait!" she cried, following him through the cabbage bed. "You cannot go until you tell me the rest!"

This time he shook her away. "One question, one answer. That's all. Now pray excuse me, my lady. I must join His Highness the Prince de Condé for our customary round of whoring and gaming."

"Then *I* shall go find the company of a gentleman who can—can be truthful and agreeable!" It was a miserable retort, and knowing it only made Mary angrier still as he walked away, toward the gate. "I'm going directly, my lord, this moment!"

"Then go," he called without looking back. "And my heartfelt sympathy to the poor, agreeable wretch you're meeting."

Beside herself with frustration, she threw open the door that led back into the inn, scattering the servants who'd been watching her and John from the window. One servant from the kitchen lingered, a bottle of wine cradled in his hands and on his face the look of a rabbit caught in a lantern's light.

"You're staring, sir," Mary said frostily, forgetting that few servants spoke English.

His eyes widened further. *"Je ne comprends pas, mademoiselle?"*

"Oh, bother, I don't understand, either," Mary muttered, and headed toward the stairs.

"Lady Mary!"

With a sigh, Mary turned back to where Miss Wood was standing in the doorway to the room where they'd eaten earlier. Hovering behind her was a widowed English lady whom Miss Wood had met earlier in the day, and clearly the two of them had been having a lovely time discussing whatever it was—songbirds, poetry, psalms?—that Miss Wood discussed.

"Were you able to catch his lordship, my lady?" she asked, smiling brightly.

"Yes, Miss Wood," Mary said grimly. "But I wasn't able to persuade him to join us tomorrow."

"Oh, no." Miss Wood clucked her tongue, faintly disapproving. "I thought sure you could convince him, my lady. Gentlemen can be so taxing."

"Yes, Miss Wood," Mary said, though she doubted Miss

Wood had any idea of exactly how taxing John had been. "I believe I'll go to our rooms and prepare for bed."

"Of course, of course," Miss Wood said. "I'll be along shortly, too. Is Lady Diana with you?"

"Not at present, no," Mary said with care, instantly fearing the worst where her sister was concerned. Until now Diana had behaved well on their journey, contenting herself with a handful of winks and smiles, and a great deal of complaint about the lack of gallant gentlemen in France. "But Diana looked so weary earlier that most likely she's already gone upstairs."

"It has been a long day for all of us, my lady." Miss Wood discreetly stifled a yawn. "We should take care to be well-rested for tomorrow. We'll want to be fresh for His Highness."

"Good night then, Miss Wood," Mary said, making a great show of yawning herself. Never in her life had Diana gone to her bed this early, something Miss Wood seemed for once, fortunately, to have forgotten. "Sleep well."

"I wish the same to you, my lady," Miss Wood said. "We'll meet over breakfast in the morning."

Mary nodded, and began toward the stairs, dawdling on the way to make sure that Miss Wood had returned to the other room with her new friend. Then she ducked down the other hall to stand outside the public room, searching among the cocked hats and hazy clouds of pipe smoke to make sure her sister hadn't gone in there among the mostly male and mostly older customers. It wasn't likely—public displays among so many men were not ordinarily Diana's preference—but this was France, and everything was different, even, perhaps, her sister.

But the only women Mary could see seemed worn and tawdry and definitely not Diana, and with a sigh of mixed worry and relief, she stepped out the inn's open front door.

"Shall I call for a chaise for you, my lady?" asked the porter, immediately slipping down from his tall stool beside the front step to bow deeply. "Or would you rather a chair?"

"No, no, thank you," Mary said, folding her arms over her chest as she backed away. What was she doing here in this near-empty street, anyway? Ladies didn't belong out alone after dark. This wasn't Aston Hall; this wasn't even England. At home Mary had known all the places where Diana and her sweethearts could most likely be found, whether a snuggery in the loft above the stable, or the folly made like a tiny Roman temple near the lake, or, most often, simply a bench in the gardens.

But where would she begin such a hunt here in Chantilly? She glanced up to the rooms she shared with Diana, hoping against hope that the candles would be lit, and her sister in fact preparing for bed. But the windows were dark, as she'd feared they'd be, and her desperation rose.

Maybe she'd have to go back to Miss Wood after all, and tell her that Diana was missing. This time it wasn't just a matter of keeping Diana's secret. Here in a foreign place, and among strangers, her sister could have blundered into real danger. They'd have to call the watch to find her, or whatever it was in France. There'd be a scandal, of course, and when Father learned of it, then their journey would be over before it had fair begun.

But what choice, really, did she have?

Two soldiers in shabby uniforms came lurching along the street, each needing the other for support.

"*Ah, ma chérie,*" said one of them as he leered at her, his breath stinking with cheap wine. "*Vous-êtes belle, ma chérie. Très, très belle.*"

"Go away," she said nervously, continuing as quickly as she could in the opposite direction. She glanced over her shoulder for the porter outside the Montmorency, but now his tall stool was empty. "That is, *va. Va!*"

"*Anglaise,* eh?" The man jabbed his friend in the ribs, and swayed toward Mary. "*Anglaise!*"

The man reached a dirty hand out toward her and Mary twisted away. Her shoe slipped on a paving stone, pitching her sideways. With no way to break her fall, she yelped and toppled toward the soldier, his face before hers greedy with anticipation.

And then another arm was around her waist, pulling her back. From instinct she struggled, trying to push free, but the man held her tight.

"There now, sweetheart, you're safe with me," John said. "Off with you now, you two. The lady's with me. *Avec moi,* mind?"

She stopped struggling, too stunned by the coincidence. Why hadn't he gone off the way he'd said he would? Why instead was he always ready to rescue her when she needed rescuing?

The Montmorency's porter ran up beside them, a large cudgel in his hand. "Ah, my lady, my lord! Forgive me my carelessness! Are you unharmed? Are you well? Such villains, such rascals!"

He shook the cudgel at the drunken soldiers, shouting words that Mary thankfully didn't know. The two men swore back at the porter and shook their fists, but staggered away.

"You are unharmed, Mary, aren't you?" John asked with concern. "No serious damage?"

"None." With a shuddering gulp to settle herself, Mary pushed herself free of John, smoothing her skirts and patting her hair back into place. She looked down as she fussed with her clothes, for if she looked up and met his eyes, she knew she'd weep from fear but also from relief. She had to think of Diana now, not herself. "I'm perfectly fine."

"You are certain?" He took her arm again, his fingers gentle and steadying.

She nodded, not trusting her voice. She must be strong. Wasn't she the practical sister, the one who arranged whatever needed arranging, the one that wouldn't squander her time on crying if anything remained to be done in the day?

Scowling, the porter rested the cudgel back against his shoulder and touched his forehead to Mary. "Forgive me, my lady, but I must beg you to take more care. We are not Paris, to be sure, yet no street is safe for an unattended lady."

"I'm sorry to have caused you such trouble," she said, forcing herself to smile. "I vow to be more cautious in the future."

"In the future," said John as he took her hand, "and in the present as well. Come, let me see you back to your lodgings. What in blazes were you doing wandering about alone, anyway?"

"I wasn't wandering," she said, struggling to keep the quaver from her voice. "I—I had my reasons, and I can't go—go back inside yet."

"They must be deuced fine reasons to put your life at risk," he said, scolding gently as he slipped his fingers more closely into hers.

"They were. They *are*." She took tiny steps, purpose-fully letting the porter get farther ahead. "I—I was looking for my sister."

"Your sister?" He stopped, and she stopped with him. "In the street?"

"I don't know where she is," she confessed, her words now tumbling out with fresh urgency. "She told Miss Wood she was joining me, but of course she went elsewhere. She always does. I don't know who she's with, let alone where she's gone, but still I must find her. I *must*."

"I don't mean to slander your sister," he said carefully, "but you suspect she's gone to meet some man?"

Mary's nod was quick and certain, for there was no use in dissembling now. She'd have to put aside her pride for her sister's sake.

"Please, John," she said, more plaintively than she intended. "Will you help me find her?"

"For you, I will," he said, though he did not smile. "Does your sister have a lover here in Chantilly?"

Inwardly Mary winced at that *lover*, hating to have the word linked so casually to Diana, and hating more to have to admit it to John. It would only be one more broken promise for Diana, one more time that she'd rationalize her behavior in another roundabout excuse.

"I doubt she knew anyone here," she said. "This is her first time abroad, too. But my sister tends to make her, ah, her acquaintances swiftly."

To John's enormous credit in her eyes, he neither laughed nor smirked. "I've noticed that one of the guards I hired seemed more attentive toward her ladyship than was proper. I spoke to him about it, of course, but that doesn't always mean—"

"My sister can be persistent," Mary said, wondering why she hadn't noticed such an attachment herself. Diana was seldom subtle. "Do you know where this man is lodging?"

"At the *Chat Rouge*," he said, pointing down the street to where the lesser inns would be. "I put the entire troop of them up in the one place. I'll return you to Miss Wood, and then I—"

"I'm coming with you," Mary said resolutely. "I couldn't

bear sitting idle. I'll want to know the minute she's found that she's safe."

He began walking toward the other inn, her hand still linked in his. "I'd rather thought you'd wish to be first to flay her alive."

"Yes," she admitted. "But only after I know she's safe."

He laughed, and she felt the subtle shift between them. He wasn't just her rescuer any longer. Now they were partners again, working together, which she found infinitely more agreeable. If she had to turn to anyone for help, she was glad—and grateful—it was John.

They walked swiftly toward the other inn. The *Chat Rouge* was a low, squat building, its dark cross-hatched timbers settling into the dingy wattle and daub. Instead of a porter outside to greet guests, here the patrons themselves had spilled outside to drink and squabble and boast and flirt, some sprawled on the long bench, others leaning against the wall. This inn catered to soldiers and other wanderers—the two men who'd accosted Mary earlier most likely had come from here—and doubtless John's hired guards felt completely at ease lodging here.

But it was no place for Diana, and uncomfortably Mary shrank closer to John's side. Even if she'd known to come here, she couldn't have ventured into this inn alone, even for her sister.

"Gaston!" John called, beckoning to one of the men in the crowd. "Gaston, here!"

Mary recognized the man as one of their guards as soon as he'd disentangled himself from one of the serving-maids. With a bottle in his hand, he came loping up to John, his hand resting easily on the hilt of his sword. Mary knew that the sword was only a sign of his trade, and that most of the other men were wearing swords or cutlasses as well as pistols tucked into their belts, but the inherent threat still unsettled her. Father and his friends only used guns for hunting, not as a constant display of bravado.

"Bonjour, mademoiselle, monsieur." Gaston swept his hat to Mary and to John. He seemed already more drunk than sober, the state of most Frenchmen. *"Comment allez-vous?"*

But John was in no humor for pleasantries. In a rough vernacular French that Mary couldn't begin to understand, his conversation with Gaston was quick and direct.

"What did he tell you?" Mary demanded as soon as the other man had turned to go back to his friends. "Has he seen Diana? Does he know where she is? Oh, tell me, John, tell me!"

But the grim set of John's face told her more than enough "It's as I feared. She's with Bauldet."

"The tall man with the reddish hair, and a scar across his cheek?" She remembered him as the most handsome of the guards, and obviously Diana had noticed him, too.

"The same," John said, already hurrying her up the street. "Bauldet went to the Montmorency to meet her, as they'd arranged. He promised to show her the canal. It's not far from here, but I wouldn't trust Bauldet for ten minutes alone with a woman."

They stopped a chaise as soon as they could, with John offering double the fare for the driver to make as much haste as his horse could muster. From the window, Mary watched as they left the town behind, the stars twinkling through the trees that lined the road. John had been right about the distance; they'd only been driving a few minutes when the chaise slowed, and drew to a halt beside a long hillside, planted with ornamental trees and flowers. John jumped from the chaise, then helped Mary down.

"Can I take one of your lanterns?" he asked, and the driver nodded from the box.

"For what you pay, *monsieur,*" he said, shifting the stem of his pipe from one side of his mouth to the other, "you may have my horse, too."

"Wait for us." John unhooked one of the small paired lanterns from the front of the chaise. "With luck, we won't be gone long."

"I thought Gaston told you they'd gone to the canal," Mary said as he took her hand and began to lead her up the hill. She couldn't tell the names of the flowering bushes, but she could smell them, their fragrance intensely sweet in the night air. "I don't see any water from here."

"You will soon enough," he said. "They say it was designed by the same gardening-fellow that laid out the flower beds at Versailles. Much to that old Louis's chagrin, though, the gardens and waterworks here at Chantilly are regarded as much the better."

"You're babbling," she said softly. "I know you're doing it only to make me think of other things, but truly, you needn't."

"I wasn't," he said, though they both knew he'd been doing exactly that. "I was preparing you for the canal, that is all. The French cannot help themselves from making improvements, even to nature herself."

They reached the crest of the low hill, and below them lay a narrow band of water, stretching out in either direction beneath the night sky. The far bank had been plowed and raised into a hill that mirrored the one they stood upon, as if the cultivated bushes and flowers were nestling the canal in their leafy embrace.

Or maybe it was simply the path her thoughts were taking tonight.

"Di-an-a!" she called, looking up and down the length of the canal. "Diana, please, it's Mary!"

With so much shrubbery and so many shadows, her sister and this Bauldet could be practically anywhere, and her despair rose. Didn't Diana realize the danger of coming to such a remote spot?

John held the lantern high, its light pitifully small against so much night. "You've done this before, haven't you?"

She sighed. She'd confided in him this far.

"I've done it more times," she said sadly, "than I can recall, and many more than I should have had to. Di-an-*a!*"

"Will she answer you?" he asked. "Will she come just because you call for her?"

"Sometimes," she said. "Most times, really. I think it's often her—her friend that shows more sense, and makes her come to me. Di-an-a, please, it's Mary!"

"Then we'll hope that Bauldet feels the same, too." He cupped his hand around his mouth, and shouted in French. "Bauldet, if you're here hiding with Lady Diana, then for God's sake come forward!"

No one answered.

"Di-an-ah!" Mary called again, walking slowly along the crest of the hill. Maybe Gaston had been wrong. Maybe Diana and Bauldet hadn't even come here to the canal, but were a dozen miles away entirely. "Diana, if you can hear me—"

"And what if I can?" Diana called back, her voice faint but distinct. With a great rustling she came from beneath the sweeping branches of a nearby beech. She held the hand of the man Mary recognized now as Bauldet, who in turn was leading his large chestnut gelding, which Mary also recognized from the road. But most importantly to Mary, her sister appeared unharmed and unravished, her white linen gown intact and in place and her person seemingly untouched.

"You're fine," Mary said with open relief. "Oh, Diana, you've come to no harm."

"Of course I haven't, you ninny," Diana said furiously, pulling her hand free of the Frenchman's to cross her arms over her chest. "Mary, why did you follow me? Why won't you ever, ever leave me alone?"

"You *know* why, Diana," Mary insisted, not wishing to spell everything out before the two men. "It never changes with you. No matter how many times you promise to behave differently, you never do."

"And who are you to lecture me?" Diana demanded. "Why do you believe that's your right, or your obligation?"

John stepped forward toward Bauldet, giving him several coins and what Mary guessed was a curt dismissal. The man tried to argue, but John cut him off. He shook his head, blew a kiss to Diana on his fingertips, and then climbed on the horse and rode off.

"You had no right to send him away!" Diana said, her wrath now turned toward John. "What did you say to him? What did you say of *me?*"

"I told him that you were the misguided daughter of an English peer, and if he valued his life and his livelihood, he'd have nothing further to do with you. Then I dismissed him from my service."

Diana shrieked with outrage. "How dare you! How *dare* you!"

"I also told him you were the bitterest poison imaginable for any man," he continued, ignoring her outburst, "and he should be grateful that I saved him when I did. As should you, my lady. Now pray join your sister in the chaise, and I'll see you both back to town."

Stunned, Mary could not believe what she'd just heard. No one except Father dared speak so directly to Diana, and she braced herself for a stupendous outburst that was sure to follow. But while her sister sputtered and huffed with indignation, she then gathered up her skirts and climbed into the chaise, exactly as John had ordered. Stunned, Mary quickly followed, pausing on the step just long enough to exchange a wondering glance with John.

"I'll ride with the driver, my lady," he said, latching the door after them. "Besides, I'm sure you two would rather be alone together."

But as soon as Mary settled beside her sister, she'd realized she'd rather be just about any other place in France than in this hired chaise.

Chapter Eight

Mary had seen storms from her sister before, but recognizing the signs of the one brewing now didn't make it any easier to prepare for. Diana had refolded her arms over her chest, her back straight and away from the cushions, her entire body quivering with fury. While John might have saved Diana's virtue and gotten her safely back into the chaise, it would now fall to Mary to weather her temper—or, more accurately, the tempest that was to come.

"You, Mary, are not my keeper," Diana began, practically spitting each word. "Nor are you Father, or even Miss Wood, to interfere in my life as if I were a child."

"Most children would show more sense with strangers than you do, Diana," Mary said, striving to keep her own emotions under control. "Aside from the risk to your person and welfare, you put your reputation in danger each time you consort with these—these men."

"*'Consort'!*" Diana's laugh was full of angry scorn. "Is that what you call it?"

"There are other words, yes," Mary countered, "but I'm too well-bred to use them."

"You're overbred, sister, like some spavined racehorse." She jabbed her fingers into Mary's arm. "At least men like Jean Bauldet don't treat me like a harebrained fool, the way you and Miss Wood do. *He* didn't care that I've no interest in musty old churches and ugly paintings. *He* wasn't disgusted because I'd rather try on new hats in a shop than read some tedious book. *He* liked me perfectly well as I *am*."

"He liked you for what you'd grant him!" Mary rubbed her arm where Diana's nail had poked her. "You know what Father would say, Diana, if he'd found you with a rogue like that one!"

"Do I?" she demanded. "Then I likewise know what Father would say if he saw how much time you've spent alone with your precious, interfering Irishman!"

Mary gasped, horrified, and prayed John couldn't hear her sister. "His lordship is neither interfering, nor mine, Diana, and it's monstrously rude of you to refer to him as an Irishman!"

Diana smiled, her pale eyes glittering in the half-light. "Why is it rude, when it's likely all you know of him for certain?"

"I know he's as much a lord as we are ladies!"

"Do you, Mary?" Diana asked. "How? He's never mentioned any friends or family, or where his family's estates might be, has he?"

"I'm not as inquisitive as you, Diana," scoffed Mary. Yet Diana's questions did echo Mary's own doubts about John, and uneasily she couldn't help but think of the rest that, mercifully, Diana did not know—his familiarity with violent acts, the gun he carried, the way he did in fact seem to be surprisingly rootless for a man of the rank he claimed for himself.

But what of the rest that Diana didn't know either—of how John had tried to rescue Monsieur Dumont from the fire, or how he'd saved Mary from the man who'd followed them in the cathedral at Amiens? Or how he'd kissed her beneath the willows, a kiss she'd never forget? Weren't such things important, too?

"I know what I need to know of him," Mary said carefully. "I don't believe in prying into his private affairs."

"But if Father and his friends are any example, Mary, then most lords lead public lives as well as private ones," Diana argued, realizing her advantage. "They sit in the House, or look after their estates. Your Lord John seems to have no other obligations but to trail about after you, spouting every manner of pretentious foolishness to beguile you, and Miss Wood, too."

"He doesn't speak to beguile me," Mary insisted. "You say that only because he's not interested in a flirtation with you."

"That's his loss, not mine," Diana said with a careless shrug. "He wears fine clothes and tosses about his money as if it's nothing, but what if that's all a sham? What if he's only an adventurer, after your fortune?"

Bravely Mary raised her chin. "If his lordship's an adventurer, then—then I'm an adventuress!"

Diana let her head drop back against the back of the seat and laughed. "How much I wish Father could hear you say that!"

"I'm not jesting, Diana!" Mary twisted around so she was facing her sister. "What John—I mean, his lordship says to me of paintings, and history, and other things—it's not meant simply to beguile. I know that much, Diana."

"Do you, Mary?" Diana asked. "Why? *Why?*"

Feeling as if she were jumping into a pool of water sure to be beyond her depth, Mary took a deep breath. "Because I trust him, Diana. I trust that Lord John has told me the truth."

"You trust him." Diana turned to stare from the window, her profile turned melancholy by the moonlight. "You scarce know the man, yet you choose to trust him, and not me. I'm warning you to take care because I'm your sister, and I worry for you, but you—you listen to him instead."

"Diana, please, I don't—"

"No, Mary, *you* don't. You've already said more than I wish to hear." Pointedly she looked from the window, ignoring Mary.

And though it hurt Mary to do so, she said nothing more in return to Diana, either, leaving the silence to swell and fill the distance between them until they once again reached the inn. The chaise slowed and stopped, the porter hurrying forward to unlatch the door.

"I didn't tell Miss Wood you'd gone off again, Diana," Mary said quickly. "I kept your secret. She thought you were with me, and I let her believe it. I didn't tell."

But Diana still said nothing, slipping from the chaise and entering the inn's front door as if Mary simply did not exist. Mary stood perched on the chaise's little iron step and watched her go, her conscience nearly as heavy as her heart.

She felt his hand close around hers, his fingers warm and ready to help her down. She'd no notion of how much he'd overheard of their conversation; she was so exhausted and confused now, she was almost past caring if he had.

"I'm sorry, Mary," he said softly, an apology that could have meant so many different things. "I'm sorry."

"So am I, my lord," she said sadly. "So am I."

The next morning, John sat inside the Duke of Aston's coach for the first time. He'd never ridden in such style before, gently swaying on the most modern leather springs and resting on cushions so soft they must have been stuffed with down.

Yet instead of relishing this luxury, the ostentation of it discomforted him. Tucked away in the glittering blue coach, he felt like some tiny enameled figure made for show and nothing else.

The coach was not the only thing that felt false to him this morning. Miss Wood was beside him, and on the facing seat were the two sisters. The ladies were dressed in fullest finery today, from the silk embroidered slippers on their toes to the curled ostrich plumes on their hats, ready to make their call upon the Prince de Condé and view his château.

Yet neither sister was speaking to the other. With stony determination, Mary stared out her window, and Diana hers, without a single syllable passing between them. John was sure he was the reason; he'd heard the quarrelling between them in the chaise last night, if not the exact words. He regretted that, for Mary's sake, and he hoped she didn't blame him, the way that it seemed. But even if she did, he didn't regret at all what he'd done to Lady Diana. Now it was up to them to mend their own fences. Two brothers would simply have knocked heads and been done with the quarrel then and there, instead of all this fuming and drama that ladies fancied.

That was hardly his fault, though he'd have to suffer with the consequences—one of which being that Miss Wood seemed compelled to act as interpreter between the sisters, as well as to fill the conversational void that their silence had created.

"You cannot believe how forward the French chambermaids are with us at the inn, my lord," she was saying to John now. "Why, consider the young creature who brought up the breakfast trays this morning. She set them down, then just stood and gawked, staring about our chamber with her jaw slack and her big moon-eyes as if she'd never before seen a lady or her belongings."

"Perhaps she hadn't," murmured John. "She could be new to her post."

"Perhaps that *is* the explanation, my lord," Miss Wood said. "If we are the first English ladies she has ever seen, then that would be why she'd stand about and gawk so, as if to be able to recall every last detail to tell those in her home."

Why, thought John dismally, was he here at all? Why had he dressed in his most elegant superfine coat and a laced Holland shirt that was already too warm for the day, and itching against his shoulders and neck? Why hadn't he held firm on his first decision not to go to the château with them?

His initial reservations hadn't changed. He could be riding into a situation that could at best be humiliating, or at worst, if His Highness the prince were in a vengeful mood, cast him into the nearest prison. The French could be a clannish lot, with their own ideas of justice. The English authorities might have declared him innocent of murder, but because the man he'd killed had been French, and an officer at that, the magistrates here in France might view the affair in an entirely different light. No wonder that when he looked at Lady Mary now, it was with something dangerously close to despair.

She was still achingly beautiful, her lovely face framed by the oversized brim of her leghorn straw, her throat and bosom a graceful curve above the low, square neckline of her cherry-and-white striped *polonaise*. But today her dark eyes were red-rimmed, either from weeping or from lack of sleep, and the bright spark that usually animated her face was so dimmed that she scarce seemed herself at all. She should be chattering about the paintings she meant to see at the château, not sitting dull and dispirited and silent as a new grave.

Well, in a few short minutes he'd likely give her and the others plenty to discuss on their way back to town.

The coach slowed as it rolled across the causeway and

over the moat, the pale, round towers of the château seeming to float on the water. John's heart began to race, and it took all his willpower to look no more than blandly disinterested in the huge house before him. It was too late to bolt now. One way or another, he'd have to play this out.

"What a beautiful estate!" Miss Wood exclaimed, the only one of them to show any emotion at all. "Have you ever seen the like, Lady Mary?"

"No, Miss Wood," Mary said, and nothing else, when she should be crying out over the turrets, the moat, the peacocks strolling about on the grass.

"The château was designed to inspire awe," John said, trying at least to fulfill his role as an educational bearleader, even as he tried not to imagine himself being clapped into the irons that the château surely still had in its lower dungeons. "That's why the forests we just drove through were kept so intentionally deep, to heighten the surprise of the château. Actually, it's not one forest, but three—Chantilly, Halatte, and Ermonville—combined into *le Massif de Trois Forêts, and—*"

The coach's door swung open to three bowing footmen in white powdered wigs and the elaborate gold livery of the Condé family. Lady Diana was handed out first, employing the small gilded step stool one of the footmen had placed in the drive for the purpose, followed by Mary and Miss Wood. As soon as they'd climbed out, the stool was whisked away by one of the footmen, leaving John to hop down to the paving stones unassisted.

So be it, John thought wryly. If inside the château everyone paid as little attention to him as they had to his explanation of the Three Forests, then he'd nothing whatsoever to dread. And if he was truly fortunate, the prince would have forgotten his name by now.

He followed the three women up the white stone steps and past more footmen. At least they'd been expected; that letter of introduction on heavy stock must have carried some influence after all. Confidence, John told himself as he joined the women. Confidence would always make others believe one belonged, even if one didn't.

They'd been greeted by the butler, or whatever he was called here in so vast a French household: a tall, grand man whose presence would have made him indistinguishable from the highest gentlemen at King Louis's court. But after his first greeting, the butler's message was hardly a welcome one.

"His Highness is not at home?" Miss Wood exclaimed indignantly. "How can that be, sir? We have a letter of invitation expressly for this day—expressly!"

She pulled the letter from her reticule and thrust it up for the butler to read.

He didn't, not even glancing down at the waving letter. "His Highness's invitation to the English ladies was for viewing his collections. His Highness is currently in residence in Paris, and is not expected back for some time."

As the misunderstanding and apologies continued, John felt the tension uncurl within him, snapping free like an unraveling rope. If the Prince de Condé wasn't here, then he couldn't very well recognize either John's face or name, let alone connect him to the old scandal that had made him such an outcast. There'd be no irons around his wrists, nor unceremonious descent into the dungeon, not this time. Most of all, Mary wouldn't know what he'd done, or be shamed by the truth. He'd be Lord John, the touring gentleman, and neither more nor less.

"Monsieur?" The butler was waiting expectantly, a footman standing beside him with an open ledger of some kind, and John realized he hadn't been listening.

He smiled ruefully, and shook his head. He'd nothing to fear now; he could play the foolish Britisher, and no one would care. "Forgive me, forgive me, I was lost in my thoughts, and my appreciation of His Highness's château. What was it you were asking?"

"Your name, *monsieur*," the butler said with another small bow. "His Highness does like to see who has visited his galleries, and which visitors are among his personal acquaintance. If you please, *monsieur*. Your name."

John could feel his smile turn brittle. There could be no real harm in giving his name, was there? The butler wouldn't know it, and the prince himself was far away in Paris. Even if one of the servants recognized him, what could he do without his master's orders?

"Tell him, my lord," Mary said softly, speaking to him for the first time that day. "Then we can go to the galleries and see the pictures."

He smiled swiftly to reassure her before he turned back to the butler. He was safe, he told himself. *Safe.* "I'm Lord John Fitzgerald. Would you like me to spell it out?"

"Thank you, no, my lord. That is not necessary." The footman's pen scratched over the page.

"You are English also, my lord?"

"I am an Irishman by birth," John said evenly, "but I now reside in London."

He didn't miss the swift exchange of glances between Mary and Diana—an "I told you so" look if ever there was one. Which was in doubt, he wondered: whether he'd been born Irish, or kept lodgings in London, or something else altogether?

"And so, my ladies, my lord." The butler finally spread his arms in welcome. "What would it please you to view? The galleries of portraits of the Condé family, the collections of

Chantilly porcelains, a tour of the most beautiful and historical chambers of the château?"

"We should like to see the portraits most, if you please,"
Miss Wood said. "Those, and the historical chambers, would
be most edifying to their ladyships."

"Very well, *mademoiselle.*" He bowed solemnly, and
beckoned to yet another footman. "Sacquin will be honored
to lead you through—"

"No, no, Miss Wood, if you please!" interrupted Mary.
"That's not what *I* wish to see. I've come to Chantilly for the
oldest Italian pictures."

"The primitive pictures, my lady?" The butler's expression was full of doubt. "Forgive me, my lady, but those are
not pictures that please ladies."

"Oh, Mary, they sound like that hideous angel of yours!"
Diana shook her head with an exasperated sigh, the plume
in her hat drifting from side to side. "Miss Wood and I agree
that we'd rather see pretty pictures than old ugly ones. You
must come with us."

John stepped forward. "Lady Mary can come with me,"
he said. "I've quite a liking for old, ugly paintings. If another
footman can be spared to show us the way?"

"Of course, my lord, of course." The butler frowned, then
waved for another footman. "Gervais is familiar with that
gallery, my lord, though I must beg you to indulge his limited
knowledge of the English tongue."

"So long as he knows the way," John said, holding out his
arm to Mary, "then we shall be fine."

She frowned down at his arm, and he caught himself
praying that she'd take it. He wasn't sure what he'd do if she
didn't.

"You shouldn't go off alone with Lord John," Diana said,
breaking her silence at last. "If it's not proper for me, then

it's not proper for you, either. Father wouldn't approve. Miss Wood, tell her so, and make her come with us."

Now Mary nearly grabbed his arm, claiming it as her own. "Father would approve entirely, Diana, because I will be making an educational study. Besides, the footman can act as our chaperone."

"Lord John, I will trust you with her ladyship's care," Miss Wood said. "I needn't remind you to guard her well. Lady Diana, you shall come with me. Unless you wish to go along with them to study the Italian pictures, that is."

"Come with us, Diana," Mary urged, clearly ready to mend the broken fences between them. "We can view the pictures together."

"I'd rather go with Miss Wood," Diana said, nursing her indignation. "At least I know when not to intrude."

Mary's fingers tightened on John's arm. "Very well, then, Diana. Please yourself. My lord, let us find these pictures."

With Gervais guiding them with a low bow every twenty feet, John and Mary followed through the long maze of grand state rooms and only slightly less grand parlors. But despite the vast display of silver gilt furniture and parquet floors and Venetian looking glasses, damask curtains and ancient tapestries, John could not be distracted from the woman on his arm.

"I'm glad you're speaking to me today," he said. "I wasn't sure if you would."

"I wasn't sure if you'd even join us," she said. "Last night you said you wouldn't."

"This morning I decided differently." He liked having her fingers curled into the crook of his arm, light and trusting.

"I am—I'm glad." She let out a tiny sigh, as if that admission had taken considerable effort to make. "I should both thank you, and apologize, for last night."

"You needn't do either," he said. "Retrieving your sister was an automatic action, like pulling a drowning kitten from a pond. You needn't thank me for that. And as for an apology—I cannot think of what you've done to make one necessary."

She bowed her head. She was swallowed up inside the wide brim of her hat, hiding her emotions as well as her face so long as she looked straight before her.

"Didn't you hear what my sister said in the chaise last night?" she asked. "I should owe you apologies until Judgment Day for that."

He rested his hand over her fingers. "I heard nothing over the horse," he said, close enough to the truth. He knew better than to entangle himself between the two sisters. "Nothing that merits an apology, anyway."

"Then you're not only kind, but deaf."

"I can be both, when necessary."

"How useful." She laughed ruefully.

"After last night, I understood more of your—your circumstances."

"Meaning Diana." She sighed. "After last night, perhaps I understand more of her, too. She is my sole sister. We have only one another to love. Yet what I consider care and devotion, she apparently perceives as cloying suppression. It's a curious dilemma."

"Not if you save her from certain ruin."

"Not if she doesn't feel it's ruin, but a kind of salvation." She sighed again, her fingertips drumming restlessly against his arm. "As foolish as Diana can be, she can also be surprisingly wise, and notice things I never saw."

"She doesn't see anything in your angel, that's true enough."

"Not at all," she agreed, "but that's not what I meant. She

sees people and their actions better than I do. For example, she has noticed that you never speak of your home or your family. She even wondered whether you go by your proper name, or another."

At once his defenses rose. "I'd never thought Lady Diana so given to suspicions."

"She's not suspicious," she said carefully. "She's observant. And just now, when you seemed to hesitate when the servant asked for your name and home, I feared she was right."

"She wasn't," he said as firmly as he could. "I was baptized John Fitzgerald, and so I'll be buried. And if I speak seldom of my family, it's because they speak seldom of me."

She turned to face him, her expression questioning. "But if they are your family, then—"

"Not all families are alike, Mary," he said, the old sadnesses and regret welling up within him. "I was the sixth son, with two sisters besides. Our house was a mortgaged shambles, my father seldom home and my mother often drunk. My breeches were patched, and in the summer we went barefoot to save our shoes, like a poor farmer's family instead of an earl's. Was it any wonder that we all scattered as soon as we could, to make our own way in a world that was bound to be more hospitable than our own home?"

He looked away, not wanting to see the pity that he was sure must be in her eyes, and pretended to admire a portrait of an earlier, blowsy Princess de Condé, swathed in emerald satin.

"No wonder at all," she agreed, evenly and without that much-dreaded pity, as if they were discussing no more than the price of eggs at the market. "You're proud of the life you've made for yourself?"

"I've no regrets," he said, and he didn't. He'd done

whatever he'd needed to do. He still did, or he wouldn't be here now with her.

"Even your—your familiarity with guns?"

For an awful instant, he thought she'd somehow learned of the duel, then realized that she'd meant what had happened in the cathedral. "If I hadn't carried that gun, I wouldn't have survived to be here now, or to have protected you in Amiens."

"True," she said softly. "Too true. And thus you are... happy? Without a family, without a real home? With only yourself to rely upon?"

"Happy enough." His family was what it was, plain and simple, and no amount of cooing and sympathy from others could go back and change his childhood. Better, far better, to concentrate on the man he'd become than to lament a distant past.

But he'd never expected what she said next.

"Then you're like my mother," she said slowly. "Exactly. I was young when she died, but still I recall her telling us tales. She was an orphan, raised by servants and a guardian she scarcely saw. Yet no matter how lonely she became, she believed that when she was grown, she'd make herself a family, full of love and happiness."

"Buttercups and treacle," he said, not hiding his contempt. "Such a pretty tale. Is it supposed to make me feel better, or worse?"

"It's not to make you *feel* anything," she said, unperturbed by his sarcasm. "I tell you only so that you can see that it is possible. Clearly you've made a worldly success of yourself. Now you must find your soul, and your love, and the happiness will follow."

Such sunny optimism did not sit well with him, nor did it have much of a place in his world, with the constant scrambling to keep appearances and a few coins in his pocket. "Is that the recipe of a practical country girl?"

"I suppose it is," she said, "if you choose to follow it."

He raised her hand to his lips, brushing his lips across her knuckles. "And if I don't?"

She might have smiled; he wasn't sure. "Then I understand you, John, just as you now claim to understand me."

"Monsieur et madame, s'il-vous-plaît." Gervais was bowing again, his round face apologetic for not speaking English as he held open the double doors to the next room. *"Voyez. Les primitifs d'Italien."*

The room was smaller than any other they'd passed through, a small cube with a single row of uncurtained windows set high to let in the sun. The walls were covered in red damask, the floor bare, with two cushioned benches in the center.

And then there were the paintings.

There were only a handful, but each one was set like a precious jewel against the patterned red cloth. The panels were surrounded by heavy frames, and glittered with gold leaf and ground lapis that represented the highest art possible nearly three hundred years before. They were serious pictures of somber, solemn saints and Madonnas, without the pagan frivolity of winking satyrs or dimpled goddesses. Yet each was graced with such intensity, such passion, that it was almost impossible to look away.

"Look, John, oh, *look!*" she whispered, her awe genuine as she went to stand before the largest of the pictures. "It could be the twin to my angel!"

"It could indeed." John came to stand beside her. This painting was really three, a standing Madonna in the largest center panel, flanked by two smaller paintings of St. John and St. Mark, with angels hovering protectively in the background of all three pictures. The panels were crowned with pointed Gothic arches, and hinged together so they might stand on their own, or, if hung upon a wall, fan out like the multicolored wings of the angels themselves.

"But look, John, really look, here at this face!" Excitedly she traced a square in the air before the painted head of one of the angels. "It's painted at the same angle, with the pose the same. The bump in the bridge of the nose, the way the curls are painted, even the dotted pattern on the halo. It's exactly the same as my guardian angel, John, exactly the same!"

"Here's the painter's name," he said, bending to read the small painted plaque fixed to the bottom of the frame. "'Fra Pacifico.' Brother Peace. Not a name I recognize."

"Nor do I," she said, still staring at the angel, "but I can find out more once we're in Italy. Still, considering how much time has passed, this picture and mine could be the only ones by the man that have survived."

"I'd venture that yours was once a triptych like this, too," he said. "The other pieces must have been cut apart and put into different frames, and sold to separate collectors."

"But why would anyone do that?" she asked. "Destroy the whole painting by breaking it into pieces?"

"Profit, sweetheart, always profit." He glanced over his shoulder, looking for their footman-guide. Gervais was standing by the door, his head drifting forward as he fought his drowsiness. Even if he'd understood their English conversation, he wasn't going to be sufficiently awake to able to recall it.

He looked back at the painting, trying to decipher the codes that the long-ago painter might have hidden within it.

"It's like a puzzle, isn't it?" he said. "We have one piece— that's your angel—and now we have this to give us more clues as to what the rest must be like."

She nodded eagerly. "One picture could be the copy of

another, I suppose, which would mean they'd be the same. But my guess is that the artist simply employed the same composition and arrangement of figures for another picture. If he'd already pleased one patron, then why not another?"

"It's certainly done often enough in London now," John said thoughtfully. "How many ladies have their face slapped on the body of Queen Charlotte?"

"Exactly," she said, her eyes bright with her enthusiasm. "These little persons here, the man and the woman showing off their fancy-dress and jewels, they're likely the patrons, just as St. Mark and St. John must be their name-saints. So while the patrons would have secured their places in heaven's favor by commissioning such a lavish altarpiece, everyone else in their parish church would have no choice but to admire their jewels and silk headdresses every time they had to kneel down and pray before the paintings. It's a tidy mix of looking after your interests in this world and the next, isn't it?"

He laughed, as much from the pleasure he found being with her as from what she'd said. He'd never known any other woman who was less conscious of displaying her intelligence. It amused him, true, but in a strange way he respected her more for it, as well.

She grinned, pleased that she'd made him laugh. "But you see, it does make sense. And if we guess that my angel was cut from the same kind of altarpiece, then it's not too much also to guess that the only thing different, really different, would be the patrons kneeling here in the corner. And if we knew them, we might have a clue as to why someone would want my part of the painting so badly."

"Badly enough to kill for it, you mean." His laughter faded, and he studied the painting's surface with fresh purpose. "It's a blasted shame no one is wearing little name-banners pinned to their chests."

"They did leave their address, though." She pointed to a tiny jumble of painted buildings behind the kneeling donors. "Now I've not been to Florence—though I mean to, on this very journey—but I've seen engravings, and doesn't this square tower here, standing taller than any of the other buildings—doesn't that look like the bell-tower on the Florentine cathedral? The *Campanile,* yes?"

"Yes," John said with surprise. "And that half-done building beside it must be the start of the cathedral's dome."

"The *duomo,*" she said proudly. "Designed by the architect Brunelleschi in the fifteenth century. You see, I *have* prepared myself for our tour."

"You have indeed," he said, impressed. "You're a clever lass, aren't you?"

"Yes," she said, without a hint of maidenly demurring. "I am. We can be nearly certain that my picture was painted by this Fra Pacifico in Florence, and that there was once a great deal more of it. But I do wish we knew who had ordered my painting, and who cut it to pieces!"

"We're not done with its cousin here quite yet." John glanced again at the footman, who was now thoroughly and conveniently asleep. With the greatest delicacy, John folded one of the triptych's side panels inward so he could see the back. This, too, was painted, but by the lesser hand of an apprentice: a landscape with a hillside village and a meandering road lined with top-heavy Lombardy pines. Charming, but ordinary, and gently he folded the panel back to where it had been.

"Your panel is plain on the back, isn't it?" he asked. "No little houses or candy trees like these?"

She shook her head. "It's painted flat green, with scribbled nonsense."

"But perhaps it's not nonsense," he said, trying to imagine.

"Now that we can guess how much of the original is missing, perhaps we could likewise guess the rest of the scribbles, and find reason to them."

"Perhaps we could," she said. "No, we *will*. I'll bring my angel to you as soon as we return to the inn, and then we can make a proper study of it together."

He liked the idea of her coming to him. They could make proper studies of a great many things, and not just the painting. This day was turning out far better than he'd dared to hope.

He pressed his forefinger across his lips for silence. "But it must be our secret, Mary," he said softly. "You must tell no one, and neither will I. Not even your sister or Miss Wood."

"Oh, no," she said. "They know next to nothing. There seems to be so much—so much danger connected with this picture, that I wouldn't dare put them at risk."

"That is good." He hadn't expected her to make that connection or the conclusion, but it was just as well that she had. "Until we decipher the depths and turnings of this mystery, we must keep it between ourselves."

"Oh, yes, of course. Of *course*." She clapped her gloved hands together, a kind of applause, and she realized that even the threat of danger was exciting to her. "Oh, John, you've no idea of how vastly special this is to me, the picture, and the puzzle, and us solving it together. I wanted adventure, and this—this is more than I dreamed of!"

Before he'd realized what was happening, she'd flung her arms around his shoulders and was kissing him with more enthusiasm than finesse. But finesse could be learned, and it most certainly could be taught, and swiftly he circled his hands around her waist and drew her close. As he deepened the kiss, slanting his mouth over hers, he could taste her willingness, taste her excitement, and he wondered if she were aware enough to taste his own in return. He'd never have predicted that the viewing of a fifteenth-century Italian triptych could make a lovely young lady so ardent, but then he'd never met another young lady quite like this one, either. Adventure, hah! He'd give her enough adventure to keep her warm for the rest of her days——

A crash in the hall startled them both and made her fly clear from his arms.

"Oh, my!" she exclaimed, hurrying to the doorway. The sleeping footman had finally toppled to the floor, taking with him a small table and a porcelain vase. Mary bent down beside the befuddled footman, sprawled with his wig askew amidst the pile of shattered crockery and marquetry. "Are you hurt? Should I send for help? Oh, how do I say it! *Comment-allez vous?*"

"*Bien, madame,*" he mumbled, clumsily struggling to push himself upright. "*Très bien, madame, merci.*"

"I'm glad to hear it," Mary said, trying to lift the man upright. "John, help me. He's larger than he appears."

"Heavier, too," John said, taking the half-stunned footman beneath his arms and with a grunt hoisting him back to his feet. Then he straightened the man's wig for him, pushing it back from his bewildered eyes and centering it where it belonged, over his ears. Considering all the poor fellow had done for him and Mary by obligingly falling asleep, it seemed the least John could offer in return.

And Mary—Mary, the dear, wicked creature, was laughing. She held one hand over her mouth as if that would be enough to stop her merriment, her eyes so full of it she was nearly weeping. Didn't she realize her own hat was crooked from when he'd kissed her? Didn't she know how deuced much he wanted to kiss her again?

"I'm going to tell the butler that I broke the table and the vase, so the poor footman won't get the sack," she said, laughing still. "The butler's sure to believe an English lady is so horribly graceless."

"He'll believe it to his peril."

"He can believe I've wings and can fly with the angels, for all I care." She reached out and took John's hand. "Come, my lord. The sooner we find the others and return to the inn, the sooner we can solve my angel's riddle."

"Ah, the riddle," he said, keeping his voice low for her alone to hear. "The riddle, Mary, will be only the beginning."

Later that evening, Mary sat beside her sister on their way from the château back to the town. The rocking of the coach along the Prince de Condé's smoothly paved road, combined with the end of the long, warm day, put both Diana and Miss Wood soundly to sleep, the governess making genteel small snores with her mouth gaping half-open. But Mary was awake—wide awake—and so was John across from her.

He had tipped his hat over his forehead as if pretending to doze with the others, but Mary could see—no, *feel*—his eyes watching her beneath the cocked brim. It was as if they were alone together, but not quite, with the risk of her sister or Miss Wood waking adding a shiver of risk. She'd never been in such an unusual situation with a gentleman before.

And yet, because it was John, and because before they'd left the château, they'd been given not tea, but a wonderful white wine that had sparkled up her nose—because of that, she felt peculiarly daring, and not quite herself. Wasn't this moment ripe to become part of her adventure? With one last glance at Miss Wood to be sure her eyes were closed, Mary pressed her lips and blew him a silent kiss.

He pushed his hat back from his face and smiled, such a slow, lazy, wicked smile that she blushed from her throat to the top of her forehead. Then, when he was sure that even in the gray light of the carriage there wasn't a scrap of her face that wasn't crimson, he winked.

She smiled back, and winked in return, even as she realized she'd have to do something more daring than a fluttery kiss. Her real quandary was, of course, that she wasn't exactly sure what that might be. She glanced at Diana beside her, trying to think what her sister would do—or at least, what she would do that Mary, fortified with bubbly wine, *might* do as well.

She shifted against the seat, moving carefully so as not to wake Diana, and as she did, a stray beam of light from the coach's outside lantern caught the toe of her slipper: green kidskin with a small shaped heel and a rosette that matched the cherry stripes of her *polonaise.*

But for now their most noteworthy quality was that they were easy to toe off. She kicked one shoe against the other and her right foot was soon free, bare except for her yellow lisle stocking. She slipped down a fraction lower on the seat, pointed her toe, and stretched out her stocking foot until it touched John's leg below the knee of his breeches.

Abruptly his smile turned somehow darker, more seductive. He moved his leg against her foot, turning her touch into a caress, her silky light stockings rubbing over the coarser thread that covered his muscular calf. She caught her breath at the unexpected sensuality of it, but she didn't pull away. This was France, not England. Any way that she touched him was part of her new adventure, and slowly she began to dawdle her toes along his leg.

"The Montmorency, my ladies, my lord!" shouted the driver, and Miss Wood instantly jerked awake.

"Oh, mercy, I must have been dropped off," she said, gathering herself with a nervous bustle. "We've reached the inn already, have we? My lord, forgive me if I woke you."

"Oh, I was waking." He made a huge pantomime show of stretching his arms over his head while he yawned, as if he'd been asleep for a week. "No trouble at all, Miss Wood."

But there *was* trouble for Mary. Furtively she was groping about with her foot for her fallen slipper with no success. Where could it have *gone,* anyway?

The door to the coach swung open, the footman first handing out Diana, then Miss Wood. Next he turned expectantly to Mary who sat frozen with indecision on the seat. She couldn't very well step out without her shoe, or walk through the inn thumping unevenly on a single heel.

"Lady Mary?" Miss Wood's face poked through the door beside the waiting footman. "Are you ill, my lady, or do you intend to be keeping the poor driver waiting until dawn?"

"She's perfectly well, Miss Wood." John reached down and retrieved the lost slipper, presenting it gallantly to Mary in the palm of his hand. "She's only thrown a shoe, that's all."

Suspiciously Miss Wood looked from John's face to Mary's to the frivolous shoe in John's hand. Mary grabbed her slipper and jammed it on her foot. With her head high, but her cheeks flushed—she'd blushed so much these last days that her face might as well be stained red permanently—she climbed from the coach unassisted, and almost marched inside.

"Don't forget to bring me the picture," John whispered, joining her in the hall. "I haven't forgotten. Not that, nor anything else."

She ducked her head and smiled, for she hadn't forgotten anything, either. She caught her skirts and hurried up the stairs. The sooner she took the painting from its hiding place, the sooner she'd see John again.

Diana was already before their door with a candlestick in her hand, fumbling in her reticule for the key to their room.

"You look as jolly as the cat who's licked the spilled cream," she said as she glanced up at Mary. "How sweet was it, eh?"

"Give that to me," Mary said, taking the candlestick so Diana could hunt more easily for the key. "And I've no notion of what you mean."

"No?" Diana asked. "I rather think you do. You see, I can be every bit as suspicious as you, Mary. And when I consider exactly what—"

"What did you see?" Mary demanded swiftly, knowing Miss Wood would be following soon. "I thought you were asleep!"

"I was," Diana said as she slipped the key into the lock and opened the chamber door. "But apparently I should have kept an eye open for what you and—oh, Mary, *no!*"

She rushed into the room as Mary raised the candlestick, and together they gasped. The room was a shambles, the bed linens torn away, their trunks emptied, their belongings scattered and tossed over the floor. Even Miss Wood's workbasket had been dumped. There was no telling what had been stolen, or left behind.

"Who would do such a thing to us?" Diana demanded furiously. "To rob us while we were away—why would anyone dare treat us like this?"

But Mary knew why, if not who. With the candlestick in her hand and a sick feeling of dread in her stomach, she raced across the room to where that morning she'd hidden the painting.

Chapter Nine

After the pleasurable day at the château, and the even more pleasurable drive back to the inn, the scene that John now faced was grim indeed.

Lady Mary, Lady Diana and Miss Wood stood clustered together in the innkeeper's office. They were there as witnesses to the thief's punishment; he'd come only to offer them support if they needed it. Though all three women had been trained to keep the emotion from their faces in situations like this, the way they stood betrayed their misery, each with her back rigidly straight and her hands clasped tightly before her, each barely touching the other but just enough to offer comfort and solace. Mary clutched her angel painting, shrouded in cloth, so tightly to her chest that John doubted any mortal could ever pry it loose.

Only he knew why. He'd sworn her to secrecy, and he was certain she wouldn't tell, any more than he would himself. But this—this was the result.

The innkeeper's face was purple with wrath, the cane raised high in his hand. "I take you into my inn, Berthe, and I trust you with my guests. Yet this is how you betray my trust? This is how you return my kindness to you!"

The girl stood before him, her hands pressed flat on the desk the way he'd ordered. John had recognized her as the maid who brought trays to the rooms, and likely tidied them as well while he was out—the same girl that Miss Wood had said had stood gawking in their room. She was neither pretty nor charming, nor even efficient, the minimal requirements of any good chambermaid, and now it seemed that she was also dishonest. But as the tears rolled down her red, swollen face, it was difficult for John to feel any sense of justice, only pity.

"Have mercy, sir, have mercy on me!" wailed the maid in French. "I was weak, sir, so weak! Believe me when I say I did not mean to sin!"

"If you did not mean it, then how did it happen?" He swung the cane down hard over the maid's knuckles. "If you did not mean it, then why did you steal from these English ladies?"

The girl wailed with pain, but kept her hands before her. "I—I only did what the gentleman told me to do!"

A gentleman? John's interest sparked abruptly. What gentleman would hire this girl to search the sisters' room? Unless he was looking for one thing, one prize, one secret.

"'Gentleman'?" The innkeeper's wife bent her face low before the maid's, her cheeks puffed with anger. "Who do you mean, Berthe? If you blame another for your crime, then you must give his name! Who told you to steal?"

"He—he said I must take what was of greatest value, *madame!*" she cried, the welts glowing on her knuckles. "I know nothing else, *madame!* Nothing! He wouldn't tell me more, I swear by the holy Virgin Mother!"

Take what was of greatest value: how could a serving girl know that that meant the painting in Mary's hands? And what bastard would dare ask her with so little risk to himself?

"You lie, Berthe!" The woman slapped the girl, jerking her face and knocking her white cap to one side. "Are you such a stupid peasant that you would obey this man instead of us? Did he threaten you? Did he promise to pay you? Is he your lover? Answer me!"

"He—he was a stranger, *madame,* at the bar!" the maid sobbed, the imprint of her mistress's hand bright across her face. "He—he promised to pay me if—if I'd do what he asked, *madame!*"

"Let her go, *monsieur,*" John interrupted, unable to listen to any more. "It's clear she's not acting on her own, but has been led."

But the innkeeper only raised the rod again. "I must ask you not to interfere, my lord. I know what is necessary to keep honesty in my house!"

"See the price of her betrayal, my lord!" Dramatically the woman tossed the bundled handkerchief onto the table, letting a pitiful handful of earrings and bracelets spill out. "This is your great value, Berthe? For this you sold your loyalty?"

Abruptly Mary stepped forward. "What she took is worth next to nothing, *madame,*" she said, her voice taut with anguish. "It's gimcrack and paste, bought for a song. Please, I beg you, let her go."

"That is true, *monsieur,*" John said, striving to be calm. "What she took has been retrieved. There is no use punishing her further. Let the poor lass go."

"What, set the thieving whore free to steal again?" The innkeeper raised the cane to strike her again, but this time John caught his wrist and held him fast.

"How much," John said, the calmness of his unspoken threat all the more powerful, "must I offer for the girl's freedom?"

The innkeeper puffed with scorn. "It is a matter of principle, my lord. If other noblemen and their ladies hear that I will keep a thief among my people, why, then—"

"Five *Louis d'or*," his wife said shrewdly. "Though if she tells of it to anyone else, I shall come myself to flail the flesh from her bones."

"Five it is." John turned toward the maid, quivering with both fear and pain. "Go collect your things, and take yourself off before *madame* makes good on her threat. Go!"

The girl rose and made a halfhearted curtsey to John before she stumbled from the room. With her gone, John finally released the innkeeper's wrist.

"You have made a bad bargain of that, my lord," he said sourly as he rubbed his wrist. "If we all die in our beds with our throats slit, we shall have you to thank."

"I think not, *monsieur*," John said, turning away toward the Englishwomen. "Come, I'll see you back to your rooms."

But Mary remained, her chin high. "Please prepare our reckoning, *monsieur*." She reached out and swept the jewelry back into the handkerchief, and then stuffed it into her pocket. "We've no wish to remain in your inn any longer than we must. *Bon soir, monsieur*."

"That was monstrous brave of you, Mary," Diana said as they climbed the stairs. "What if that man had taken the rod to *you*?"

"He wouldn't have dared," Mary said, so fiercely that John believed her entirely. But he also believed that her decision to speak in the maidservant's defense had come from much the same guilt as had his: that the young woman's theft had some connection with her painting.

"Wait for me," he said to Mary. "I'll only be a few minutes."

Word of Berthe's dismissal, as well as the circumstances

of it, had already run through the rest of the staff, and it took only a few questions for John to find the maidservant. She was sitting on the bench before the stables, waiting alone for her brother with her few belongings bundled in her lap. As John came closer, she looked up at him, then quickly away.

"No more trouble, my lord," she mumbled in her peasant French, hiding her face inside the lappets of her plain cap as she stared steadfastly into the street. "*Madame* said I was to speak to no one of this."

"I want no more trouble, either, Berthe." By the light of the lantern behind her, John saw how bruised her hands and face already were. He took a coin from his pocket and dropped it into her lap.

She gasped, and shook the coin away from her skirts to the ground as if it were a hot coal. "I won't be had for money, my lord!"

"That's not what I want, Berthe," he said. "All I wish is to hear more of the man who asked you to steal."

She stared up at him, clearly trying to decide whether he could be trusted.

"I'll be grateful for anything you can tell me, Berthe," he said softly. "I'd like to see the real villain punished, instead of you. The young ladies agree with me."

She sighed, and reached down to find the coin from the dust at her feet, tucking it away in her bundle. "He *was* a villain, my lord. Handsome, like you, but mean. He told me if he didn't do what I said, he'd see I lost my place. I did, but then I lost it anyway."

"Did he tell you his name, Berthe?"

She shook her head. "He wouldn't. He knew I'd tell if he did. But I knew he was from Paris, my lord, and a gentleman from how he spoke. He was tall and pale, with black hair and eyes."

Like every other Frenchman in Paris, thought John. "Yet he didn't tell you what to look for in the young ladies' room?"

"He said he couldn't. He said it was a secret. He said even His Majesty the king would want to know it."

It had to be the painting; even allowing for the man's exaggerating by mentioning the king to impress the girl, it still couldn't be anything else. "So you took the jewelry."

Her shoulders sagged. "I thought I'd done right, my lord, taking those red jewels with the letters on them. I thought that's what he wanted. Anything with an *F,* he said."

"Do you know your letters enough to judge, Berthe?" he asked gently, knowing the odds against a country-born maid-servant being literate.

"He showed me the letter. He drew it out, so's I would recall it." She bent over, and with her fingertip in the dust, traced an elaborate *F* with a curled tail.

The *F* had stood for Mary Farren, of course, the Duke of Aston's family name, the center of the cipher on the stolen pendant. He realized that it also stood for his own name of Fitzgerald, though that was neither here nor there.

"Did he say what the *F* meant?" he asked. "Did it stand for a name?"

"He did, my lord, though I can't recall it exact," Berthe said slowly. "He said it quick, so I shouldn't. But it was a foreign-sounding name, my lord. Not foreign like yours, my lord, nor them English ladies, but not French."

Not English, not French. He glanced back down at the curving letter she'd marked, the dramatic curves and flourish that were purely Italian. She'd helped him more than he'd expected, certainly more than she could realize, and he reached into his pocket for two more coins.

"Thank you, Berthe," he said, "and God bless you."

Miss Wood answered the door to the sisters' room. Behind

her, John could see their own maid Deborah as well as two others from the inn, sorting and packing everything that Berthe had scattered. Diana was helping, too, though with far less enthusiasm.

"I'd like to borrow Lady Mary, if you please," he said to the governess. "We saw a painting similar to hers in the Prince de Condé's collection, and we'd agreed to discuss the resemblances after dinner."

There were dark rings of exhaustion beneath Miss Wood's eyes; the day had taken its toll on her, too. "I suppose for a few moments, my lord. But pray do not keep her ladyship too late. If we're to leave in the morning, we must be ready tonight."

Diana gasped, hurrying to the door. "Oh, now that is not fair, Miss Wood, not fair in the least! You would let Mary go with Lord John, and yet when I—"

"Lady Mary is not you, my lady," Miss Wood said severely, taking Diana by the arm to let Mary pass, "nor is his lordship in any way like the men of your acquaintance. Now come with me, so they might have the time they desire to discuss the picture."

"I'm glad you're here," Mary said to John as she slipped through the door, the picture in her arms. "Where shall we go?"

He cocked his head down the hall. "My room is free."

"Your room? Alone? I shouldn't, and we shouldn't, and you are ill-mannered so much as to suggest such an improper choice." She smiled wearily. The evening had cooled, and she'd wrapped a thick, dark shawl around her shoulders that seemed to diminish her even more. "But after that odious scene with the keep and his wife, I believe we're entitled to a bit of impropriety."

"Oh, even Miss Wood said so," he said, then turned more

serious as he touched his fingertips to her cheek. "Besides, I spoke with the maidservant, and I'd rather not tell you what she said where we could be overheard."

"No." To his surprise, she led the way down the hall to his room, leaving him to follow. For her sake he was glad they met no other guests. It was one thing to court a ruined reputation, even in France, and another to court it before witnesses.

Once inside his room, she propped the painting in the only armchair and stood beside it with one hand resting protectively on the top of the frame. The light from the fire's flames danced over the image, animating it in an otherworldly way.

"Can I offer you anything?" he asked. "Tea, or wine, or—"

"That poor girl was looking for this picture, wasn't she?" she said, her voice tinged with both anger and sadness. "That man—that *evil* man!—didn't tell her what she was hunting for, and then left her to suffer the consequences. To be beaten like that for garnets and brass!"

"I'm not sure he knew himself," John said, crouching down before the painting. "He told her to look for something of value with the letter *F* upon it. He made the mark to show her, too. Do you still have the pendant with you?"

She reached into her pocket and handed him the necklace. He held it flat in his palm, tipping it toward the firelight. Mary was right about its value—silver and brass, studded with garnets and winking marcasite—but what interested him was the heart-shaped piece in the center, engraved with an elaborate *F*.

"This letter for your name is the reason Berthe took the jewelry," he said. "That's what she was hunting for, and when she found it, she believed it to be the valuable piece, doubtless seeing rubies and diamonds instead."

She hugged the shawl around her shoulders, twisting her hands in the ends as she bent down beside him. "So if we find those same *F*s somewhere on the painting, then this man was likely looking for my angel."

"I believe we will." He turned the panel around to study the haphazard marks written on the back, but Mary turned it back.

"I *know* we will, because I already have." She pointed to the angel's halo. The wide band of gold leaf was impressed with a thick decorative border, and incorporated into the filigree design was a recurring pattern of elaborate capital *F*s. "There's more here, too, along the hem of his gown."

"When did you notice that?" he asked, incredulous. "It's so subtle, the letters seem only another part of the design unless one is looking for them. Then they stick out plain as day."

She grinned. "I saw it at once, in Monsieur Dumont's shop. I thought they stood for Farren, which was part of the reason I bought the picture. I told you, it's my own guardian angel."

"I'm rather afraid he had another charge before you," John said, once again turning the panel over. "And I don't believe he did very well at his guarding then, either."

"You mean whichever family it was whose name begins with *F*," she said promptly. "We know they're from Florence. We know they commissioned Fra Pacifico to make this picture and likely the rest of the triptych that it's been cut from, and so we know that they were wealthy."

"We don't *know* any of that for certain, sweetheart," he cautioned. "We don't know any of it."

But John did know, and given all the other ways Mary had surprised him with her knowledge, he'd half expected her to realize it, too. The initial had to belong to the infamous

Feroce family. All the evidence together pointed to it: the painter, Florence, the date of the panel.

Every true bearleader or five-*centesimo* street *ciceroni* in Florence could tell Mary the story. The Feroces had been rivals of the Medici for control of Florence, both politically and financially. Only the invasion of the French King Charles VIII and his army in 1495 had destroyed the empire they'd so ruthlessly built. All of the Feroce men and their wives had been killed or executed by the French, their palazzos looted and burned, their fabulous possessions—jewels, silver, paintings, tapestries—scattered in a thousand different directions across Italy, and beyond. Never found was the chest of gold that the last Signori had supposedly prepared for the flight he never made, a king's ransom in gold that existed through the centuries only as a tantalizing mystery.

Could this painting hold the secret to that long-lost fortune? The gold alone could be worth an unimaginable sum, riches beyond counting in the modern world. Could the Feroces have remained true to the meaning of their name—"the ferocious"—and wielded their power through the centuries, even in death?

He glanced at Mary, poring over the painting as if her life depended upon it. Perhaps it did. Yet he wouldn't tell her about the Feroces, not a word. He'd keep that secret to himself as his own reward, just as he'd let her keep the painting once he'd learned its riddle.

That was only fair, wasn't it? She was a duke's daughter, a prize in her own right with a dowry to match, while he— he was worth little more than the letters in his name, his title an empty mockery without an income to support it. This long-lost treasure could give him a lasting estate for all his days, and for his heirs. He'd finally be accepted wherever he chose to go, a lord among lords, without any taint or scandal to his name. Money was always the true fuller's earth for any reputation, taking away every stain. With the Feroce gold, he could do anything.

Even ask for the hand of the Duke of Aston's daughter.

"We can guess, Mary," he said, "and we've made very excellent guesses at that, but we don't know for certain, not yet."

"Oh, you're too serious." She leaned closer, ostensibly to study the panel beside him, but also to brush against him.

At least that was what he hoped. He didn't know that for certain, either.

He frowned at the marks on the back of the panel, trying to concentrate on them instead of how her body, soft and warm as a kitten in the dark shawl, was pressing against his.

Earlier in the day, he would have wanted nothing more, but the mingled sense of excitement and foreboding he'd felt now had changed that. He didn't believe that an object could be cursed, any more than he believed in witches and warlocks, or even angels, for that matter. But with the Feroces involved, he couldn't deny that the mystery surrounding Mary's painting seemed to be a dark and dangerous one indeed, and until it was solved he wouldn't feel easy about their safety.

"Now that we've a notion of the final size of the picture, perhaps we can guess if these marks have any meaning," he said. He'd never again be able to see any kindness to the angel's face, not with the past he suspected it of having. "It could be that the marks are the beginnings and the ends of letters, or fragments of words."

Thoughtfully she nibbled on her lower lip. "Of course it would be Italian words, and old ones at that. We wouldn't necessarily know them. At least I wouldn't."

"If they're very old," he said, "I doubt I'd know them, either."

"But you're our bearleader," she said, half teasing. "You're supposed to be wise and learned in everything."

He laughed. He'd almost forgotten his assumed role as their guide. "Only a temporary position, sweetheart, and one born more from necessity than actual knowledge."

"You've been...splendid," she said, her voice lingering over the compliment. "I only pray that you won't abandon us once we reach Paris."

"I'll stay on so long as you require my service," he said, as aware as she of the double meaning to every word. When they'd first left Calais, he'd blithely told himself he'd travel with the three women only until he'd gotten the painting or seduced the older daughter, whichever happened first before Paris. Now they'd be in the capital by early afternoon tomorrow, and those first goals had oddly grown more distant, more unattainable. Yet the stakes had also been raised. If he solved the painting's riddle, he could be infinitely richer than the value of the picture alone. And if that happened, he might be able to claim the girl and her fortune as his own not by ruining her reputation, but honestly, as his wife. "So long as I'm wanted."

"Of course you're wanted," she said, as if there'd never been any doubt. He should have been gratified, but given his current thoughts, he wasn't. He wanted more than teasing. He wanted her.

"What of the genuine bearleader you hired?" he asked. "Monsieur Leclair, wasn't it? If he came as highly recommended for his erudition in French history as Miss Wood says, then it would be a pity for you to cast him aside."

"But Miss Wood is always watching our accounts," she said, "and since you have made a gift to us of your guidance and wisdom, why, she'd scarcely wish to turn you away."

Her frankness made him laugh. "You'll keep me about because I labor without hope of reward?"

"You're a gentleman," she said promptly. "You don't expect to be rewarded."

"My dear, I am one gentleman who does in fact toil and scrape for every last crumb of my bread," he said. "*That* is the true definition of practicality."

She bowed her head, smoothing her hair behind her ears. "I must sound like the most ignorant, spoiled, useless creature in the world. Of course you must make your way. You told me your circumstances before, and I beg your pardon a thousand times over for forgetting. If your private affairs require your attention in London, why, then surely you must go tend to them."

"No apologies, Mary, not from you," he said, reaching out to smooth back one stray lock that she'd missed. Would she understand as easily if he never told her of a Feroce treasure? Would she be so obliging if he kept it all to himself? "I'll be honored to continue with you to Paris."

Her eyes betrayed her uncertainty. "Truly?"

"Truly," he said. "Honored, and pleased by the company, too."

"So am I," she said, hugging her arms around herself and making a little shrug of relief. "I suppose we should return to our discussion as to the language represented by these fragments."

"Italian would be my guess," he said, "though they could be French, if the painting was brought to France long ago. And you, Mary Farren, are unlike any other lady I've ever had the delight to meet."

She looked up at him from beneath her lashes, seemingly unaware of what she was doing to him.

"Thank you, John." She didn't say it coquettishly, but as a matter of ordinary good manners. "I do thank you. Now, I've seen old Italian writing that's similar to this. One of my father's friends collects old letters by famous folk, and he showed me ones he had by a Roman poet."

So it was to be all business for a bit. He could be businesslike, if that was what she wished, and so he nodded sagely. "I've seen the same. It's rather like the way English people wrote in Shakespeare's time, with squat, stubby letters."

She nodded with enthusiasm. "And recall, too, that likely the person who wrote this did it in haste. There'd be no writing-master leaning over his shoulder."

John pointed to a fat, sweeping arc. "So that this could be part of a letter?"

She nodded. "And the mark, here, could be another. But this—doesn't this look like a number? A two, and a four, or a twenty-four?"

"A two, and a four." He sat back on his heels, thinking. "It could be a quantity, a sum, a fee, an address. It could, in short, be anything, or nothing."

"But it's a beginning, John," she said, echoing the way he'd sat, her striped skirts settling around her bent legs across the floor. "An excellent beginning! Think of how much we've discovered today!"

"And in the manner of all good mysteries, every question we answer begs three more." He stood, and offered her his hand. "Rise, my lady. I can't leave a peer's daughter sitting on the floor."

Ignoring his hand and his gallantry, she scrambled to her feet on her own. "It should be easy enough to find a list of ancient Florentine families, John. With all the collections and libraries in Paris, we'll be able to learn all that's known of Fra Pacifico and his patrons, and then once we reach Florence itself, why, we—"

"Slow, slow, Mary," he said softly. "Don't rush your

journey. Like all good things in life, this will be over soon enough without your wishing."

"I know." She gazed up at him, her dark eyes luminous by the fire's light as she searched his face. "I've waited so long for all of this, you see, that I can't help but look forward. I know I should pause and remember everything for when all I'll have is looking backward. It's the dreadful part of my practical nature. I cannot help it. I plan and plan to make things as right as they can be, and then, before I realize it, they're over and done."

"Then it's a habit you must break." He ran his fingers lightly across her jaw, turning her face up toward his. He couldn't remember the last time anyone had looked to him like this, as if he really did know the answer. "How can you have all this infamous adventure that you so crave if you're squandering all your time worrying over libraries and family names?"

Her smile was slight, melancholy with a regret at odds with her usual efficient cheerfulness. "I wish I could do as you say, and make this day last and last, and never be forgotten."

"That's not much of a wish, considering how it's entirely in your power to make it so."

"Not alone, I can't." She blushed at her own boldness. "Oh, goodness, I cannot believe I said that!"

"Why, when it was true?" He chuckled softly, lowering his face close to hers. He was going to kiss her, and she would welcome his kiss, and the fact that they both knew it only added to the delicious anticipation of these last hovering moments. "Or was I only one more part of your ever-practical planning?"

"Oh, no, John," she said. "I could never have planned you."

"Nor I you, sweetheart," he said as his lips found hers. At once she slipped her hands around his shoulders, letting the shawl slip to the floor behind her, and he folded her into his arms like a homecoming. He liked how she arched against him, her breasts rising high above the neckline of her gown, and the muffled creak of the stays that narrowed her waist.

He slid his hands lower over her hips to where the whale-bone ended, and even through the layers of petticoats he could feel the soft swell of her hips, the rich invitation of warm flesh. He didn't know if it was because they'd been interrupted this afternoon at the château, or everything else that had happened since, or simply that the better he knew her, the more he wanted her, but as he held her now, he felt his need for her fire and grow to a new urgency.

He turned her into the crook of his arm so he could kiss her harder, more relentlessly, thrusting his tongue deep within the velvet of her mouth. She made a small, happy growl that he hadn't expected, a sound that vibrated between their joined mouths. So she felt it, too.

"You're beautiful, Mary," he said, his voice rough with need. "You've no idea what you do to me."

He rocked her farther back, and slipped his hand inside her bodice, easing the neck downward until the ripe curve of her breast came free. She gasped with surprise, but he kissed her more to reassure her as his fingers caressed her breast, warm and full in his palm. He rubbed his thumb across her nipple, feeling how she trembled as the small nub tightened. His lips left hers, trailing kisses down her throat. Her skin was warm with her fire, her heartbeat pulsing on the side of her neck. Lower still he moved, until his mouth latched on to her nipple, licking it, grazing it lightly with his teeth, then suckling hard to draw the most sensation from her.

"Oh, John!" she gasped raggedly. "What you do—what you do!"

She twisted against him, struggling for the same thing he wished. She clung to him for support, her fingers digging desperately into his shoulders, and he wondered if her legs had the strength to support her.

Perhaps this was the night for them. He had her here in his room, now, where they wouldn't be disturbed. They'd never have such freedom in Paris, not once they were in separate lodgings. He'd no doubt she was still a virgin, but he'd also no doubt that he could give her such pleasure that any reluctance or second thoughts would be soon forgotten.

"I—I shouldn't," she whispered, her eyes still shut as she warred with her conscience. "Miss Wood trusts me."

"Miss Wood's not here, sweet," he reasoned. "It's you I'm kissing, not her."

"But I—you—must stop."

"You don't want me to do that," he whispered in return. "Not my adventurous lass."

A breathy sigh was her only answer. It was easy enough to lean her back that extra fraction, and catch his arm beneath her knees. Easy enough for her, too, to loop her arms more tightly around his shoulders to steady herself, her face flushed in the firelight and her hair coming unpinned and tumbling haphazardly down her back.

Four steps, no more, and then they were at the bed, and that was easiest of all. He laid her down, watching her hair fan over the coverlet as she sank into the feather bed, her breasts bared and her lips parted with desire for him, for *him*.

The rope springs of the bed creaked beneath his weight as he joined her. He bent to kiss her again, even as he was tearing his arms from the sleeves of his coat. He lay beside her, gathering her up against him to relish the teasing feel of her bare breasts against his chest, the delighted little catch in her breath.

He tossed back her striped skirts, sliding his hand along the length of her legs, the skin of her thighs like velvet above her garters. From her hip, it was easy to slide his hand forward, over her belly and the thatch of dark curls, and lower, lower, to the sweetest place between her thighs. She was wet for him already, astoundingly, wonderfully, all the proof he'd ever want that she desired him as much as he did her. She gasped at his touch, but didn't pull away, instead arching up against him. As gently as he could, he eased his fingers between the slick folds, stroking her until she gasped and trembled.

"I can't keep from you, sweetheart," he said, kissing her again and again as she lay beneath him. "Did you know that, Mary Farren? My Mary! You taste like heaven, and I'll never get enough."

And then, like that, she was gone, slipping from beneath him and stealing away all that fire, all that passion, all the kisses and promise of so much more. Instead she was sitting on the edge of the bed with her legs over the edge and her knees firmly together, repinning her hair with shaking hands.

"I cannot do this, John," she said without looking at him. "I'm sorry, but I cannot."

He came to sit behind her on the bed, his hands on her shoulders as he kissed the nape of her neck. She couldn't leave him, not like this.

"Don't be sorry, sweet," he whispered. "Stay, and I'll make you fair scream with pleasure. You can't even know what—"

"But I do, John," she said, her voice full of anguish that he didn't understand. "For me to be here with you like this— Diana was right, it isn't fair. Not to her, not to the trust Miss

Wood and Father have placed within me. How can I lecture my sister on how she should behave with gentlemen, and then be here with you?"

"It's not the same, Mary," he whispered, coaxing her. He slid his hands beneath her uplifted arms, filling his hands with her breasts. "It's you and it's us."

She groaned, and her eyes fluttered shut as she let her head fall back against his shoulder.

"But—but that's my reason, John," she said haltingly, distracted by his caress exactly as he'd hoped. "To behave with more passion than—than sense is not how I *am*."

"But it is, Mary," he said, letting the breath of his whisper be another kind of caress across the sensitive skin below her ear. "This is how you are with me. Full of fire and longing and ripe to—"

"No!" The single word seemed torn from her, and she pushed herself away from him and from the bed. Swaying before him on unsteady feet, her hair still half-unpinned, he could see now that she was crying as she tugged her bodice back into place over her breasts, breasts whose rosy, tight nipples still craved his touch.

"Mary, Mary," he began again, following her, reaching her, not wanting to lose her. "You know in your heart you wish this as much as I."

But she only shook her head, her hair trailing across her teary face. "I do, John, I *do,* and that is exactly why I must not. I may yet be a virgin, but being innocent is not the same as being a simpleton. I know what I wish to do on that—that bed with you, and that the pleasure you're promising me will likely be beyond anything I can imagine."

"Then why stop, sweet?" he asked. "Why not—"

"Hush, hush, I beg you, and hear me!" she cried, her voice breaking with tears and emotion. "What you've given me now, how you've kissed and touched me, is headier than the first sip of wine to a drunkard. I want more, and I want it from you. But I know the consequences, John. I'm too—too practical to pretend otherwise."

She was letting her tears flow freely now, sliding down her cheeks unchecked as she struggled with her hair.

"I'm sorry, John, so sorry for us both," she said. "But know that in exchange for this night with you, I must risk conceiving an unfortunate child or contracting the pox. I'd cheat the gentleman I've yet to meet who will someday honor me as his wife, and I'd burden myself with a shameful dark secret the rest of my days. And I cannot do it, John. I cannot, and still be true to myself."

"What if I won't let you go, Mary?" he demanded, coming to take her into his arms again. "What if I know better what both of us want?"

"Because you can't," she said sadly. Slipping free of him, she bent to gather her discarded shawl from the floor, and used one corner to wipe at her tears. "That's who you are, too. And I am sorry for it all, John, more sorry than I ever can say."

He felt hollow, bereft, his heart racing and member still hard and aching for a release that now it would not find. She stood before him, her beauty all the more tantalizing for her melancholy and her refusal, even for her reasons. He'd never wanted a woman, any woman, more than he did Mary Farren at this moment. Yet damnation, she was right: he wouldn't take her against her will or her conscience. He'd come to respect her far too much for that. She was the daughter of a duke, and entitled to choose how and when she gave up her honor, and he couldn't fault her that it wasn't in a post inn in Chantilly, to a mercenary Irish lord.

She stepped close and kissed him again, her lips barely

brushing over his in farewell. "If you do not wish to come with us tomorrow to Paris, I will understand, and make proper excuses for you. I'll understand, but I'll not forget. Good night, my lord, and God bless you and keep you safe."

She took the painting from the chair, slipped through the door, and was gone. He was either a far greater gentleman than he'd ever realized to let her go, or a far greater fool than he'd ever feared.

Archambault sat in the tall-backed armchair at his open window, allowing himself the considerable pleasure of a small glass of burgundy wine with the clear salted soup that was his dinner. The physicians had long ago forbidden him wine or spirits, but today he'd felt so much improved that he'd decided his own course. He had gone out in his carriage for a drive, and had been able to salute and amaze old acquaintances who'd likely already given him up for dead. He'd even let himself be briefly carried into his oldest haunt, Madame du Fontenelle's *salon,* to hear his poetry read and to have praise lavished upon him—as if such meaningless blandishments held any of their old allure for him now.

He couldn't say what had caused the change. Was it this brilliant summer day that had warmed him better than any fire, or the taste of the wine now on his tongue, or the letter that had arrived last night? He'd venture it was the letter, for the news in it had been cheering indeed.

The lost painting of his Madonna's triptych had been found.

Of course he would not rest until this last panel hung in place beside the other two, but now he knew it still existed. Miraculously, it, too, had survived the centuries. After the disaster in Calais, Archambault had employed a new agent especially known for his subtlety and cunning.

In short order the man had learned the painting had been bought by a young English lady traveling through the country. He'd spoken to servants in the inns where the lady had stayed, and who could describe the painting in the young lady's arms. He'd even learned from a footman at the Château de Chantilly that the young lady had viewed another triptych by Fra Pacifico, and recognized it as a twin to the one in his posses sion.

Yet the agent's news wasn't entirely without fault. Three times, in three different ways, he'd tried to arrange the capture of the painting without success. The lady had proved most resourceful in thwarting these attempts, and a gentle-man traveling with the lady's party had helped as well.

But he could overlook all this because the painting and the lady were both coming to Paris. They could even be here now, and gallantly Archambault raised his glass toward the open window in a silent toast to her. One way or another, he'd get it from her now. His agent had said she was very young, very beautiful, and Archambault smiled wearily to think of how little that now mattered.

He turned in his chair so he could see the two parts of the triptych already in his possession. Sunlight slanted over the wall, making the Holy Mother's cloak glow around her. There was real beauty, the beauty of faith and grace, and he couldn't wait to see the third panel in place. An angel, the agent had said. An angel much like the one in Chantilly, and Archambault tried to imagine how the reunited triptych would look on his wall. He'd keep his promise to the Blessed Lady after all. With her glory restored, he could die in peace.

The sun had slanted lower over the chimney pots, the once-warm air now feeling chill on his shrunken shoulders. He rang for his servant to close the window, and slowly, stiffly pushed himself from the chair. He couldn't stand straight, not when the pain returned with this sudden, blinding keenness.

"Have mercy on my miserable soul, oh, Holy Mother," he prayed, his voice strangled to a whisper and his eyes squeezed shut against the pain. "Soon I'll come to your embrace, but not yet. Please God, not yet."

Chapter Ten

The packet office clerk turned doleful as he saw John coming to his grated window yet again.

"I am very sorry, my lord, very sorry indeed," the clerk began before John had even reached his window. He patted his snuff-colored wig with both his hands, and sighed mournfully. "But tides and wind bow to no man, my lord. So it has been since the beginning of time, my lord, and so it will be until the end of it."

But John had already heard this particular homily twice before, and he'd no wish to hear it again. "All I care to know, sir, is when I might reasonably expect to board the packet for Dover."

"The boat with the mail will leave within the hour, my lord, and attempt to reach the packet," the clerk said. "But that will be an arduous passage across a rough sea, with no guarantee of success. Better you should wait here, my lord, and take your ease until the tide turns this afternoon, and the packet can run into the quay."

Better struck John as entirely relative. It was indeed far better to wait here on shore than to venture out with the mail in an open boat, soaked with spray and dependent upon the strength of the men at the oars for his survival. Better to stay in this office as the clerk had bidden, where tedium would be preferable to drowning.

But was it better to remain here in Calais, in the same country with the one woman he ever really wanted, body, soul, and wit, who in turn didn't want him? How could he turn his back on her and her wretched painting, when the very waves conspired to hold him back? Was it better to sit in this small, stuffy room and meditate on how badly he'd mis-stepped with Mary Farren, or to plunge into the rough waves toward London and the certainties of his old life before Mary had turned it upside down and wrong side out?

Damnation, he was beginning to sound like some third-rate touring company of *Hamlet* with this better and best. He glanced out the window to the harbor, the water spanked and churning with choppy whitecaps. Better, far better, to live than to drown, and with a muttered oath of frustration, he went to the end of the waiting room benches and sat by himself.

Near the benches stood a crooked shelf piled with old newspapers to help those waiting for the packet pass the time. Desperate for amusement, John rummaged through the stacks. All the papers were months old, fly-spotted and rippled from the damp sea air. Yet just as John was ready to shove the whole grubby mess back on the shelf, a short article caught his eye, and held it.

A Sale of HISTORIC SIGNIFICANCE in Rouen
When the effects of the late Widow Mme. Germaine were put up to auction by her nephew M. Paul Germaine in this city recently, a hidden TREASURE was discovered, and sold. An Italian picture showing a group of

kneeling Worshippers was revealed to be a RARE PAINTING by a Monk of Florence known as Fra Pacifico. Though dirty and in ill-repair, the picture was recognized for its true VALUE by the agent of a great nobleman of PARIS as being portraits of his Italian cousins, shown in the antique dress of their time three hundred years ago. The painting having been believed long LOST, its recovery was greeted with REJOICING by the nobleman, who gave 200 gold pieces, a great sum beyond the picture's value, for its safe RECOVERY & RETURN.

****

It had to be the partner to Mary's angel, the other side of the triptych. It couldn't be anything else, not by Fra Pacifico. But if this nameless nobleman had been so quick to pay such an outrageous price, would he also be capable of murder to possess the other panel? Was this man the one behind the attempts to steal Mary's angel from her? John had told himself that if he'd given up Mary, he'd give up pursuing the painting as well. It seemed right that way, fitting.

But what if he'd abandoned her, his Mary, when she might need him the most?

"My lord, I can see the packet coming into the dock now," the clerk called. "The boarding orders should be handed down from the master within the hour."

"Hang his orders," John said, tucking the newspaper into his coat. "I'm bound for Paris instead."

Mary sat on a small folding stool in the long gallery of the Palais du Luxembourg. There were only a few other people here visiting the collection this morning, their footsteps echoing in the grand empty halls. Miss Wood sat farther down the gallery on a bench before a statue of Jupiter, while in the other direction Diana seemed more occupied in gazing out the nearby window into the gardens than appreciating the classical art around her.

But Mary was determined to *learn;* this was why she'd wanted so much to come abroad, wasn't it? With an oversized sketchbook in her lap, she sketched the large marble statue of the goddess Artemis and the stag before her, her pencil moving across the page with conscientious purpose. The best advice for English ladies viewing foreign art was to make a concentrated study of the painting or the statue, the theory being that the more one looked at a piece, the more one understood it. Sketching statues and other *objet d'art* had been highly recommended to Mary, not only for focusing her study, but also as a way to amass a portfolio of sketches to display to her father and neighbors at home in Kent.

With a sigh, Mary paused to consider her drawing. At home she'd always done well enough with watercolors of fields, streams and woods, but this morning Artemis was proving far more of a challenge than amorphous oak trees and distant cows.

She'd drawn the statue's head first, and she thought she'd captured the spirit of the profile rather well. But then she'd had trouble making the head align properly with the body below it, giving the poor goddess of the hunt such a peculiar kink to her neck that any real archery would be a challenge indeed.

"Well, now, my lady, that is fine!" Miss Wood said, coming to stand behind her, the white cuffs of her sleeves rolled up to keep from being soiled by her drawing pencils and chalks. "Pray be sure to write the name of the statue and the date at the bottom, so you'll always be able to recall when it was done."

"I'm not sure it's worth the trouble of remembering,"

Mary said, frustrated with her own lack of talent. "Look at my poor Artemis, Miss Wood! Her arms are too long and her legs are too short, and her bow and quiver are small enough to be suited to Cupid instead of any huntress."

"Don't be so critical of yourself, Lady Mary," Miss Wood said kindly. "It's only your second day in the galleries. We must all learn to train our eyes to see what's before us, without letting our thoughts wander to idle distraction."

Distraction. Oh, yes, thought Mary glumly, that was a good word for it. It wasn't that Paris had disappointed her. She'd never seen so lovely a place, full of magnificent houses, churches, palaces, and other public buildings, and beautiful bridges arching over the river Seine. Three days before, they'd settled into their lodgings at the Hotel d'Imperatrice in the Rue Jacob, a convenient place popular with the English gentry, and for their four guineas a week they had two bedchambers, a dining room, a small parlor, and apartments for their servants, as well. The beds were cleaner than any others they'd found in France, the bugs fewer, and the furnishings grand. Their new bearleader, Monsieur Leclair, an affable if long-winded Frenchman with excellent English, had taken them for their first tour of the city. They hadn't begun to make calls and present their letters of introduction, yet already they'd received invitations to suppers, *salons,* and other amusements.

Yet despite all these pleasurable diversions, Mary and Miss Wood both understood that there was only one real distraction able to keep Mary's thoughts from her work, and that was John Fitzgerald. It wasn't his presence that was the distraction, because he had yet to appear at the Hotel d'Imperatrice.

Mary didn't even know if he'd come to Paris or not. The last word she'd had from him had been a short, charming note left with the innkeeper and directed to Miss Wood and Diana, as well. He'd been called away on an urgent matter, and regretted not saying farewell in person. He would always treasure the memory of the lovely ladies, and their journey from Calais. He hoped one day that they would meet again, either in London or abroad. He wished them well, and Godspeed.

Only Mary knew the real reason for his sudden departure, but the knowledge only made his absence harder, not easier, to bear. A hundred times a day, she'd thought she'd glimpse him on the street. She'd jump at every knock at their door, and her heart would race at every letter or invitation that was delivered. Though she kept the angel painting tucked inside her bedsprings for safekeeping, the same hiding place she'd used all along, she still took it out when she was in her chamber, and each time she did, she thought of John. No wonder she couldn't think of a more accurate definition of a distraction.

"Why don't you try another sketch of a different statue, my lady?" Miss Wood suggested. "There are so many to choose from, and with each drawing you attempt, you're sure to improve, and be more satisfied with your result."

"You are right, of course." Resolutely Mary flipped the page in her sketchbook, burying the unfortunate Artemis and, she hoped, her thoughts of John, as well. "There is no fresher beginning than a clean white page."

"True words, my lady," Miss Wood agreed, and sighed. "I know these galleries would be so much more entertaining with Lord John's company. But gentlemen must tend to the affairs of the larger world, and leave us ladies behind."

But John didn't leave them, Mary thought miserably. She'd been the one who'd left him, and now she'd likely never, ever see him again.

"Instead we must be grateful his lordship could spare as

much of his time and knowledge as he did with us," Miss Wood continued. "Now we must simply devise our own amusements without him."

Mary lowered her head over the page, hoping to hide her flushed cheeks. She couldn't tell if Miss Wood recognized the depths of her wretchedness, or if it were simply a hideous coincidence that she'd mention John now, when Mary was missing him so much.

"I'm sure we can entertain ourselves most admirably, Miss Wood," she said, making sharp, determined strokes across the page. "We have done so before we'd met his lordship, and there's no reason why we won't now that he's gone. Oh, a pox on this, that's ruined."

She scowled down at the thick awkward line she slashed across the page, a line that could never be corrected. Where was her concentration, her resolve, now? She ripped the sheet from the sketchbook and tore it into quarters to stuff in the back, then abruptly rose from her folding stool.

"Diana, show me what you've sketched," she said, leaving Miss Wood behind as she came to stand beside her sister.

But Diana quickly covered her sketchbook with her arms, hiding her drawing.

"Oh, you don't wish to see," she said. "My pictures are never very good."

"They're bound to be better than mine this morning," Mary said, reaching for her sister's book. "Come, let me see what's so dreadful."

Diana shrugged with a cheerful resignation. "Very well," she said, raising her arms and sitting back. "If you really wish to."

"Oh, *Diana*," Mary said, more disgusted than surprised. "How could you squander your time like this?"

While her sister had unfolded her stool before a handsome

ancient marble of Jove, she might as well have been before a milliner's shop instead. Her entire sheet was covered with drawings of the oversized hats favored by French ladies, head after head bedecked with clustered ribbons, trailing veils, and huge curled plumes.

"I drew what interested me," Diana confessed, not in the least remorseful. "From this window, I can see the ladies in the park, and lah, what fantastical hats and bonnets!"

"Is that what you meant to take home to show to Father?" Mary asked, incredulous. "Will this be the proof of how you were improved by traveling abroad—a portfolio of *hats?*"

"I didn't ask to be improved," Diana said. "I rather liked myself the way I was."

"But to waste such an opportunity for education, for knowledge!"

Diana tossed the sketchbook on the floor and stood. She plucked at the ribbons of her own hat, plumping the bow beneath her chin.

"It's you who wishes to look at grubby old things, Mary, not I," she said. "And I should think that after Lord John decided he'd had enough of your dry sort of education, why—"

"That's quite enough, Lady Diana," Miss Wood said firmly, taking Diana by the arm. "Perhaps a short stroll with me outside will clear the frivolity from your head, so you might better concentrate on your sketching. At least it will permit your sister to continue her studies undisturbed by you."

"Then everyone will be most blissfully happy," Diana said, gaily fluttering her fingers by way of farewell as Miss Wood marched her from the gallery. "Apply yourself, Mary, and when you're ready, I'll tell you how best to dress your next hat!"

"You do that, Diana," Mary said wearily, more to herself than her departing sister. "You just do that."

She took up her sketchbook and pencil again and sat back down on her stool, sweeping her skirts neatly around her feet. She would try Artemis's stag alone this time, and attempt to capture the look of wildness that the sculptor had given the animal's eyes. She needed to concentrate harder on her task, that was all.

Yet even as she began drawing the stag's crown of antlers, her thoughts wandered back to what Diana had said, or had at least begun to say before Miss Wood had interrupted. Mary had believed that John had liked her cleverness. She'd thought he'd enjoyed working together with her to decipher her painting's history and meaning.

But what if she'd misunderstood him and his actions? What if in truth he'd found her as tedious as most other younger gentlemen did, too erudite, too practical, to be the amusing female companion every man desired?

On that last night in Chantilly, she'd tried to be more like Diana, only to feel as if she'd betrayed herself as well as John. There'd been no doubt that she'd wanted John—she'd been shocked by the intensity of her desire for him, and the fiery sensations that he'd raised in her body—but at the last moment, she couldn't abandon her values or her old practical self for the sake of a night of pleasure. Reviewed over and over in her head, the experiment could only be called a miserable failure.

And now it was done; it was done. So much for her attempt at adventure, or the passion that Diana relished so effortlessly. There was no point to missing John any longer. All around her were other women and men, going about their lives, and so should she. She must think of the rest of her journey like the blank white sheet before her, waiting for her to make a fresh start. She took her penknife from her pencil box, shaved a new point on her pencil, and concentrated studiously on the marble stag before her, determined to begin again. The nose was long and pointed, the nostrils flared, the ears pointed and—

It could not be possible.

She inched up from her stool so she could peek through the tangle of the stag's legs. Surely this was just another imagining. Surely he couldn't have come here to find her. Surely…

John was walking toward her, sauntering almost, keeping an easy rhythm with a walking stick in his hand as he came down the center of the hall. The gallery was long, a series of arched windows interrupted by tall pilasters. Shafts of light angled through the windows across the tiled floor, and he passed through them in a regular pattern: three steps in shadow, then two through the brilliance of the sunlight. Though his steps were measured, his expression beneath his black cocked hat was anything but calm: fierce and determined, and set upon reaching some distant goal.

Could she be that prize?

She gulped and ducked back down. How horrible if he'd caught her spying like that! Her wide-brimmed hat with the striped ribbons, though not so big as the ones Diana had drawn, was still bound to show behind Artemis and her stag. She must pretend she hadn't noticed him, that she was so dedicated to her drawing that nothing could distract her.

Her heart racing, she bent over her sketchbook, pencil in hand. It wouldn't do to have him see an empty sheet, either, and with quick, mechanical strokes she forced herself to return to drawing the stag.

What was he going to say to her? What would she answer

in return? Oh, please, please, let her for this once say the right thing!

She heard his footsteps stop, then saw the well-polished toes of his shoes and the tip of his walking stick just before her. Did he clear his throat to draw her attention, or were his words as sticky as her own were bound to be?

"Good day, Lady Mary."

She made herself finish the line she'd been drawing, then counted to five before she looked up.

"Lord John," she said, wishing she knew how to make her voice sound less eager. "Good day to you."

He nodded, his fingers flexing on the gold-headed crown of his walking stick. "I trust you are well?"

"Oh, yes, thank you," she said. They could have been reciting lines by rote from a play, and not very convincingly, either. "And you, my lord? You are well?"

"Quite well." He glanced around her. "You are, ah, unattended?"

"My sister and Miss Wood are taking a bit of air," she said. "They should be returning directly. You know how little empathy Diana shows for art."

For the first time his mouth twitched into something resembling a smile. "Her ladyship has always demonstrated different sensibilities."

"Yes, she does." She felt herself blushing, foolishly reduced by even that half smile, and again she took shelter inside her wide-brimmed hat, looking down at her sketch.

"Might I see your drawing, my lady?" he asked, almost painfully respectful considering all they'd done together last time they'd been together.

She nodded, and tipped it for him to view.

"The stag, is it?" He glanced between the statue and her sketchbook.

"Of course," she said, a bit wounded that the subject wouldn't be more self-evident. "I've only begun the head so far."

"Ah, yes, so you have." He studied it a bit longer, his expression more concerned than appreciative. "I can make out the antlers now."

"I don't believe you'd discern the antlers from the hinder legs, my lord," she said with a sigh. "Not from my drawing, anyway."

"I did not say that, my lady!"

"You didn't have to, because I did." Idly she began drawing stars around the hapless stag's head, as if it were a constellation in the sky. "I draw for myself, my lord. And I've never purported to become either a copyist or a forger."

"That is wise," he said, so solemnly that at first she couldn't tell if he were jesting or not. "Because your true talent lies in your eye, not your hand. Your gift is your rare appreciation and sympathy for pictures, and your love of their meaning."

Mary stared, overwhelmed. She'd never before heard such words from a gentleman, and she'd take them a thousand times over compared to one more tired comparison of her eyes to the stars. It was a genuine, unexpected, delicious compliment that only he could offer, fitted to her and no other.

And no matter what else either of them now said, she'd never, ever forget it.

"If I'd been born a gentleman, that's what I would do with my life," she confessed in a breathless rush, a secret she'd never told another. "I'd study pictures. I'd build my own collection, and perhaps advise others on their own purchases. I'd make the acquaintance of living artists, too, to learn more of their gift. And I'd live not in London, but on the Continent, and it would be my *life*."

And he didn't laugh. "You still could," he said. "You have the eye, the gift. Turn your back on all the bachelor-peers clamoring for your hand, and choose the life you want."

She shook her head, unwilling to trust even the dream of such a glorious future. "Father would never permit it."

He shrugged. "It's your life, not his. Please yourself first."

She gazed up at him, and felt her own smile build slowly, unfurling like a spring flower. "You cannot know how much I missed you since we—we parted in Chantilly."

"But I can," he said softly, "because that is how much I missed you, as well."

She looked back down at her drawing, unable to let him see the confused emotions that she knew must be on her face. "I didn't believe I'd ever see you again."

"Ah, Mary," he said, clearly choosing his words with great care. "Like you, I'd thought it would be wisest if we parted. I told myself it was the best course for both our situations, and our stations. Yet damnation, each mile I put between us made me want you more, not less. You've become too dear to me, Mary, too much a part of me in ways I can scarce understand."

"I felt the same way," she confessed in a whisper. "I felt the *same*."

He nodded, but didn't smile, as if not wanting to risk interrupting his speech before he'd finished. "I was waiting in Calais to board the packet. The harbor was too rough for the packet without the tide, and I'd no wish to test my luck with the boat. Fate must have kept me there, sweet, because that's when I saw this."

He reached into the front of his coat and drew out a yellowed scrap torn from an old newspaper. "Read this, Mary. Read it, and tell me your thoughts."

She took the scrap, spreading it flat with her fingers on

her sketchbook. "Fra Pacifico! Why, this sounds exactly like the third panel of the triptych we saw at Chantilly, the one with the donors. Oh, John, do you think this could be part of the same set as my angel?"

"I'd venture the odds are high that it is, wouldn't you?" he asked. "What I'd give to learn the name of that French nobleman who bought it!"

"This says the sale was made in Rouen," she began, unable to keep the excitement from her voice. Five minutes once again in his company, and here was more adventure than she'd seen in the past three days. "If we can contact whomever made the sale to ask the buyer's name—"

"I already have, sweetheart." He took Diana's abandoned stool and brought it to sit beside Mary. "The buyer wrapped himself in secrecy. He bought the picture through an agent, had the man pay cash, and revealed nothing of himself. The owner of the auction house doubted the agent himself knew more than what was reported in the paper."

Mary leaned closer, her arms folded over her sketchbook. "But why such secrecy?"

"He has his reasons, I suppose." John leaned forward, too, his hands resting one on top of the other on the head of his walking stick. "He might simply be a very private gentleman who prefers to keep his affairs from public conversation. He might intend the painting as a special gift for another. He might be shamed by the vast sum he bid, far beyond the picture's value, in order to stop other bidding before it began."

"Were there other bidders?"

"The auction house's owner said there was no other interest in this particular picture at all. Originally it wasn't even included in the offering catalog, but jumbled in with a miscellaneous lot. 'Old-fashioned and unappealing' was how he characterized it."

"Well, then, there must be another path for us to try." Swiftly she scanned the article again. "It says here that this Frenchman lives in Paris, and has Italian relatives. Surely that—"

"Will be impossible to trace," he said, firmly enough to leave no doubt. "Half of France has an ancestor from Italy."

"But if we asked here in Paris—"

"We'd come up with too many names to sort through," he said. "Italian blood is everywhere here, especially among the noble families. For that matter, there's plenty of it flowing through high-born Englishmen, too. Remember that our own old King Charles II had an Italian granny named de Medici."

"Oh, there must be some other clue!" she said, tapping her knee with frustration. "I wish I'd known this other picture was for sale at auction. *I* would have bid on it, and outbid this French rascal, too. To have two paintings of the three!"

"Our mysterious nobleman may already have the center panel, and now one of the sides as well," he said. "We don't know for certain. You may have the last piece of his puzzle."

"I won't let him have it, either," she said fiercely. "Whoever he is, the angel is mine."

John smiled, a quick flash of pride for her determination. "Our thoughts run the same course, Mary, but this nobleman might think otherwise. He has an advantage over us, too, since he knows who you are, and that you have the picture he wants."

"Then he must keep on wanting," she said. "He can't just go about taking things from other people because he wants them, John."

"In England, no," John said. "But in France, the nobles have more power to do what they want. And depending upon how highly placed this rascal is at court, he may be able to do exactly that. Where is the picture now?"

"In a safe place," she said, hedging. She didn't know why she still didn't want to confide any of her hiding places to John. Diana knew, of course, since they shared the same room, but only if she'd paid attention each night, which, Diana being Diana, was no certainty. Mary had trusted John with most everything else, but still she clung to this last little secret, as if telling anyone—even John—would somehow weaken her possession of the picture, or make it less hers.

His face was full of concern. "Perhaps you should take it to a bank for safekeeping until this is resolved. That way, not only will the picture be safe, but you as well."

"I'm not frightened, John," she said firmly. "I'm my father's daughter, and I'll not be intimidated by any bullying Frenchman."

He grunted, and she could tell he was unhappy with her. Well, so be it; she wouldn't budge. The painting was special to her. She'd paid fairly for the painting, and she was determined to keep it.

"I'm not frightened," she said again. "Truly."

"I am." He rose, and offered her his hand. "If you're feeling so deuced brave, would you come along with me? I've heard there's another painting here in these galleries somewhere by your Fra Pacifico, and I thought we'd try to find it."

It should have been a pleasant invitation to walk in the gallery and admire the art they both enjoyed. But his expression was so dark it was almost forbidding, turning his invitation into a dare.

Did she dare go with him? Did she dare accept his admission that he'd missed her as much as she had missed him, or should she remember the other side of him that knew of guns and murder and other things he himself had hinted at? Did she dare put aside the misgivings she'd earlier felt about being alone with him, and nearly—very nearly—lying with him in the inn at Chantilly? Did she dare begin again with him as if nothing had happened or ever would, when they both understood that what they'd felt in Chantilly was still running beneath the surface of this summer day, eating away at the ground beneath their feet?

"I'm not frightened," she said, a third time. But was it to convince him, or herself?

"Then you'll come?" he asked, his extended hand almost a command. "I'm told the painting's not far. A lady's portrait."

"I will." She'd take those dares, all of them. She wrote a quick note of explanation to Miss Wood on a fresh sheet of paper, and propped the sketchbook against her stool as a makeshift sign. Then she rose without taking either John's hand or his arm, choosing instead to walk by his side, without touching. As she fell into step beside him, down the long gallery of blank-eyed white statues, she didn't look to see his reaction.

It was, she decided, much safer like that.

"I told you it wasn't far, Mary." He stopped at the door of a smaller chamber off the main gallery, waiting for her to enter first. She felt foolish for hesitating, even the second she did, finally sailing in with her head high. This was John, who'd already risked his own life to preserve hers. Yet still she caught herself noting that here was no door to the chamber, only a short passageway, with others visitors walking back and forth. She'd be safer here than on any Parisian street—with John, or without him.

But the little gallery wasn't as empty as she'd thought. While she hesitated, a servant slowly pushed a wheeled chair through the doorway, a frail gentleman swathed in shawls and coverlets hunched over in the seat. The gentleman's face was ashen gray, his cheeks carved with deep lines of either great age or great suffering, and painted with the garish daubs of red and white affected by French gentlemen as well as ladies. His wig and clothes were costly, and over his black velvet gloves he wore a large diamond ring on his little finger. Bent as he was, he still had the aura of nobility and importance, and as the servant wheeled him by, Mary automatically stepped to one side in respect.

"No ceremony, mademoiselle, I beg you," he said, his voice a wheezing croak. "My only friends now are old pictures."

"Yes, monsieur," Mary said gently. "Certain pictures can bring enormous comfort."

"Exactly so." He twisted his head to gaze up at her. "How clever you are for so young and beautiful a girl!"

It was a harmless, idle compliment, and yet the leering appraisal in the invalid's rheumy eyes made Mary take another step back. He began to laugh at her discomfort, then disolved into a wracking cough that made him press his handkerchief to his face as the servant hurried the chair away.

At once John took her by the arm and led her into the small gallery. "I thought that old rascal was dead by now, gone to the demon that surely sired him."

"He was like the devil." Mary shivered, glad to be away. "Did you see the look in his eyes when he looked at me, John?"

"Be grateful that's all he could do," he said. "He's the Comte de Archambault, Mary. Does the name sound familiar to you?"

Mary frowned, thinking. "Vaguely, though I cannot place it exactly. Is he a famous nobleman at court, or perhaps a *philosophe*?"

"Oh, he's famous, yes, even by Parisian standards," John

said, his voice so full of contempt that she knew far worse was to come. "His family's as ancient and venerable as they come, but he's proof enough that even the bluest blood thins over time. You can see how debauchery's destroyed him."

"He's...*debauched?*" Mary looked after the invalid with interest, if not sympathy. She didn't think she'd ever seen anyone who could be described that way. Now she remembered where she'd seen his name, however: he'd been a regular feature in the lowest London scandal sheets that she and Diana would sometimes see in other people's houses. He was often linked with behavior so wicked that his name had been abbreviated with asterisks to keep the publisher from being taken to court.

While Archambault was obviously suffering for his past, even in her innocence Mary had sensed something corrupt about him, a taint of lingering sinful cruelty in the set of his mouth beneath the expensive curled wig, the suggestion of an illicit, unwanted caress still in the curve of his long fingers with their too-large diamond ring.

"So you know him, then," she said. "Strange he didn't acknowledge you."

"I?" John shook his head, clearly surprised she'd ask. "No, I'm far too humble for his exalted acquaintance."

"Likely too decent and honorable as well," she said loyally, "if what is said of him is true."

"Likely what's said is only the half of it," John said, his expression set. "He's not ten years older than I, yet he's as broken as a man of eighty. They say he's turned repentant now that he must stare death in the eye, that he's burned all his licentious poetry and sent his mistresses packing, in the hopes of salvation for his soul. No wonder his only remaining friends are pictures."

"Pictures don't care who looks at them," she said softly.

"Ah, well, he can't hurt you or anyone else now," John said. "Not in this life, anyway."

"God willing." She took a deep breath, determined to forget the wicked comte and concentrate instead on the beauty of the paintings around them. This room was different from the other galleries she'd seen, where one enormous painting was hung in stately splendor on a single damask-covered wall, topped with a row of smaller ones by the same artist that were hung so high visitors had to crane their necks to see them.

Here the paintings were smaller, set in narrow gold frames and crowded onto the four walls so closely that they nearly touched, martyred saints beside stern *condittieri,* sweet-faced Virgins next to nightmarish visions of devils, dancing ladies atop heroic battles. It was almost as if this were a closet for storing the pictures, rather than for displaying them to any advantage. Because she liked these smaller, older pictures so much more than the large, florid ones of the last hundred years, the carelessness of the arrangement made her sad.

"I'd guess the caretakers here have no more regard for older pictures than the auctioneer in Rouen," she said sadly. "They're all jumbled together, like buttons tossed from a seamstress's jar."

"They're also all Italian, from Florence, Rome, Venice, Padua," he said, his gaze sweeping across the rows of pictures as he searched for one in particular. "The French as a people so love themselves that they find it impossible to admit there's anything a foreigner might do better than they. There's the one. That must be by your Fra Pacifico."

He took her hand and led her to the far corner of the room. At once she saw which picture he meant: as familiar as she was now with her angel, there couldn't be any other that had the same rare beauty.

This was a portrait of a young lady, her profile sharply outlined against a turquoise sky. Her hair was braided and twisted and threaded throughout with jewels and strands of pearls into an elaborate coronet on her head, and her red velvet gown with its high, tight bodice was fantastically embroidered in gold threads, and embellished with more jewels. While Mary's angel was crowned with gold leaf to give him celestial magnificence, this lady's jewels and velvet were to display her family's power here in this life, perhaps as an advertisement for possible suitors.

But what she shared with the angel, and what caught Mary's eye first, was the fierceness of her gaze. There was none of the melting soft expression of the ladies and Madonnas around her, no doe-eyed sweetness. She was a warrior-princess in her own right, her dark eyes flashing and those elaborate braids writhing with an almost malevolent vitality. From the set of her jaw to the tip of her elegantly arched nose, she was full of the same challenge and fire as her own militant angel.

"How could he paint such pictures, and be called Fra Pacifico?" she wondered, leaning close to take in the picture's magic. "Brother Peace, indeed. Look at her! She could have been a Caesar in her own right!"

"She's like a lioness," John said beside her. "Certainly the pagan among so many Christians. I'll wager this is the one that Archambault came to see, as wicked as he is himself."

"Hush, John," Mary said, shocked by his casual irreverence. "She was likely some respectable Italian matron, the noble queen of a great family."

"More likely she followed her own will and passion to the torment of her father and the sorrow of her mother," John said, clearly as drawn to the picture as she was herself. "Look at her face—more Mars than Venus!—and tell me she didn't cause far more trouble than she soothed."

Mary smiled wryly. "I never said she didn't cause trouble."

"You didn't because you couldn't, not and speak truthfully." While they'd been admiring the picture, he'd gradually drifted closer to her until now, when he set his hand lightly on the back of her waist, it seemed the most natural thing in the world. "She must have been rather like you in that way."

"Like *me?*" Incredulous, she twisted around to look at him directly. "It's my very nature to solve problems, John, not to cause them. Everyone in my family would tell you the same."

"Then perhaps I'll follow my own observations," he said. "And mind you, I'm not complaining. Your troublemaking can be quite entertaining."

"Stuff and rubbish," she said, turning back to the painting. "I'm just going to pretend I didn't hear that. I wonder if this lady belonged to the family that commissioned my angel."

He made an odd strangled sound in her throat that Mary suspected was swallowed laughter. She could feel the vibration of it through his palm on her back. How could he possibly believe she was a troublemaker?

"It would make sense if she were of the same family," she continued, ignoring him as best she could. "I wonder what her name was?"

"It's lost to time now," he said, at last regaining his composure. "'Portrait of a Young Lady' isn't much to go by."

"If only we had the panel with the donors' portraits, then we'd know everything!" she said. "We'd know who commissioned the pictures, what the marks meant on the back, what this lady's name might be, what—"

"In short," he interrupted with droning mock sagacity, again working hard not to laugh, "we'd be the wisest persons on earth, with the answer to every great secret in our grasp."

She ducked her chin. "So you *are* teasing me, my lord."

"Only cautioning, Mary," he said, "as one trouble-maker to another."

His gaze shifted from the picture to her with such unabashed fondness and admiration in his eyes that she began to think teasing might not be so bad at all.

"I did miss you," he continued. "Damnation, I can't even begin to explain all the ways, just that to not have you with me felt wrong."

She understood this, for she'd felt much the same way. All the little wars she'd had in her head, the doubts and the questions she'd tried to reason through—everything came back to the same place. To be with him felt right; to be apart felt lost, lonely, *wrong*.

Was this what poets and other romantic folk called love? He'd spoken nothing of that yet, but she'd heard that this was a most difficult word for gentlemen to say. She wished she'd some married lady friend she could ask for advice; with such a question, neither Miss Wood nor Diana—especially not Diana!—would do. Was love the passionate excitement that swept through her when John held her and kissed her and touched her in such a wonderful fashion? Or was love this quieter sense of understanding, and of belonging to one another? Was either one of them love, true love, or merely friendship and attraction?

He leaned closer, and she knew he likely meant to kiss her. She knew, too, that she'd just as likely kiss him in return, and that they'd both enjoy it, for that was another way they seemed to belong. But in her present confusion, she wasn't sure if kissing might not be too great a pleasure and too much a distraction, and so she turned her face away from his, and back toward the young lady's portrait.

And then she saw the letters.

They were hidden in the embroidery of the lady's sleeve, so buried in the painted gold thread that most would not see them. But because Mary had already seen the same design on the angel's robe, she recognized it now: interlocking *F*s, over and over, in and out.

"John, look," she whispered, tracing the design with her finger held over, not touching, the picture's surface. "It's the same as on the border of the angel's robe. So she did belong to the same family as my angel, in fact as well as in spirit!"

"I see it, too," he said slowly, whipping off his hat to come even closer. "The same pattern of *F*s."

Mary gasped, her hands fluttering with surprise. "Oh, John, there's more! Look, here, worked into the lace that's edging her shift! 'Isabella Maria di Feroce.' It must be her name, John. It *must*. Isabella di Feroce! Why has no one else ever seen this before?"

But John didn't share her excitement. His expression troubled and grim, he drew her into his arms, not as an embrace, but as if to protect her.

"No one has ever seen it, because no one has looked as you do," he said, his voice reduced to a raspy whisper. "And what you've found—ah, Mary, Mary, this could be the greatest trouble you've ever made."

Chapter Eleven

When Mary had sat in the old schoolroom at Aston Hall, planning and plotting their itinerary, she'd included museums, cathedrals, palaces and castles. She'd never thought to include a library, yet here she was with John beside her, hunched over a long reading table in the Bibliothèque Nationale de France. It was, she supposed, a historical landmark of much fame, for Monsieur Leclair had been able to lecture her a good ten minutes over breakfast about the library's great age and even greater collection, and the generosity of Louis XV to open it to the use of the public in general and scholars in particular. This was edifying to Miss Wood, of course, but all Mary herself cared for was to learn more of the Feroce family of Florence.

Fostered by the elegant portrait of the young Isabella they'd seen at the Palais du Luxembourg, last night Mary had let herself dream of the lady's charmed, beautiful life in a medieval *palazzo*, full of art and music. Yet as she and John pored over the musty, dusty volumes brought to them by the equally musty librarians, Mary soon learned that there was little charming about the Feroce family.

In their prime in the 1400s, they had virtually ruled Florence by sheer will. They had been greedy and violent. They had claimed whatever they coveted, and they had murdered or poisoned anyone who stood in their way. True, they'd served as patrons to artists like Fra Pacifico, but they were more proud of the skill of the master torturer in their *palazzo*'s dungeon, and the numbers of women they'd raped. When at last the French armies had captured Florence, no one had grieved when the Feroces had fallen with the city, too.

"Did you know any of this, John?" she whispered to him as she turned yet another gory page full of thumbscrews and disembowelings. "These Feroces were awful people."

John nodded, and shrugged. "You'll hear worse once you reach Florence. Every guide has a favorite gruesome story. The Feroces make such splendid villains because in the end they were given exactly the fates they deserved."

"Drawn and quartered, with their heads on spikes along a wall." Mary couldn't help but shiver. "I'm glad we live in more civilized times."

He raised a single skeptical brow, but to Mary's relief, he said nothing more. She suspected he could if he wished, given the hints he'd dropped about his past.

"Didn't I tell you Isabella would be a match to the French soldiers?" he said instead. "Not every lady could dispatch a half dozen of the enemy herself with only the stiletto knife hidden in her bodice."

"She does seem to have been rather—rather skilled." It was hard for Mary to reconcile the young lady in the portrait with this bloodthirsty history. "It may be just as well she seems to have disappeared."

"Amen, said the French."

"Be serious, John." Mary pushed the book she'd been

reading toward him. "It says here that while Isabella and her two sisters tried to flee, her sisters were both captured and killed, but Isabella was never found. How dreadful to lose both sisters like that! I cannot imagine losing Diana in such a fashion."

"She tries to lose you at every opportunity."

Mary narrowed her eyes at him. "That's not what I meant, as you know perfectly, perfectly well."

"Forgive me, then." He lightly ran his fingertip down the bridge of her nose. "Tell me more of Isabella, and I'll promise to attend to her instead of you."

Mollified, she contented herself with a small huffy sound of disapproval, and no more. How could she be cross with him, really? "After the French captured Florence, Isabella was the only one of her family who might have survived."

John sighed, resting his head on his hand. "So no doubt she was able to run off with her father's famous treasure."

"Oh, yes, the treasure," Mary said excitedly. "The great cache of Feroce gold! That's mentioned in every book."

"And by every street guide in Florence," John said, smiling at her eagerness. "No one ever found it, nor is likely to now. Mary, if I don't have some of that wicked Parisian coffee soon and one of their sweet biscuits with it, I vow I'm going to perish here in this damned library."

"Oh, John!" She brushed aside his protests with an impatient wave of her hand, unwilling to be distracted when it seemed the end of their mysteries was so tantalizingly close. "How can you think of coffee now? How can you not be excited, when we've almost found the answer?"

"I am excited, sweetheart, because you are," he said, "but I'm also more cautious. All this history is only speculation and conjecture, while the people who've tried to steal your angel from you have been exceptionally real. I care far more for you than a cartload of phantom gold, Mary, no matter how many ways your clever head can twist about the Feroce stories."

"But if my angel could make his way clear to Monsieur Dumont's shop in Calais, John," she argued, "then why couldn't the Feroce gold come here, too?"

"Because gold spends more easily than a painting, sweet." He reached out and closed the book shut to end her history lesson. "What you should care for the most is that with the whole villainous family gone centuries ago, the Parisian nobleman has no better natural claim to the other two panels in the Feroce triptych than you do."

"No," she said, tapping her open hand resolutely on the leather binding of the now-closed history book. "He most certainly does not!"

"Mary, Mary," he said seriously. "A measure of your old practicality, if you please. Don't let your cleverness let you mistake foolishness for bravery. Challenging any Feroce descendant is not wise, no matter how justified you may believe yourself to be."

"I will not be bullied, John," she said. "You more than anyone must know that of me by now."

"Alas, I do." He took her hand and lifted it to his lips, turning the palm upward so he could kiss it. "And so long as I'm with you, Mary, I must do my best to see that no one harms either you, or your angel."

The servant drew the razor deftly across John's jaw, the familiar scrape and tiny pull of the blade over his skin a reassuring sensation. It would be easy to give in to the feeling of well-being, to sit back in the chair and doze, the way he often did while being shaved.

But tonight was different. He'd need all his wits, and a

sizeable amount of luck. Tonight he was going to take a step that would change his life forever, and risk everything he was in a way he'd never thought he'd do. If he was successful, he'd be happier then he'd ever dreamed, and blessed far beyond what by his birth he deserved. And if he failed—ah, he wouldn't consider that unless it happened.

Tonight he would ask Lady Mary Farren to be his wife.

His heart lurched at the thought alone. That was how it should be, wasn't it? He'd never loved any woman before this, and he still wasn't sure how it was done. If he were honest, he'd likely never loved anyone. Oh, there'd been women he'd liked well enough, and cared for, too, with the trinkets they'd wanted, but what he felt for Mary went far beyond that.

He loved her beauty, and he desired her beyond reason, that was true. Her lithe, pale body haunted him at night, and he couldn't forget how eagerly, how passionately, she'd responded to him that night in Chantilly.

Yet he was fascinated by her cleverness, as well, and how often her thoughts seemed so completely in step with his own. She called herself a practical country girl, and he liked that directness in her, without the silliness of other girls her age. She didn't smile easily, or laugh at nothing, which in turn made her smiles and laughter feel like the rarest gifts on earth when he'd earned them.

When fate had brought her to him in Dumont's shop, he'd thought she'd be a passing amusement, nothing more. When there'd been a chance of finding the Feroce gold through the painting she'd bought, then he'd charmed her with hopes of claiming the picture and the treasure for himself.

But the more time he'd spent in her company, the more he'd come to realize that the real treasure was not the gold, but Mary herself. She'd left his room that night in Chantilly, and while he'd been frustrated and disappointed, he'd most of all admired her for being strong enough to recognize her own worth, and in turn making herself all the more desirable to him. When he'd come across the old newspaper in Calais, his first thought had been for her safety, not for his hope for personal profit. He'd raced back to her in Paris as fast as he could, and finding her there in the Palais du Luxembourg, safely surrounded by statues and sunbeams, he'd been so overcome with emotion that he must have sounded like a dithering idiot.

It wouldn't be easy, of course. Nothing worth having was. The distance between their ranks was vast. Her family was powerful; his was negligible. He had no fortune beyond his own wit and charm, while hers was old and venerable and based on land and property and wise investments. He could guarantee that her father would not approve, nor did he believe Miss Wood would, either.

But it all came down to love. He'd never thought he'd feel like this, but then he'd never found another woman like Mary. He was in love, and that was the beginning and the end of it. He dared to believe she loved him the same way. He wanted Mary always with him, and so long as she said the same of him, then they'd find a way to be together.

On the table beside his bed was a small leather box, and inside that his silent accomplice, a ring with diamonds and a sapphire as rare as she was herself. She had asked him to meet her at Madame du Fontenelle's weekly *salon*. Ordinarily he avoided such tedious, self-important gatherings like the pox, but for her sake he'd go. He'd coax her away from the company as soon as he could, into the garden if the du Fontenelles had one, and ask her.

And pray with all his heart that there, beneath the stars, she'd say yes.

* * *

"I wish you'd put that wretched picture away, Mary," Diana said as she hooked her pearl earrings into her ears. "After what you told me of that horrid family who commissioned it, I don't know how you can abide having it watching you."

"The family was horrid, not the angel," Mary said, smoothing the wide blue silk sash around the waist of her silver-sprigged muslin gown. "How could the angel be wicked when he was painted by a holy man?"

"A Romish monk, you mean." Diana leaned closer to the mirror, patting a bit more powder over an imagined blemish. Their maid Deborah had finished helping them into their gowns, just as the hired hairdresser had given them each great poufs of powdered hair with long lovelocks over their shoulders, in the height of current French fashion. Soon their carriage would come to take them first to collect John from his lodgings, and then to the house of Madame du Fontenelle. The invitation had been an unexpected surprise, and an honor, too, for Madame's *salons* were famous even in London for the brilliance of the company.

"When Fra Pacifico painted the picture, Diana," Mary said, standing before the angel where she'd propped him up on the mantel, "there *wasn't* any other Christian church but the Romish one. Not that it matters to the quality of the painting."

Diana shrugged, twisting one elaborately curled lock of her hair around her finger. "Not that it matters, period. Honestly, Mary, you would have done far better to come with Miss Wood and me to see the balloonists in the park instead of trudging off to a *library*."

"I wanted to go to the library," Mary protested. "John wished it, too."

"Then you should have both come with us to see the ascensions," Diana continued. "I've never see anything like it, all those bright silk balloons floating high in the sky! And do you know what a gentleman told us? It's scandalous, really, and Miss Wood was distraught that he'd shared such a story, but I laughed."

"What did he tell you?" Mary asked warily, almost afraid to hear it. Gentlemen often confided scandalous tales to Diana's ears—too often, really. "Do I really wish to know it?"

"Oh, Mary, it's *Paris!*" she exclaimed, leaning closer in confidence. "This gentleman told us that certain ladies take their lovers with them aloft in the gondolas of the balloons, and then they make delirious love to one another up in the clouds, high over the city! Perhaps you and Lord John should try *that* instead of an old library!"

"Oh, hush, Diana, please," Mary said, more exasperated than scandalized. "It's not like that between John and me."

"No?" Diana asked, arching a single brow. "Then why isn't it?"

"Because it's better than that," Mary said staunchly. "Because John and I are friends, too, not just like your tawdry balloonists, and because he cares for me as I am, and because he is more dear and special to me than—than anyone."

"'Friends.'" Diana's sigh was full of pity. "You mean he has no interest in you as a woman?"

Mary flushed, remembering Chantilly. "What I mean, Diana, is that I love him. There, I've said it, and I'm glad."

Diana's eyes rounded with surprise. "You *love* him? Lord John Fitzgerald, our delightful makeshift bearleader? Oh, Mary, from you that's news indeed!"

"I love John," Mary repeated, liking the sound of her declaration now that she'd made it. "I love him—I love him!— and I don't care if you know it."

"It doesn't matter if I know it," Diana said. "The real question is whether Lord John does. Have you confessed this to him? Does he know it, too, or are you pining away in silence?"

"He knows," Mary said slowly, thinking. "That is, he *must* know."

"Meaning you've never bothered to tell the poor gentleman." Diana came behind her, looping her arms around Mary's shoulders.

"If you truly *do* love Lord John, Mary," she said, directly to her ear, "then you must tell him. He can't be expected to guess. Men aren't that clever. Tell him tonight. Heaven knows there should be plenty of opportunity, if there's as much conversation at a *salon* as everyone has warned us. You must tell him so he can tell you he loves you in return, and then he can kiss you properly, and whatever else you please."

"Lady Mary, Lady Diana!" Miss Wood called, opening their chamber door for a moment. "Please collect yourselves, my ladies. The carriage is at the door for us."

Mary slipped away from Diana and lifted the picture from the mantel, hurriedly hiding it up inside the bed's rope springs. She took her cloak from the bed and swung it over her shoulders, tying the silk bow beneath her chin as she rejoined Diana.

"Tell him, Mary," Diana said softly. "That's not a secret you should keep to yourself."

"But what if he doesn't say he loves me, too?" Mary asked anxiously. "What if he lets me speak, and—and that is all?"

"Oh, he loves you," Diana said, giving Mary's cheek a small pat for reassurance. "I shouldn't worry about that. I've seen it since Lord John found us near Abbeville. Now come, the sooner we leave, the sooner you can tell him."

* * *

The Comte de Archambault was holding court tonight in a tall-backed armchair with wide wings to keep away drafts, and a fur-lined coverlet around his legs. Athenais du Fontenelle had seen to that, making sure, too, that he'd be seated so close to the fire that anyone else would have melted from the heat like a wax figure. But to Archambault it felt no more than a pleasing warmth, barely enough to keep his shivering at bay, and he'd thanked Athenais for her thoughtfulness. Madame had smiled and curtseyed prettily, and thanked him for gracing her *salon*. There was old history between the two of them, when they'd both been young and beautiful and passion had flowed like a merry stream between them.

Now he could see the melancholy in her still-lovely eyes when she gazed at his ravaged body, the realization that youth and love had not been enough to stop age and suffering. Poor Athenais! She'd none of the comfort that he had from the paintings that hung beside his bed, none of the peace he could find in the face of the Blessed Mother.

Now he sipped at the barley-water in his wineglass, pretending to listen as one more callow young creature professed his admiration for Archambault's poetry. Wine, or company: he could only stomach one in the course of a day, and this babbling whelp was making him doubt his choice. He closed his eyes and feigned a passing weakness, sending the would-be poet scurrying away and bringing Athenais back to him.

"What now, old fox?" she whispered with amusement, bending beside his chair. "You can fool the others, but not me."

He slitted his eyes open. "Are the English girls here yet?"

"Not a fox, then, but a goat." She chuckled, delighted. "I invited them as you asked, and they have come, with a dowdy

governess and a handsome young gentleman in tow. One girl
has already vanished with the young gentleman, as to be
entirely expected, but the other still remains here in the
room."

Archambault smiled. "Is she beautiful, this daughter of an
English duke?"

Madame poked his arm gently with her folded fan. "*Such*
a goat you are, Archambault! Shall I bring her to you, so you
may judge her yourself?"

He nodded, and closed his eyes again as Athenais left him
to find the girl. Ah, surely the Holy Mother was watching
over him tonight, to make this so simple!

"My lord, might I present Lady Diana Farren?"

He opened his eyes slowly, savoring the moment. How
many more times in this life would he have the pleasure of
a lovely young woman's company? She *was* beautiful, too,
even if it was in the English manner of blond hair and red
lips, without style or elegance. But there *was* a voluptuous-
ness about this girl that surprised him, a ripeness unusual
among the priggish British. How could she be the keeper of
something as ethereal, as sacred, as the long-lost Feroce
angel?

"You look lost, my dear Lady Diana," he said in English,
motioning feebly toward the stool that had been placed for
her beside his chair. "Pray sit with me, and I'll do my best
to decipher this room full of pretentious boors for you."

Her face brightened, clearly relieved to find someone who
spoke English, and sat beside him without further persua-
sion. He understood her confusion, poor child: Athenais's
guests prided themselves on being incomprehensible in any
language.

"Forgive me, my lord, for not returning your kindness,"
she said, "and speaking your French so well as you speak my

English. Alas, I fear I never did apply myself to my studies in the schoolroom."

"Oh, no, of course not," he agreed. "Leave that to dry old scholars like myself."

"Not so very old, my lord." She smiled and opened her fan, expertly using it to draw attention to her bosom. He approved. Somewhere in her veins must be a drop of Parisian blood, but ah, what a trial the coquette must be to her ducal father!

"You are kindness itself, my dear." The familiar pain rippled through his belly, a reminder he must heed. He was here tonight with a greater purpose than an empty flirtation with some well-bred English minx.

"But you've found other pleasures in France, yes?" he continued. "Our parks, our shops, our galleries for art have amused you?"

She sighed glumly. "I have seen far too much of the tedious galleries, and far, far too little of the shops."

"Yet I have heard you've already made a splendid purchase, a painting of such rarity as to please any *connoisseur.*"

She stared at him so blankly that he feared he'd been misinformed. Then suddenly she smiled, her fan fluttering with renewed vigor.

"You must mean my sister's painting, my lord," she said, "though how you would have heard of it I cannot fathom. She bought it in Calais, and an uglier bit of rubbish you cannot imagine. Yet she insists upon setting it out on the mantel whenever we are in our chamber, so that that dreadful angel seems to stare at us."

Archambault's weakened heart lurched in his chest. "An angel, you say?"

"An *ugly* angel," she said with a toss of her hair. "My sister says it's only because the picture's so old and the artist didn't know any better. Yet still she insists on hiding it at night and each time we leave our chamber, as if it were actually of value to anyone but her."

"Does your sister know the picture's artist, my lady?" he asked, praying that the excitement he felt wouldn't kill him outright. "That can affect the value."

She shrugged carelessly. "An Italian monk, my lord," she said. "I disremember his name. Oh, but I do recall what she told me today. She learned that the picture belonged to a perfectly barbaric old family from Florence that believed in war and torture and stealing and who knows what else. I know the name, I do: Feroce. That was it. The Feroces. Have you ever heard of them, my lord?"

"Yes, Lady Diana," he said slowly, carefully, so he wouldn't betray himself. "You see, I am descended from the Feroces through my grandmother."

"Oh, my lord, forgive me!" Flustered by her gaffe, she snapped her fan shut and bowed her head, her cheeks red. "I did not know, else I would never have—"

"You needn't apologize, my dear," he said, forcing himself to smile. "Being my ancestors does not improve their reputation. By all accounts they *were* perfectly barbaric, as you say. They deserved the violent deaths that ended their line. Only one young woman escaped the slaughter, and came here to France, with a painting much like your sister's among her belongings. There were two other sisters, with other paintings, that were not so fortunate, and vanished."

He'd been fascinated by this story of Isabella Feroce ever since he'd been a boy, when his grandmother had told it to him. He'd loved the young woman's courage and her defiance, and even now when he looked at the picture of the Holy Mother, he thought, too, of Isabella. She'd married into the Archambault family for power, not love. It would have been her goal, her dream, to restore the triptych, just as it was his. Isabella had risked her life; he would soon give his.

But young Lady Diana had no such fascination with his family's history. Her gaze had wandered away from him, toward other, younger men across the room, and it was clear enough she'd stopped listening.

"That's most interesting, my lord," she said absently. "But I see that my governess is beckoning to me, and I must go to her. I trust you'll excuse me, my lord, if you please?"

"Certainly, my dear, go, go," he said with a final exhausted wave of his hand as she hurried away. He sagged back into the armchair, his eyes squeezed shut in a grimace of pain. He'd already known he was dying; he hadn't realized he'd become a bore as well.

But soon none of that would matter. He'd have the last painting. Because of this foolish girl's chatter, he almost had it now.

And soon, so soon, peace and grace would be his forever.

Mary stood to one side of the doorway, unable to calm herself no matter how fast she fluttered her fan. For years, she'd imagined herself at a Parisian *salon,* as far from the dull fox-hunting blather and smug county society around Aston Hall as her imagination could contrive.

Based on what she'd read and heard, she'd pictured it to every last detail in her head: beautiful ladies and well-dressed gentlemen, their expressions serious and their voices passionate, yet still respectfully hushed, as they gravely discussed great philosophical questions. She'd imagined herself as honored simply to listen, and only daring to venture her own opinion if it were a topic she'd understood completely.

There'd be no gentlemen who'd drunk too much punch, the way there always were at her father's parties, no ladies shrieking with silly laughter, no dogs wandering through the room to steal scraps from the plates of the inattentive. At a *salon,* everything would be dignified and elegant.

And so here she finally was, in the drawing room of one of the greatest *salon* hostesses, Madame du Fontenelle. The drawing room was achingly beautiful, filled with delicate gilded chairs and marble-top chests with porcelain inserts, tall Venetian looking glasses and lavish paintings by fashionable artists like Fragonard and Boucher. The company was as elegant as she'd always pictured, and as precisely dressed as most French seemed to be.

"What a pack of tedious bores," John whispered, standing beside her. "I know you wished to come here tonight, but could there be anything less entertaining than this?"

She raised her fan to hide their conversation. She'd never seen him look more handsome than he did tonight, his unpowdered hair standing out among so many white wigs, and his tanned face, browned by their time on the road, contrasted with the fashionable *salon* pallor. But he was in an odd, brooding mood this evening, more withdrawn than usual. She wondered if this were like Chantilly all over again, a place he'd rather not go for unspoken reasons. She'd promised herself that she'd tell him tonight that she loved him, but there was no way she'd speak her heart unless his humor improved.

"Hush, John, hush now," she chided gently. "We're guests. You can't say such things."

Unconvinced, he coughed, using his cupped hand much as she'd used the fan. "I can, because it's true. I know the members of every French *salon* believe themselves to represent the true genius of their age, but listen to them! They're jabbering away like monkeys in a cage, not caring what the other fellow is saying so long as his own voice is the loudest."

"Oh, John, please," she murmured uneasily, hoping no one could overhear. Yet the sorry truth was that John was right: her beautiful vision of a French *salon* still looked beautiful, but the sound of it was as raucous as any hunt breakfast, with every gentleman shouting and waving his hands to make his opinion heard. "It's a considerable honor for us to be here. Madame Fontenelle invites only the most brilliant persons to her *salons*."

He looked at her, and shook his head, as if to say she'd never understand. "Look over there. There's that decrepit rascal Archambault, his armchair so close to the fire he might as well be sitting in the flames."

At once Mary recognized the comte from the gallery, and felt the same shiver of uneasiness at his presence. "I'd thought we'd never see him again," she said. "At least I'd hoped we wouldn't."

"The devil watches over his own," John said. "Thus here he remains for now, the most honored centerpiece of this fine *salon*."

She looked away, uncomfortable gazing any longer at such a man. It was one thing to read a pious tale of morality on a Sunday afternoon, and another to see the sad results of sin in the wasted flesh before her.

"Perhaps his presence here will serve as a warning to others," she said, striving to put the best face on it. "Even if it's too late for him to lead a better life, there may be others here who'll see him and reconsider their own actions."

"I'm sure there are, though whether they wish to be reformed is another question entirely." He slipped his fingers into hers, as if to reassure himself in a way she didn't entirely understand. "You don't belong here with such people, Mary."

Had Archambault unsettled him, as well, she wondered, or was this more of him simply not wanting to be here tonight?

"We can't leave so soon, John," she said, though she realized she, too, now wished she could do exactly that. She glanced around the crowded room, hoping to spot her sister. If there were in fact so many dissolute gentlemen here, the last thing she wished was to abandon Diana.

"Your sister will be fine," John said, reading her fears as clearly as if she'd spoken aloud. "That's what Miss Wood is for, isn't it?"

"But it would be rude to leave now," she protested. "We've only just arrived."

"Then let's find the way to the garden," he said, his hold on her fingers tightening. "There must be one for a house this size. I don't believe I can survive another five minutes in here."

He led her through the crowd of guests, cutting a path with his body for her to follow. The tall arched door to the back garden was already open to let in whatever breeze might pass by. They slipped outside, and Mary breathed deeply of the cooler air as they stood on the white marble step.

The garden was long and narrow, and enclosed by high brick walls, and mirrored the drawing room inside for formality. Espaliered pear trees were pinned to the wall, their branches bent into an unnatural symmetry against the bricks. The walks were regular, too, a grid of pale paths centered with a sundial whose shadow now stretched long in the moonlight before the facing marble benches.

"Look at that," John said with disgust. "Only those damned spindly elms. Nary a shadow to hide a squirrel."

"But a squirrel could hide behind that garden shed, there beside the far wall," Mary said, glancing around at the other guests around them who'd likewise left the crowd inside. "Perhaps even two squirrels."

He grumbled restlessly. "Next you'll be suggesting the privies."

"John, please," she said softly, curling her arm around his. "I—I've things to say to you, and I'd rather not have an audience."

"I've things to say to you, too." He took her by the hand and marched down the steps, moving so fast she had to skip to keep up.

"John, slower, if you—if you please!" she said breathlessly, trying to pull him back.

He stopped abruptly beside the sundial, his frown magnified by the moonlight. "You've always kept pace with me, Mary, or even gone ahead. Since when have I been too fast for you?"

"Since now," she said, pressing her hand to the sudden tightness in her side. She was loath to admit that she was more tightly laced to fit into this gown than she usually was for walking with him, but she was going to have trouble enough finding the proper words without being strangled, too. "What I've to say is—is important, but it can—can wait another half minute."

"Very well," he said, releasing her hand. He patted the front of his coat, then turned suddenly self-conscious, and tapped his fingers on the fixed brass gnomon of the sundial instead. Slowly he made a half circle around the marble pedestal, until he was standing opposite her with the sundial between them. "Then I'll speak first."

"No!" She'd no idea of what he meant to say, but she knew if she didn't speak her own thoughts soon, she could well lose her nerve. The thumping of her heart in her chest no longer had anything to do with whalebone or lacing. "That is, John, I should like to go before you, if you'll agree."

"Of course I'll agree." His grin flashed in the moonlight, taking her so completely by surprise that she realized it was the first time he'd smiled all night. "I'll always agree to you, sweetheart."

He leaned across the sundial. He threaded his hands into the back of her hair, cradling her head and drew her forward. The powder from her hair dusted around her, and she gave her head a little shake. His mouth met hers over the dial, over the silent hours of day and night, and when he kissed her, she tasted not only his desire for her, but something more.

"I love you," she breathed as their lips parted, her eyes still shut. The words felt so light in her mouth that she wondered if she'd truly spoken them aloud, or only dreamed it. "I love you, John."

"Mary." That was all he said, a rough whisper that answered her own. "No wonder I couldn't keep away from you."

"Because I love you," she said again, and finally dared to open her eyes.

His hair was blowing lightly across his forehead, his lips curved in a smile, his eyes half closed, yet still so intent on her that she shivered. She felt his hands in her hair and the breeze on one side of her face, she heard the carriages in the street beyond the wall, and the laughter and raised voices from inside the house, and the unbridled emotion that rippled through her own voice.

No matter what else happened in her life, she would remember this, leaning over the sundial to reach him while time stood still.

"I love you, John," she said again, her voice trembling with all she longed to say to him. "What I feel when I'm with you, or worse, what I feel when we're apart—I can't explain except to say that it's like magic, as if you're the one gentleman put on this earth to please me in exactly this way, and no other could ever, ever—"

"Then marry me, love," he said. "Marry me, and be my wife."

Chapter Twelve

John couldn't stop now, even if he'd wanted to.

"Be my wife, Mary, and my love forever," he said, his voice so rough and rocky to his own ears that he prayed she'd understand it was from uncertainty of her response, and not doubt in his decision. "Marry me, and we'll never be parted again."

He reached inside his coat for the leather-covered box with the ring. Damnation, why couldn't he make his hands stop shaking? That wretched jeweler must have put this tiny, stubborn latch on the box just to plague him. What must she be thinking to see him turning so clumsy, his hands turned to stone mitts, fumbling and bumbling like this?

And why the devil wasn't she saying anything in return? She'd already told him she loved him. What more was he supposed to say?

Finally he wrestled the box open, the moonlight twinkling on the cut stones. He'd meant to put the ring on her finger, to hold her hand in his and pledge himself to her. But because she hadn't accepted—*blast, only a word, Mary, yes or no, to tell him where he stood!*—he set the box on the sundial with the lid open. The moonlight winked and danced on the cut stones, determined to catch her eye even if he couldn't himself. Only then did he realize he'd set the box on the Roman numeral twelve. Midnight or high noon: either one could be his hour of destiny.

"You're serious," she murmured, her eyes lowered on the box. "You tease me so much, John, I thought this was only another—"

"I've never been more serious in my life." He wished he could see the expression in her eyes, almost as much as he wished she'd say something else. Only one word, really, the one that mattered. "If it were a jest, Mary, would I have brought you this ring?"

"It's—it's very beautiful," she whispered. She stared warily at the ring without touching it, as if she somehow feared it. "But then, you've always astounded me with your kindness."

Kindness was the not the word he wanted to hear. "I know I must seem a wanderer to you," he said gruffly. "I've no family to recommend me, or welcome you home. But I've more love for you than any other man could dream of offering, Mary, more love than a hundred men combined!"

"Love." She sighed. "What Father wishes is my happiness."

John doubted that, and to his despair he could feel her slipping away. His Grace would expect far more in the way of material goods for his daughter's future, and in the end she'd expect the same.

Yet still John blundered onward, as unable to stop as a runaway horse. "As for our home—we can make that wherever we wish, Mary. Wherever *you* wish, I mean. You could have your studio, your gallery. You could study art, and become the great *connoisseur* you want to be. I can't give you a house in Bedford Square or an estate in the country, but I'd grant you that dream, Mary, if that was what made you happiest."

"You must know that I'd never judge you by your fortune, John," she protested, misreading his assurances. "That's not why I—why I said what I did."

"Then I swear I'll do whatever is in my power to please you," he said solemnly, "every day we share together."

"I never imagined that you'd do otherwise." She took a deep breath, and finally raised her gaze to his. "You've surprised me. Here I thought I'd be the one to speak plain, and to offer you my love, yet here you—you meant to offer me so much more."

"Damnation, Mary, this isn't a wager!" Desperate to make her understand, he reached out and seized her face in his hands so she could not look away. "I love you, Mary. There, I've said it aloud, and I've never said it to another woman in all my life. *I love you.*"

Framed by his hands, her smiled wobble uncertainly. "I've never told it to another man, either."

He felt a lurch of emotion deep in his chest. To most women, such words came as easily as asking for another dish of tea, but just as Mary didn't laugh or smile idly, she wouldn't pledge herself to him without meaning it, or without all of her country girl's heart.

"Then we're even, Mary, as even as a man and a woman can be," he said, his voice rough and low with his urgency. "That last night in Chantilly, Mary. You remember that, don't you?"

"In your room," she whispered. "How could I ever forget that?"

"I'm not asking you to forget, Mary, but to remember," he said, his fingers sliding deep into the rich waves of her hair. "Remember what we did. Remember how that felt, Mary?"

"Oh, yes, John," she answered, her eyes widening. "You can never know how difficult it was for me to walk away from you that night!"

"Then remember how I touched you, and kissed you?"

From the house came a woman's shrill, shrieking laugh. Instinctively Mary turned toward the sound, but John pulled her face back toward him.

"Forget them," he ordered. "Think only of us. Remember how I made you tremble and shake and moan my name?"

"You did," she said, the words scarce more than a sigh of longing. "What you did!"

He could feel the heat of the flush rise along her throat to her cheeks, and hear the quickening of her breath. He wanted her to recall every detail, every exquisite sensation with the same intensity that he did. Hell, if he could make her come with words and memory alone, then he'd do it, if it would convince her to be his wife.

"Remember how your blood turned to fire in your veins and your heart raced in your chest? Remember how your breasts felt heavy and full in my hands, aching for my touch, and when my lips on—"

"I remember." She swayed toward him over the sundial with her eyes heavy-lidded and her lips parted as if begging to be kissed again. "I *remember.*"

"I knew you would." He trailed one hand along her throat, his fingertips barely grazing across the vein that pulsed with desire, and lightly back and forth across the pale ridge of her collarbone. "Then you remember, too, how I caressed you and stroked you until you trembled with joy, such joy that you—"

"That I left," she said, so breathless now she could hardly speak the words, "else embrace my own ruin."

"Yes." He trailed his fingers lower, across the twin curves of her breasts above the tight-laced bodice. She was trembling, and when for the briefest, teasing moment he dipped his fingers into her bodice between her breasts, she gasped aloud.

"Whatever joy you felt that night is nothing to what I'll give you as my wife," he whispered fiercely. "Every night, Mary, passion and pleasure so great you'll scream with it. That's the power of what we have together, sweetheart, what we'll never find with anyone else. That's real love. You left your home to find adventure, Mary, and by God, with me, you'll always have it. Marry me, sweet. Say yes, and be my partner, my love, my own dear, clever wife."

Slowly she reached up to touch his face, her smile wobbling and her eyes bright with unshed tears. "Ahh, John, how could I not—"

"There he is!" a man shouted behind them from the garden door. "That's Fitzgerald, the bastard!"

"What the hell?" John murmured, looking past Mary, who'd now turned, too.

A tall gentleman was striding down the steps toward them. Two footmen, each holding raised candelabra for light, hurried to follow on either side of him. Drawn by the excitement, other guests streamed from the house, chattering among themselves with excitement.

John grabbed Mary and pushed her behind him, shielding her as much as he could.

"What is it, John?" she asked, more curious than anxious as she tried to see around him. "Who is that ill-mannered French gentleman?"

"I suppose he has reason to feel ill-mannered toward me," John said, steeling himself for what was coming. He'd always known this would happen sooner or later. But why here, before Mary, and why now, right as she'd started to answer him?

"How could anyone feel ill-mannered toward you?" Mary asked indignantly.

John took a deep breath. "Because last spring I killed his brother in a duel."

The man stopped abruptly before him with a curt, angry bow. Below his wig, his face was mottled with fury, his mouth a tight slash across his narrow face.

"Fitzgerald," he said. "I should have known you'd be out here in the garden, hiding behind petticoats."

"Turgeon," John said. He would not let himself be defensive, nor would he let his temper rise. "If you've something to say to me, then say it, and leave."

"You're a fine one to give orders, my lord Fitzgerald," Turgeon said, his face twisted into a contemptuous snarl. "That's something a gentleman should do, an officer, not a cowardly, whoring bastard like you."

"You can slander me with every foul name to Hell and back, Turgeon, and I'll not take offense," John said. "Your brother had his satisfaction, and I mine. Let it end there."

"Since when is murder satisfaction, my lord?" demanded Turgeon, raising his voice to be sure all around them heard, and the delighted gasps and oaths proved they had. "You murdered my brother, naval captain Jean Turgeon, just as surely as you seduced and ruined his wife!"

"Your brother challenged me, Turgeon, and I fought him fairly," John said, refusing to raise his voice to match the other man's. There was no need; at the time, the duel had been the talk of both London and Paris. John had tried merely to wound the other man, a grazing shot to the arm that would satisfy the requirements of honor. But at the last minute Turgeon had lunged to one side, and John's ball had caught him squarely in the chest. The inquiry afterwards had determined the same, and no charges had ever been filed against John. He'd left England on his own accord, hoping to leave the scandal behind as well. Likely every person now clustered in this garden knew every detail—except, of course, Mary.

"Honor was served, though with lamentable results," he said gravely. "There were seconds, a surgeon, and any number of spectators who'll tell you the same, as did the results of the formal inquiry. There was no fault found, and no charges."

"Oh, yes, a pretty tale!" Turgeon's words were slurred just enough to prove he'd fortified his challenge with drink. "Do you have the same sort of easy, empty explanation for what you did with my brother's wife? How you seduced her, ruined her, and convinced her to leave my brother?"

"She had already left your brother when I met her," John said. "Every officer in the fleet knows how he ill-used her, in public and in private. All I did was offer her my friendship."

There was nothing new to this sad story, either. Marie Turgeon had been introduced to him in Brighton as a wealthy widow. Their affair had been light-hearted and insubstantial, a diversion by the sea to them both, and as soon as John had learned her husband had not been killed in the American war, he'd broken with her. But while he had not broken Marie's heart, he had wounded her pride, and in her anger she'd gone back to her husband, demanding he seek vengeance, with disastrous results.

"Is this true, John?" whispered Mary behind him, the shock in her voice clear. "Did you really do—do these things?"

"Tell her the truth, Fitzgerald!" Turgeon said, turning

shrill. "Tell her how you coldly murdered my brother, without regard for honor or decency!"

"This is not how it seems, Mary," he said carefully. "I will say nothing of the lady, or against her. But anyone who witnessed the duel can tell you that Captain Turgeon's challenge was unnecessary and tragic, and that I acquitted myself as honorably as was possible."

"Liar!" Turgeon shouted, and pulled his sword from its scabbard with a sharp scrape of steel. "Would my brother have demanded satisfaction from you if you'd not coldly seduced his wife?"

Instantly the crowd around them scattered like startled pigeons across the garden paths, with oaths from the gentlemen and frightened little shrieks from the ladies.

"For God's sake, Turgeon, have you lost your wits?" John could think only of Mary behind him. "This is a garden, not a battlefield! Put your sword away at once!"

But Turgeon held the sword before him, the blade leveled at John. "I'll put it away when you agree to give me satisfaction, Fitzgerald."

John didn't answer, hoping Turgeon would see his own foolishness and withdraw. This was why he never wore a sword if he could help it, not even a dress sword. The pistol beneath his coat, yes, he'd always carry that, but a sword seemed to attract bravado and dangerous bluster like a lodestone.

"Don't do it, John," Mary whispered behind him, her fear palpable. "Whatever other wickedness you may have on your conscience, please, please, don't!"

She loved him, she cared what became of him, she loved him! Without turning, he blindly reached for her behind his back to reassure her. Yet it wasn't as simple as that. She'd said more: *the wickedness on his conscience.* What had that meant? What must she think of him now? Damnation, before this, she'd been so close to accepting him!

"Speak, damn you!" Turgeon demanded, nervous sweat glistening on his forehead. "Not to the chit, you coward, but to me!"

John's head jerked forward. "She's not a chit. She's the daughter of an English peer, and worth a thousand of you, Turgeon."

"And I say she's an English whore," Turgeon said with a nervous little flick of the sword, dancing back and forth on the balls of his feet. "A whore, with a bastard-coward like you for her pimp. Will that do it, Fitzgerald? Will you give me what I want now?"

John sucked in his breath, holding it for what seemed like an endless minute. If he let himself be drawn into another duel for the sake of Mary's good name and his own, then he would be party to another wasteful death, or even squander his own life now for another man's vanity. He couldn't do that to Mary, not when he'd just offered her his love, not when she'd already spoken of the wickedness on his conscience. Yet what would she think of him if he failed to defend her honor, or his own?

"No," he said at last, not bothering to hide his weariness. "No more, Turgeon. Your brother's death was enough."

The other guests gasped with shock, and exclaimed with amazement. For a gentleman, a lord, to refuse a challenge like this—no one had ever heard or seen such a scandalous thing!

"Damn you, Fitzgerald!" Turgeon shouted, his eyes bulging with frustration. "You owe this to me!"

"I owe you nothing," John said, and turned away, to find the solace and sanctuary of his Mary.

He turned, but she was gone, vanished as completely as

if he'd imagined her, and with the crowd still surging and shifting around him, he was once again alone.

Two hours later, Mary was back in their rooms, her gown put away, her face washed, and the powder brushed from her hair. She and Diana both were ready for bed, but from the appearance of Miss Wood as she stood before them—her hands clasped so tightly that the knuckles were white and knotted, her mouth pinched tight, her back so rigidly straight it almost arched backward—there'd be no question of sleep for any of them for a good long while.

"I will speak as plain as plain can be, Lady Mary," the governess said. "I can scarce conceive of a worse situation than the one you contrived for us this evening."

"Yes, Miss Wood." Mary bowed her head, more miserable than contrite. She was sitting cross-legged on the bed beside Diana, her dressing gown pulled down tight over her hands and knees, as if trying to hide herself away from everything that had happened this night. "That is, no, there's no worse situation."

"Of course there could be a worse situation, Miss Wood," Diana said, slipping her arm around Mary's shoulders. "That horrid Frenchman who challenged Lord John might have pulled out huge pistols instead of his sword. He could have fired them at Lord John, and we could have been hurt—or killed!—by accident. That would be much, much worse."

"My lady, that is preposterous," Miss Wood snapped. "Not only is such fantasizing preposterous, but it is also not useful to your sister's situation. To *our* situation."

"But in some way she is right," Mary said, appreciating Diana's support. "Lord John could have been killed by that man, right before our eyes!"

"There seems to have been a great deal going on right

before our eyes," Miss Wood said, "and the eyes of everyone else in attendance at Madame du Fontenelle's *salon* as well."

Unable to keep still, Miss Wood began to pace back and forth by the bed, short, brisk steps that echoed her anger and frustration. "I trusted you, Lady Mary. I permitted you great freedom with Lord John, believing you both would return my trust. I thought you shared with him a harmless interest in scholarship and art. Instead it appears that he is neither an honorable gentleman, nor trustworthy with women, while you, Lady Mary, have deceived and betrayed my confidence in you by conducting an—an intrigue with this unfortunate rascal."

"He's not a rascal, Miss Wood!" Mary cried. "He's exactly the same gentleman as he was before!"

"I'm sure he was, my lady," Miss Wood said sternly. "But the question remains as to exactly what manner of deceitful gentleman that could have been."

Mary looked down at her lap, fighting back her tears. She loved John, and he loved her, enough that he wished to marry her. How could he be a rascal? Wrapped in her handkerchief and tucked deep in her pocket was his betrothal ring. In the flurry and crush in the garden, she'd impulsively taken the little box for safekeeping, and, to be truthful, because she'd wanted it. Two more minutes alone with him and she would have accepted his proposal, and the ring would now be on her finger instead of orphaned in her handkerchief.

Two more minutes, perhaps even less. But what would happen now? She'd panicked and run away. She'd been the coward, not John, and the practical, sensible country girl that she'd always claimed to be had disappeared. She'd been so overwhelmed by what she'd seen and heard that she'd panicked and fled back to the safety of Diana and Miss Wood, standing just outside the garden door.

She'd meant to stay away from John only for the time it would take to settle herself. She'd meant to go back, and tell him again how much she loved him, and how honored she would be to become his wife. But Miss Wood had insisted that they leave at once, before any further damage could be done to Mary's tattered reputation. The carriage ride home had been filled with stony silence, a pall made all the more painful for Mary because she'd never before been the target of Miss Wood's disapproval.

But where was John now? And what must he be thinking of her? That she'd run away and abandoned him when he'd needed her most? That she couldn't possibly love him as much as she'd claimed? That she wasn't nearly brave enough to be his wife?

Coward, coward, *coward!*

"Consider what he freely admitted tonight," Miss Wood continued, each step of her pacing another recrimination against John. "He engaged in an intrigue with a married women that led to that gentleman's death in a duel. A *duel!*"

"He told me it wasn't as it seemed!" Mary protested, ready to be his champion. At first she'd been shocked, too. The other gentlemen she'd known never admitted to doing anything nearly so scandalous as this. But then she remembered how John had been forced by circumstance to make his own way in the world, and how he'd clearly had experiences in his life that she hadn't. "Father always says there are two sides to every story, and I'm sure there's another to this one!"

Miss Wood stopped pacing. "His Grace your father was not referring to a situation that involves murder."

"And why not, Miss Wood?" asked Mary. "Lord John said he'd been found innocent by the inquiry afterward!"

"But if dueling has become a pattern of his life, my lady, why, then—"

"He refused, Miss Wood!" Mary cried. "This gentleman challenged him to fight a meaningless second duel, and because he'd no wish to risk killing again, he refused!"

"Then why didn't he accept this gentleman's challenge, my lady, and defend your honor?" Miss Wood said, her outrage bubbling up fresh. "He'd defend himself against insult, but when you, the eldest daughter of His Grace the Duke of Aston, were called a—a vile name, he outright declined, leaving all in the garden to believe it true, and repeat to the rest of Paris! That I should hear a lady in my charge publicly reviled in that fashion, without a gentleman defending her—oh, it is beyond bearing!"

"But *I* understood why he didn't, Miss Wood," Mary said swiftly. "The Frenchman was only trying to goad his lordship into fighting. It had nothing personal to do with me, and I'd be far happier that he refused to fight."

Miss Wood gasped. "However can you say such a thing, my lady?"

"I can," Mary said, her voice rising with emotion, "because standing firm and refusing to be pushed into something he knew was wrong was much, much more noble than fighting for a misplaced sense of honor. How honorable can it be to die? If anything had happened to him because of me, I'd—I'd never, ever forgive myself!"

"What has he done to you, my lady?" Miss Wood asked, horrified. "What other lies has he told you? Oh, my lady, to think that he's beguiled you into caring for him this way!"

"He hasn't beguiled me into anything!" Mary lunged forward across the bed toward the governess, driven by the urgency to make her understand. "He cares for me as I am, and I for him!"

Unconvinced, Miss Wood only shook her head. "Don't deny it, my lady. I know what I saw in the garden, and what

I see now. Why else would you defend his shameful treatment, if he hasn't coaxed and cozened his way into your affections?"

"It's not like that, Miss Wood, not at all!" She swung her bare legs over the side of the bed, and the little lump of the ring box in her dressing gown pocket knocked against her hip. No matter how much Miss Wood quarreled with her now over John, she still didn't know that he'd proposed, or more, that Mary had meant to accept, and the realization gave Mary a small bit of comfort on a comfortless night.

"John—Lord John—is a good man, Miss Wood." That was all Mary would say for now. Perhaps by morning, Miss Wood would have calmed herself. Perhaps, too, John himself might appear. "That hasn't changed, and it won't."

"Oh, Lady Mary, listen to yourself!" Her round face full of fear and despair, Miss Wood seized Mary's hands in her own and held them tight. "All I care for is your safety, your welfare! It's my own fault, of course, for letting you spend so much time in this—this *rake's* company, but now I am determined to make things as right as I can for your own good."

"He's *not* a rake, Miss Wood, and he's—"

"No, my lady, my mind is set in this," Miss Wood said with ominous conviction. "We will no longer be receiving his lordship. You are not to write to him, and if he writes to you, his letters shall be returned to him unopened."

"You cannot do that to Mary, Miss Wood!" Diana struck her fist on the coverlet. "Oh, that is most barbarous cruel!"

But Mary said nothing. She knew that once Miss Wood had made up her mind, no persuading or begging in the world would make her change it. Yet just as surely, Mary knew that she'd see John again. She refused to vanish from his life. Though she wasn't sure how or when they'd next meet, they *would*. She'd never rebelled so openly against Miss Wood

before, but then she'd never had so important a reason for re-
bellion.

"It's not cruel, Lady Diana," Miss Wood said. "It's necessary. After tonight, there will be no place for us in polite
Parisian society. Therefore we shall be leaving for Italy
tomorrow, as soon as it can be arranged."

"Tomorrow!" Mary pressed her hand over her mouth.
Tomorrow was only a few hours away, leaving her almost no
time to see John.

"Yes, tomorrow," Miss Wood repeated sternly. "I'll have
Deborah come pack your things first thing in the morning,
and order the coach and horses to make ready."

"What about the guards that Lord John hired to ride with
us?" Diana asked with a great show of innocence. "He was
so thoughtful to consider our safety! We must arrange for
them, too, shouldn't we?"

Miss Wood frowned. "We'll take nothing more from his
lordship. I'll speak to the innkeeper here to see if he can
arrange a different escort. One last word, Lady Mary. Before
we leave, I intend to write to your father to advise him of this
shameful business, for I do not want him to learn of it from
common gossip or in the papers."

"I don't want that, either, Miss Wood." Mary could
imagine too well what Father's reaction would be to so scandalous an evening. He'd asked her to keep Diana from
trouble while they were abroad, not to revel in it herself. At
least she could count on Miss Wood to write a version placing
them all in the most favorable light. If she wished to keep
her position with the family as a responsible governess, she'd
make Mary's transgressions sound like the merest peccadillo.

Miss Wood gave a final nod, as if everything were settled.
"Then I wish you both good night, my ladies. Be ready to
rise early, for we'll have much to do."

The bedchamber door was barely closed behind her before Diana had grabbed Mary's arm. "Tell me all, Mary! Did you tell him you loved him, as you said you would? Oh, Mary, I want to know everything!"

Mary took a deep breath. "I told him, yes, and he told me he loved me in return."

"I knew he did!" Diana crowed. "I knew he *would!*"

"And then he asked me to marry him."

Diana squealed, so loudly that Mary clapped her hand over her mouth. "Hush, hush, or Miss Wood will return to see if you're being murdered!"

Diana pulled Mary's hand away. "Did you accept him?"

"I didn't have the chance to say anything before that awful Monsieur Turgeon interrupted us." Mary pulled the jeweler's box from her pocket, opening it so her sister could see the ring inside. "Here's the betrothal ring he brought."

Diana's eyes widened. "Oh, that's very fine, Mary. His intentions are monstrously serious, with stones like those. But why isn't it on your finger?"

"I told you, I hadn't the chance to accept him. He'd set the box on the sundial, and with all the fuss going on around us, I took it for safekeeping, so it wouldn't be lost or stolen."

"You didn't accept him, yet you took the ring anyway?" Diana cackled, and clapped her hands. "Ah, Mary, there is hope for you yet!"

"What I wish is for there to be hope for John and me together." Mary scrambled from the bed and pulled a gown from the clothespress.

"Where are you going?" Diana demanded with obvious excitement. "You're going to John, aren't you?"

"Of course I am," Mary said, shrugging free of her dressing gown. "I'm not going to sit here like an old stewing hen and wait for Miss Wood to carry me off in the morning.

His lodgings aren't far from here, in the Rue Ste. Pierre. Here, be useful, and lace my stays."

"He'll only have to unlace them later," Diana said, scurrying to help Mary dress. "Are you going to elope with him?"

"Elope?" The word hung in the air between them. "I don't know. I haven't considered that."

"Well, you should," Diana said. "If he wished to marry you earlier tonight, then he'll likely wish to marry you still a few hours later. If you go to him now, at this hour, you really shall be as good as ruined if anyone learns of it. You do know that, don't you?"

"I do," Mary said slowly. "But mainly I wish to apologize to him for running off so abruptly. Then I want to tell him I'll accept his offer, if he'll have me."

"*Have* you?" repeated Diana, incredulous. "Of course he'll have you! You're beautiful and charming and clever. You're the daughter of a peer, and you'll have at least £20,000 a year settled on you. What other reasons would he need?"

"That he loves me, and I love him, and we wish to be together," Mary said firmly as she reached for her cloak. "*That* is what matters most."

"Then you're still my same sister Mary after all." Diana sighed, and to Mary's surprise, there were tears in Diana's eyes. "John does love you. I saw that in his face from the first. No gentleman has ever looked at me the way he does at you."

"Oh, Diana." Her own eyes filling, Mary hugged her sister close. "One gentleman—the right gentleman—will look at you like that soon, I'm sure of it."

"Someday," Diana said, trying to smile through her tears. She took the ring from the bed. "Here, don't forget this."

Mary looked at the ring, the blue stone winking at her with

such promise, before she gently closed the lid, and slipped the box into her pocket. She could have worn it, but she wanted John to put it on her finger himself. Soon, he would, and her heart beat a little faster.

"You do know the exact address of his lodgings, don't you?" Diana asked, fussing with details to soften the larger moment of their parting. "And do you have French money for the hackney? The porter at the door downstairs can find you one, but you'll have to pay him yourself."

"I can do it." Mary bent to look beneath the bed. The painting was still there where she'd left it, a lumpy, flat bundle tucked into the rope springs. She thought of taking it with her, then decided to leave it. The picture would likely be safer here. Whatever happened next, she could always come back for it tomorrow. "You must look after my angel for me, until I can take him."

"You and that ugly old angel," scoffed Diana, her smile wobbling. "Who else would want him, anyway?"

"He can be your guardian for tonight." Mary wrapped her arms around Diana one last time, holding her close. Nothing would be the same after tonight; everything in her life would change. "Take care, Diana."

"You, too, Mary," whispered Diana. "Now go, and love him, and be *happy*."

Chapter Thirteen

Slowly John climbed the stairs to his rooms. Since he'd left Madame du Fontenelle's house, he'd tried hard to drink himself into oblivion. Yet no matter how much wine he'd drunk, he still found himself appallingly sober, with every detail of the evening limned forever into his memory.

Little things, like the impossible blue of the sapphire in the ring as it sat on the sundial, and how the lightest of breezes had rippled through the leaves over their heads, and how the panicking fear in Turgeon's pale face as he'd challenged him had been exactly the same as his brother's in the last seconds before John had shot him.

Yet he'd virtually no memory at all of Marie Turgeon, whose pretended widowhood had led to such sorrow and havoc.

Better for John to think of the little things that mattered, the better things: the bowed arch of Mary's lips, the feathered shadow of her lashes over her cheeks, how her breath had quickened and the raw longing had showed in her eyes when he'd reminded her of Chantilly, how she'd swayed toward him over the sundial's face, defying logic and gravity as she seemed to float toward him.

Little things, little things that should be forgotten. Yet when all the memories were set together, they combined like a bundled sheaf of tiny darts to stab and slash him to the quick.

She'd sworn she loved him, yet when he'd needed her most, she hadn't been there. She'd seen him at his worst, and she'd fled. How could he expect her to share his future forever, when he'd so much past to bring with him?

But he wouldn't trouble her again. His belongings would be packed by now, for he'd sent word to his manservant earlier in the evening. He'd leave Paris in the morning, as soon as the light broke, and head back to Calais, and Dover, and London. He'd go north, while she'd go south, with her angel picture tucked beneath her arm. It seemed particularly ironic—and fitting—that amidst the chaos in the garden, someone had filched the sapphire ring meant to signal their betrothal.

And that would be the end of his single, disastrous attempt at love.

"My lord, my lord, if you please!" The innkeeper came thumping up the stairs after him, huffing and puffing with exertion. "A word, if you please, before you enter your rooms!"

John didn't pause. "What, are they full of cockroaches and rats, your charming custom of sending me off in the morning?"

"No, my lord." The innkeeper ignored the insult, trotting along beside John. "You have a visitor waiting within, my lord."

"In my rooms?" John stopped abruptly. The last thing he wanted tonight was company. "Damnation, man, what would possess you to let anyone—"

"She begged me, my lord," the innkeeper said, his eyes

lowered. "She appears to be a lady, young and very beautiful, though in considerable agitation, and I—"

But John had already raced ahead. He was insane to hope it was Mary, to believe that she'd come here at this hour of the night, yet he couldn't open the door fast enough.

At the sound of the door, she swiftly rose. She'd been sitting in the chair before the fire, and she stood with such a singularly graceful motion that it stopped him there in the doorway.

"John," she said, her voice no more than a whisper. She was clutching the back of the chair so tightly that he suspected if she let go, she'd tumble to the floor. She was wearing a pale blue gown with a matching short jacket that he remembered from traveling, and she'd untied her wide-brimmed hat and tossed it on the bed. Her hair was mussed around her face, her eyes enormous with uncertainty. "I wondered if you'd ever come back."

"If I'd known you were waiting," he said slowly, "I would have come at once."

The innkeeper cleared his throat. "Is everything, ah, satisfactory, my lord?"

"It is," John said. "Now leave us."

The man shut the door, closing them in together. John didn't move, not wanting to frighten her, and waited for her to come to him.

But all she did was look down at the floor. "I came to apologize for leaving you as suddenly as I did."

"Is that all?" he asked, though he wasn't sure himself what more he expected. She'd come to him; that should be enough.

"If you forgive me," she said carefully, "why, then it's a beginning."

He decided to tell her the truth, for he'd no reason to dissemble, and a thousand others for being honest. "When I turned, you were gone," he said gruffly. "I thought you'd stay."

"I did, as well," she confessed. "But I was surprised by what I'd heard, and in my uncertainty, I went to Miss Wood. She wouldn't let me return to you, but made me come away with her and Diana."

"Ah." Why hadn't he thought of that? Why couldn't he think of anything else to say now?

"I'm sorry," she said. "I should have stayed. I was a coward to run away."

"Never a coward, Mary," he said. "Nor should you apologize to me. I should have told you all that myself."

"You should have told me when you were ready," she said softly, then paused. "The other woman—Madame Turgeon—were you, ah, fond of her?"

"Oh, Mary," he said, wishing for all the world he could have undone everything he'd done with Marie Turgeon and a score of others like her. "She was nothing to me, nor I to her. But I'm not without fault, Mary, nor have I always turned from temptation as I should. I'm not proud of it, either, but before I met you—"

"Hush," she said softly, resting her fingers across his lips to silence him. "You can confess it all if you wish, but it doesn't matter to me. Having a man's life and a ruined marriage on your conscience, even one taken in an affair of honor—that's a terrible enough burden to carry."

How could she have guessed that? His dear country girl— how could she have known how heavily that needless death weighed on him? After a lifetime of keeping everything to himself, the relief she was offering was still more than he could bring himself to accept, too much for him to deserve.

Had she any idea of how much he loved her?

"I should have defended you," he said gruffly instead. "I shouldn't have let Turgeon call you that, even in spite."

"What, and risked your life or his over a foolish word?" She shook her head. "No, that would have been a thousand times worse. I know I'm not what he called me, no matter how scandalized Miss Wood was that you refused to be my champion."

"I should have guessed Miss Wood believed in champions."

For the first time she smiled, albeit a half smile with little humor to it, and still directed more to the floor than to him.

"For the ladies in her charge, Miss Wood expects nothing less than Sir Galahad on a snow-white charger," she said. "After what she heard in the garden, she decided you were a rascal and a rogue. She doesn't much care for you any longer, John."

"Hah," he said, not really giving a damn if Miss Wood liked him or not. "But do you?"

Finally she looked up at him, almost startled by his question, as her smile spread slowly over her face.

"Oh, yes," she said softly, her expression full of giddy wonder, as if realizing this for the first time. "Very much."

She looked down again, fumbling with something in her pocket. At last she held out her hand to him, turning her palm up so he could see the sapphire ring.

"So you had the ring all along," he said. "I thought someone else had carried it off."

"I wouldn't have let them." She raised her chin a fraction higher as she came toward him, her hand with the ring still outstretched. "It's still yours, until you give it to me."

"Then let me do it now." He took the ring, and knelt before her. "I'll never be Miss Wood's Galahad, but I can do this."

"I don't want Galahad," she said, her voice squeaking and breaking. "I want you."

"Then have me," he said, his own voice rough with emotion as he took her hand. Her fingers were shaking, the skin moist, and it touched him no end that she'd be so nervous now, too. "Be my wife, Mary, and take all I have to offer with my love."

"Yes," she whispered. "Oh, John, yes!"

He slipped the ring on her finger, and rose, sweeping her into his arms. He wasn't sure if she kissed him first, or he kissed her, only that he'd missed her more than he'd ever thought possible. He kissed her deeply, relishing her taste and her passion. In her eagerness, she bumped against him and they nearly fell, and she laughed into his mouth, and then laughed again with pure delight. He understood; he'd never been happier. They could be husband and wife for a thousand years, and he'd swear he'd never tire of her.

"Wait, John," she said, at last untangling herself from him. Her cheeks were flushed, her hair coming down, and he loved her all the more for her disarray. "Please, please. There's one other thing I should have said before."

He bent to kiss the hollow of her throat. "Then why say it now?"

"Because—because it must be said."

He loved making her flustered like this. "All that must be said is that I love you."

"Well, that, too, but—but there is more, John." She took his face in her hands, holding it steady before her. "I will marry you, yes, a hundred times over, but I've one condition."

"A condition?" Doubt sliced through him. "What the devil do you mean, Mary?"

"I mean that I want to marry you tonight," she said, and his doubts fell away. "I don't want to wait for you to come back to Aston Hall to meet Father. I don't want to wait through a long engagement, or for a wedding to be arranged, or banns to be read and guests invited. I want to marry you tonight, John, so I don't have to wait for *anything.*"

"Tonight." He looked at her beautiful, flushed face, letting the reality of what she'd just said sink into his lust-clouded head. She wanted him so badly that she'd marry him here, in Paris, without waiting for the duke's blessing. "You are sure of this, sweetheart?"

"Of course I am sure," she said, with her usual sensible confidence. "I know it will cause another terrific scandal, but I'll be so happy that it will be worth it. *We'll* be happy."

"There will be a scandal, yes," he said softly. "What made Miss Wood squawk last night will be nothing to this. I want you to be certain I'm worth it."

She smiled, and kissed him. "You're worth any scandal, and more."

"Am I worth your father cutting you off?" he asked with great care. It could well happen; in a way, he'd be surprised if the duke didn't summarily punish her for making such a sudden match. And there'd been a time when it would have mattered to John himself, a time when he wouldn't have taken any lady without a sizeable portion to her name, nor was it so long ago that he'd been considering wooing Mary only for a chance at claiming the Feroce gold. Now, loving Mary as he did, he'd take her in her shift alone. "Am I worth being banished from Aston Hall, and from your sister's company?"

Her eyes shined with a gleam of unshed tears, but her voice was firm. "Father has always told me to do what will make me happy," she said. "*You* make me happy, John, and I cannot imagine my life now without you in it. We'll open a picture gallery in Rome. We'll become famous for it, and show the world. Ah, John, I'll go with you anywhere to become your wife, your partner, your love!"

"My own dear, brave Mary," he said, kissing her again. "I don't think we'll have to go far at all."

She grinned. "But I wished to be adventurous, John. Surely there must be some version of Gretna Green for lovers like us in Paris."

"I like the way you say we're lovers, but I don't believe we'll have to travel so far as Scotland." He kissed her again, then eased himself free to go to call for his servant in the next room. At once the man appeared, sleepy but dressed, for he'd been waiting to retire until after John had returned for the night. "Go down to the innkeeper. Tell him to wake Dr. Pennington. Tell him it's a matter of great urgency. Oh, and tell the innkeeper we'll be needing him, too."

"Who is Dr. Pennington?" Mary asked as soon as the servant had left. "And why shall we need the innkeeper at this hour?"

"He's an eminently respectable clergyman on his way from Lancastershire to Rome to study ancient Christians," he said, taking her hand. "I met him yesterday in the public room, and I think he'll do for us."

"Let me get my hat if we're going out," she said, pulling away from him back toward the hat on the bed. "I can't go bareheaded."

"We're not going out-of-doors," he said, guiding her toward the door. "We're going to be married."

"Hold, another minute." She wriggled her hand free of his, worked the sapphire ring free off her finger, and pressed it back into his palm. "This is fine enough to serve both for promise and for wedding."

He raised her now bare hand to his lips. "How useful to have such a practical wife!"

"I'll fair *astound* you with my practicality, my lord," she teased. "You'll marvel at how you ever managed without me as your paragon."

He laughed, even though he suspected what she'd said would prove wonderfully true. He wanted to be astounded by her, and he wanted to marvel. What man wouldn't want that from his wife and lover?

"Then come along, my paragon," he said, his hand on her waist, "before you change your mind again."

Ten minutes later, they were standing before Dr. Pennington. The clergyman was solemn if sleepy in his crimson dressing gown and a paisley silk nightcap, his *Book of Common Prayer* open in his hands. At his side was his wife, and across from them were the innkeeper, and John's man-servant, there to serve as witnesses.

"You are certain you wish to be wed, my lord?" Dr. Pennington said dolefully, the firelight catching the white whiskers on his unshaven jaw. "This is most irregular, you know."

"Oh, hush, Doctor," Mrs. Pennington scolded. "What's more irregular is these two young persons alone together in an inn in Paris at this hour of the night. If they wish to redeem themselves in the eyes of the church by marrying, then it is your duty to do so."

Dr. Pennington groaned. "I know my duty, my dear. It's the legality of the ceremony I question, without the proper banns or notice. With titled personages, there are often large fortunes and estates involved. If the lady's father should choose to—"

"My father would be more distraught to learn I was not wed," Mary said shyly, with a demure dip of her head. "If he were to learn that I'd come to Paris with Lord John not as his wife, but as his—"

"You have put my concerns completely to rest, my lady," Dr. Pennington said hastily. "Shall we begin, then?"

Shall we begin? Mary heard Dr. Pennington's words,

letting their significance sink slowly into her consciousness. This was a beginning, not just of the ceremony, but of her new life as John's wife. She'd no longer be simply Lady Mary, a small filial satellite to the Duke of Aston. She'd become Lady John Fitzgerald, a wife, a grown woman at last in the eyes of the world. She'd be the mother to his children, if they were so blessed, and the mistress of their household. She'd have responsibilities she'd never had before. She'd share all her husband's fortunes, the bad as well as the good.

Most of all, she'd have his love.

She smiled up at him now, his face hazy through the veil of her tears. He looked very serious, as he should, his handsome face solemn as the words that would change their lives rolled along over them.

For the second time that night, he lifted her hand and slipped the sapphire ring onto her finger. Now it was for keeps, as gamblers said at the gaming table.

For keeps, and forever.

Dr. Pennington cleared his throat with a low rumble. "It is customary to kiss your bride now, my lord."

She blinked to clear her eyes. She wanted to see everything as it should be, to remember this part forever. John's expression was still grave as the stone carvings they'd seen at the cathedral at Amiens, and she realized he was studying her with the same intensity that she must be gazing at him. Touched, she smiled, and he smiled in return, the gravity banished from his face as completely as storm clouds by the summer sun.

"Lady John," he whispered as he bent to kiss her. "I wanted to be the first to say that to you. My wife, my friend, my love."

She closed her eyes as they kissed, a pledge for their future together. When she'd dreamed of her wedding, as all girls do, she'd never pictured so hasty a ceremony, before witnesses she didn't know, in a room in an inn in Paris. But she'd never imagined she'd feel such love for her new husband, either, and as she flung her arms around his broad shoulders, she laughed through her tears, happier than she'd ever been.

"Well done, my lord, well done!" Dr. Pennington clapped John on the back with a heartiness he hadn't demonstrated during the ceremony. "I wish both of you great joy."

"Offer them a glass of cordial, Doctor," prompted Mrs. Pennington. "We must drink a cheer to their health and prosperity."

"Oh, I don't believe his lordship will have need of any such fortification for the task ahead." Dr. Pennington chuckled, patting the sides of his dressing gown, while the innkeeper guffawed loudly. "Not with such a lovely young wife to inspire him, eh?"

"Hush, Doctor, hush!" Mrs. Pennington waved her hands before her, as if to shoo such slyness away. "The poor ladybride doesn't need to hear any such foolishness from you!"

But to Mary's relief, the foolishness was mercifully brief. In lieu of proper marriage-lines, Dr. Pennington wrote a letter of testament that she and John and the witnesses signed as well. They all drank the toasts with the sweet orange cordial, and Mary dutifully presented her cheek for each of the men to kiss in turn. The wedding trip was short, too: hand in hand, running up the stairs and back to John's rooms.

She kept her arms looped around him while he fumbled with the key at the door.

"If we were common folk," she said, "you'd have to carry me over the threshold of our cottage."

"We were wed at three in the morning above a tavern," he said, finally turning the key and pushing open the door. "I don't believe we could be more common than that."

"Except that I'm with you, John, and you're with me." She kissed the side of his neck, laughing because it was the closest part of him that she could reach. "And there's nothing—*nothing*—common about that."

He answered by catching his arm beneath her knees and lifting her up, as she made a little shriek of surprise. She clung to his shoulders, laughing, as he kicked the door shut behind them. He carried her across the room and laid her on the bed, dropping down beside her with his head propped up on his bent elbow.

"You are absolutely right, Lady John," he said softly, trailing his fingertips in a lazy path from the hollow of her throat to the curve of her breasts above her shift. "There's nothing common about us at all."

"No," she said, more a breathy sigh. She lay very still beside him, feeling the teasing touch of his fingertips gliding over her skin as she watched his face. There'd be no stopping this time, no holding back. Whatever they began, they'd finish, and that thought, combined with his teasing touch, was more than enough to make her heart quicken. "You are…a most singularly rare man, John Fitzgerald."

"And you are the likewise rare, my lovely wife." Idly his hand glided lower, cupping the side of one breast, and despite the layers of gown, stays and shift, her nipple still tightened in anticipation. "We shall be happy together, you and I."

"I shall be happier still if—if you continue," she said, her body twisting restlessly.

He hooked one finger into the ribbon that zigzagged along the front opening of her bodice, idly pulling the ribbon through the eyelets. "What exactly do you wish me to continue, Lady John? As a greenhorn husband, I'll have to be trained, you know."

"'Trained,' hah," she scoffed. "You've already more skills

and talents than husbands twice your age. I told you you were rare, didn't I?"

"That's right, you did." He leaned forward to kiss her, so lightly that his lips only grazed hers. "But I'd like to hear it again, just to be certain."

She linked her arms over his shoulders, pulling him down and holding him there for a more lasting kiss.

"There," she whispered fiercely. "*That* is what will make me happy. I know what we began in Chantilly, and what I put a stop to. But you've punished me ever since, John, by making me simmer and suffer through the longest, most heartless seduction ever endured by a woman."

He laughed, a warm, deep sound that vibrated between them, and finally pulled the ribbon-lacing free, letting the two sides of her gown's bodice slip apart. "Ah, sweetheart, you don't begin to know how I can make you simmer."

"Then show me, John," she pleaded, tracing her fingers around the outside of his mouth. "Prove to me what you know, and show me."

"And you said I didn't need to be broken to your ways," he said, easing her now-open bodice down her shoulders. "Don't you know where such orders will get you, Mary?"

His smile had grown darker, and her thoughts raced back to the night in Chantilly. She helped him now, shrugging her arms free of the sleeves of her gown, and rose up onto her knees to untie the back tape on her petticoat.

"Help me, John, please," she said, wrestling blindly with the double-tied bow. "It's all tangled."

"So it is, pet," he said, moving to kneel behind her. "Be still now. I can't possibly untie it if you keep wriggling like a naughty puppy."

Dutifully she went still. "Now who's giving orders?"

"Only when necessary." Deftly he'd untied the tape at her

waist, letting her skirts drop around her knees. She lifted one leg, then the other, so he could pull the yards of muslin free, and tossed it to the floor.

"Now my stays," she said, looking over her shoulder to him. "Diana did them up for me, so they won't be hard to unlace."

"But perhaps I don't wish to unlace them, not yet." He kissed the back of her neck, his hands settling upon the narrowest part of her waist. "I like how you're so small here, and then so full below."

He slid his hands from the tightly laced stays, over the flaring tabs that had supported her skirts, to the full, unbridled curves of her hips.

"There, you see, you like that, too," he whispered just behind her ear as he noted how her breath had shortened. "It's all about the contrasts, my love, soft flesh against hard. It's why men always find women so endlessly fascinating."

He repeated the motion again, riding his palms from her waist to her hips, and each time drawing her more closely to him until at last her bottom was pressed close against him. The gauzy Holland linen of her shift provided no real barrier at all, and she could feel the rigid length of him through his breeches. It seemed very large and very hard, and the more he pulled her against him, the faster her breath came—and, she noted absently, so did his. Instinctively she spread her thighs more widely apart as she kneeled, and leaned forward to press more closely against him.

"Ah, so you've learned wriggling with a purpose now," he said raggedly. "No wonder I wished to wed you. I always knew you were a clever lass."

He slid his thumbs up the stitched channels, ridged with whalebone, along the back of her stays. He caught the narrow shoulder straps of her stays and the linen of her shift together, and with teasing leisure slid them over the tops of her arms. As if to distract her, he nipped the side of her throat, making her shiver and tip her head back against his shoulder. His hands slid lower, lifting her breasts free of the stiffened stays, free of the lace-trimmed shift. Her breasts filled his palms, the crests tightening at once as he caressed and teased the tender flesh.

"Your breasts were made for my touch, Mary," he said, his voice rough as he pulled gently on her nipples, drawing them out, making her gasp with delight. "These are perfect breasts, neither too small nor too large, exactly as I like them."

"And I—I like what you're doing, John," she said, her words splintering with pleasure. Unable to keep still, she arched her back against his chest, pushing her breasts more deeply into his hands and rubbing her bottom against him. This was like Chantilly, only a thousand times better, because she didn't have to heed her conscience, didn't have to think of consequences. All she needed to do was to feel the tension he was building in her body, the way her blood seemed to race and her skin seemed to glow, and how the heat was growing low in her belly, between her parted thighs.

"That's good," he murmured, his hands leaving her bared breasts to slide down the front of her stays. "*You're* good."

As if he could read her thoughts, his hands slid lower still to the tops of her thighs. Impatiently he shoved aside the hem of her shift, leaving the heat of his bare palms on the sensitive skin inside her legs. She gasped again as his fingers explored her, reaching higher to part her opening and dip inside her. She felt inexplicably swollen and wet, but because it was John, she wasn't ashamed. He stroked her and she cried out, twisting and pushing against him as the tension spiraled higher and higher still.

"I—I want you, John," she begged, too lost to even know exactly what she wanted. "I want you."

"I know, sweetheart," he growled, "and damnation, I want you, too."

He jerked aside the back of her shift, and now when he pulled her hips back against his, it was skin against skin, the heat of his hard, velvety flesh searing hers. She pitched forward onto her hands to give him more, but he grabbed her arm to pull her around.

"Not like that, sweetheart, not the first time," he said, flipping her onto her back. "I want to see your face when I come into you."

Feverish with longing, she watched as he tore his own clothes away. Gently he eased her knees apart, and lowered himself over her. She held her arms out to him, drawing him close as he stroked her one last time, readying her. With a moan of delight, she lifted her hips against his touch. This time, it wasn't his finger, but his manhood, infinitely larger, thicker, harder as he pushed into her. She gasped and stiffened, surprised by the difference, and braced herself for the pain that she'd always heard must follow.

"Don't hold back, Mary," John ordered, his voice taut and strained. "Don't pull away from me now. Ride it, sweetheart. It's yours for you to claim. Ride the pleasure, and take it."

He pushed in deeper and she caught her breath. The sensation was unfamiliar, yes, stretching her in this strange way, but it didn't hurt. She rocked her hips upward, taking more of him in, and he groaned.

"That's it, Mary," he said hoarsely. "Move with me."

He thrust harder, and as he pulled back, she gasped, for the sensation was the same as when he'd touched her with his fingers, only better—infinitely better.

"What I feel, John," she said, panting as she drew her knees up higher to curl her legs around his hips. "What—what you make me feel!"

It didn't take long for her to learn his rhythm. Her body was shaking, every muscle taut. She pushed her head back against the bed, her eyes squeezed shut as she clung to him.

"Look at me, Mary," he gasped. "I want to see the moment when you become my wife."

With her last scrap of reason, she forced her eyes open to see his face over hers. "John," she whispered. "Oh, John—I cannot stop!"

"Don't stop, Mary," he said, his head thrown back as he plunged and ground into her. "Don't—ever—*stop*."

She cried out one last time, a wordless exclamation of joy as her body seemed to explode. Her release left her reeling and weightless, and was so sudden and complete that she'd no words to describe it. With a guttural roar, John followed, sinking deep into her with one final thrust.

"I love you, John," she whispered afterwards as they lay together, their limbs still tangled intimately together. She'd never felt so content, nor so wanton, either, to lie here half-dressed with her naked husband. She kissed his shoulder, tasting the saltiness of his skin.

"My Mary." He curled his arm around her waist, pulling her onto his chest. "I love you, too."

She propped herself up on her arms to look at him. His smile was as satisfied as a man's could be, his eyes half-closed and his hair tousled. "My *husband*. No one could quarrel with that now."

He chuckled. "True enough, Lady John. How vastly clever of you to notice."

She smiled, more full of love and tenderness than she could explain. It wasn't just the power and joy of their love-making that had changed her forever; it was knowing that this night she could have conceived his child, the greatest blessing imaginable to their union, and their love. She was his, and he was hers, and nothing now could ever change that.

He touched her cheek. "Are you happy, love?"

"Oh, yes," she whispered. "More happy than I ever can say."

He smiled, and she basked in the surety of his love. "So am I, Mary," he said softly. "So am I."

"Oh, John, I'd no notion it was so late." Sitting across from him in the hackney, Mary gazed from the window at the clock that hung over the door to a watchmaker's shop. With the help of one of the inn's maidservants, her hair had been restored and her gown pressed, and in her lap was his first gift to her as his wife, an outsized bouquet of white roses, tied up with a blue ribbon. But anyone who saw the heavy-lidded look of her dark eyes, the flush of her cheeks, or how her lips looked swollen, almost bitten, would know at once that she'd spent a long night in bed, a night that had involved very little sleeping.

How was it possible to love anyone this much, his Mary, his wife?

"We'll be there in plenty of time, sweetheart," he said. "We're just around the corner from your inn now. And consider how much your sister must have enjoyed being able to tell Miss Wood for once that you were the wicked one."

Beneath the sweeping brim of her hat, her mouth curled into a smile, and to his delight, she winked. "Not wicked, John. Adventurous."

He laughed. "I'll take either version, my love, and count myself a most fortunate man."

But Mary wasn't listening. She was leaning from the window, her face tight with concern.

"There's some misfortune at our inn, John," she said anxiously. "Look. The steps are covered with soldiers. Oh, John, if something's happened to Diana or Miss Wood while I've been away—"

"Don't worry until you know for certain," he said firmly. "Odds are this is nothing that affects either your sister or governess."

Yet the porter had scarcely opened the hackney's door before Mary had clambered down without waiting for the step, and begun accosting the soldier posted as a guard at the door.

"What has happened within?" she asked in breathless French. "Tell me, oh, please tell me! I've family within!"

"I'm Lord John Fitzgerald," John said as he joined her, taking her hand, "and this is my wife. Her sister is a guest at this inn, and we must—"

"No one enters, *monsieur*," the guard said. "We have orders that no one is to be admitted, on account of the English ladies that have been stolen away."

"English ladies!" Mary repeated, grabbing John's arm. "Their names, *monsieur*, you must tell me their names!"

The guard shook his head. "All I can tell you, *madame,* is that they are the daughters of a great English lord, the Duke of Aston."

"But that is *my* father!" Mary cried. "I am Lady Mary—"

"Lady Mary!" Miss Wood rushed from the inn and threw her arms around Mary. With her was another soldier, an officer. "Oh, my lady, my lady, I thought I heard your voice! Praise the heavens, you're safe! Now where is Lady Diana, so that I—"

"She's not with us, Miss Wood," John said, shepherding them inside and away from the curious on the street. "Now tell us what has happened."

"It is clear enough, *monsieur,*" the officer said importantly. "The English ladies have been abducted with the hope of ransom. We expect a note at any time."

Miss Wood was shaking, her round face pale, and she clutched Mary's hand as if she feared she'd disappear again. "If you're safe, then perhaps Lady Diana is, too. Perhaps I won't have to summon your father. Perhaps her ladyship has simply gone to—to meet a gentleman. But who could that be? She scarcely spoke to anyone at the *salon* last night, on account of her poor French."

"She spoke to the Comte de Archambault," John said. "We saw her sitting with him, near the fire."

"The Comte de Archambault is a great lord in this country, *monsieur,* and a favorite of the court," the officer said, close to scolding. "The Comte would never be involved with such a crime."

Mary glanced at John, remembering what he'd told her both of the comte's past and how in France, there was a different justice for the rich and titled, and her fear for her sister grew. "Tell me when you discovered us gone, Miss Wood."

Miss Wood nodded, her eyes welling with tears of desperation. "I went with the maidservant to wake you this morning for breakfast, my lady, and oh, what we saw! You and your sister were both gone, and the room torn apart, and—"

"The angel," Mary whispered, horrified. She'd left the picture in Diana's casual safekeeping, never intending for it to bring her sister to harm. Beside this, her own scandal of eloping seemed petty indeed. "Oh, John, come with me, quick!"

They ran up the stairs to the bedchamber she'd shared with Diana, and past another soldier who'd been posted at the door. The room was a shambles, their clothes and belongings scattered everywhere, just as Miss Wood had said, and just the same as had happened in Chantilly. Mary ran straight for the bed, crouching down to look beneath the mattress.

The rope springs had been cut. The picture was gone.

She rocked back on her heels as if she'd been struck. "They've stolen my angel."

"They have your sister, and your picture," John said grimly, holding his hand out to her. "We must go at once, Mary. We're going to call upon Archambault, and we haven't a moment to lose."

Chapter Fourteen

Archambault sat in his chair beside the fire, so close that stray sparks and cinders had jumped past the andirons to leave charred pinpricks on the heavy wool coverlet that swaddled his legs. That was the way of it now: he could sit in the flames themselves and still feel no warmth, as if the iciness of the grave had already claimed his limbs.

He should never have gone to Athenais's *salon* tonight. He felt so weak he wondered if he could ever leave this chair again, so exhausted that he was beyond sleep. Only the pain in his belly was sharp, sharper than he could ever recall it before, twisting and gnawing and worrying at this guts like a starving, mongrel dog. He'd not much longer now, days, even hours. He knew that, in his soul even more than his body. His life was nearly done, and he'd no choice but to accept it.

He looked across the room to his Madonna. He could almost swear she was smiling at him, encouraging him, promising him the sweetest welcome once he slipped free of his tortured, broken body. His reason wanted to laugh with its usual scorn, and remind him such effects were only the trick of the shifting firelight coupled with the wasting weakness born of his illness.

He smiled in return, and raised a shaky hand to receive her benediction. Surely she must know what he'd ordered done for her tonight; surely she must be pleased. To once again be complete, whole again in all her majesty after so many years of mutilated disgrace—how could she not reward him with her grace?

He heard the carriage in the street, stopping before his house. The angel had come at last, and he twisted toward the door, anticipating the servant's knock before it came.

"Enter, enter, you fool!" he called, his voice crackling with impatience. "Bring the picture here to me at once!"

The servant entered and hurried forward, holding a crudely wrapped bundle before him like an offering.

"Open it, damn you!" Excitement gave Archambault strength, and he pushed himself forward in his chair. "Show it to me now!"

Quickly the man unwrapped the picture, and held it up.

"That is it," whispered Archambault, devouring the picture with his gaze. It was as perfect as he'd imagined, as rare as he'd dreamed it would be. "That is Our Lady's angel."

The servant bowed. "Shall I place it with the others, my lord?"

"Turn it around first for me to see." Archambault scowled at the picture's back. The painting of Florence that would have matched the other panel had long ago been broken away to leave only raw wood, marked with some sort of base, defiling scribble. But tucked beneath the heavy gold frame—a travesty, that—were the original brass hinges that had once linked the side panel to the central one.

"Knock off that frame," he ordered. "Destroy it if you

must, but take care not to harm the picture. Carefully, you moron, carefully!"

With surprising ease, the man prised the panel from the frame, using the wrapping-cloth to dust it clean.

"There," breathed Archambault. "Freed at last. Now put him where he belongs, in exaltation of Our Blessed Mother."

Dutifully the servant carried the panel across the room. It took him only a few moments to hook the smaller panel to the larger one.

"Fancy that, my lord," said the amazed servant as he stepped back. "All those years apart, and they go together like it was nothing."

"Of course they go together," Archambault whispered in awe. "Such are miracles in this world."

He had never seen Our Lady glow with such joy. The angel beside her once again was set to guard her with his militant courage, and worship her as she deserved.

Archambault could feel her joy and her grace, like a precious balm to ease his pain. He could feel his body lightening, rising above his suffering. Soon she'd call him to her, and he'd go, all his old sins forgotten and forgiven.

"Forgive me, my lord," the servant said, "but what shall we do with the girl?"

Unwillingly Archambault jerked from his reverie and the sweet promise of deliverance. "What girl? Damn you, you make no sense."

"This girl, my lord," the man said uneasily, pointing toward the doorway. Archambault had been so lost in the picture that he hadn't noticed the other man standing there in the shadow of the hall, a limp, bundled figure tossed over his shoulder. "She was in the room with the picture, my lord, and she threatened to make a fuss. We could've silenced her for good, my lord, but we thought you might find a use for her instead."

"A *girl*," Archambault repeated, unable to keep the cynicism from his voice. "Show her."

Not so long ago, he would have found such a gift irresistible. She must be beautiful, or else his men would simply have killed her outright. They knew his tastes. To bind this girl to the posts of the bed, to amuse himself by breaking her spirit and her body to his whims, to finally take her with or without her consent: he'd always relished the captive game. But no longer, alas, no longer.

Unceremoniously the man dropped the girl onto the floor at Archambault's feet, and tumbled her free of the dirty tarpaulin.

"For God's sake, you idiot," Archambault said with disgust. "That's not some 'girl,' as you called her. She's a high-born chit, the daughter of an English duke. Did you strike her? Is that why she's unconscious?"

"We had the sleeping drug in the carriage, my lord," said the first man. "From the old days. She'll wake soon enough, my lord."

Archambault sighed. The "old days," when he'd send his men out to find some hapless fair innocent in the streets or parks to amuse him and his friends, seemed very old indeed now. "Put her on the daybed until she does."

"We could take her back," the other man suggested. "Or leave her some place common, to be found, the way we used to."

"Not with this one," Archambault said wearily. "They'll be hunting for her."

Was it so much to ask for a few hours more of peace in this life? He watched the girl's head drop back over the servant's arm, her golden-blond hair hanging loose. She'd told him her name. Diana, wasn't it? She hadn't even been the sister who'd kept his angel from him. But with any luck, he'd be gone himself before she woke, and beyond caring for whatever scandal she'd brought with her. He turned back to the triptych.

"Go," he told the servants. "Leave us."

They hesitated. "Forgive me, my lord, but what if she wakes?"

"Then she wakes," Archambault said. "Leave me now."

He didn't know how long he sat there before the girl stirred, and groaned. There was sunlight peeking through the curtains, the dawn of a new day he hadn't expected to see.

She pushed herself up from the daybed, huddling on the edge. "Where am I?" she asked, her voice thick. "Who are you?"

"I am the Comte de Archambault," he said. "We met last night. You are at my house."

"Why?" she asked, still confused as she pulled the tarpaulin around her shoulders to cover her night rail. "How?"

"You ask too many questions," he said, "and I am too tired to answer them."

She peered at him, struggling to shake away the fog of the drug. "I recall you now. You're the old gentleman who's so ill."

"Your servant, my lady." He leaned his head back against the chair, watching her through half-closed eyes as she looked curiously around the room. She wasn't cowardly, he'd grant her that much. Soon she'd see the painting in place. He hoped she'd behave well about that, too.

"There's my sister's angel," she said slowly. "Now I remember. There were men who came in from the roof, men who—"

"Who came for the angel," he said. "You see that all along it wasn't your sister's, but mine."

She rose and went to stand before the triptych, the grubby

tarpaulin draped around her shoulders like a trailing cape. "So it was part of a larger picture. My sister thought so."

Archambault smiled, and the Madonna smiled back at him. "It's the Feroce altarpiece, my dear. I spoke of it to you earlier. It's been broken apart for nearly three hundred years, and now at last it's restored."

"That may be true," she said, "but my sister paid good money for that angel. It's still hers, and you stole it from her."

To Archambault's horror, she stepped forward and began to wrestle the angel from the center panel. Without a thought, he reached down into the cushion of his chair, pulled out the pistol he kept there, and aimed it at the girl. It took both hands clasped together to hold it steady against the arm of the chair, and the click of the flintlock made her turn.

"I'm a dying man, my dear," he said. "Killing you would be nothing on my conscience."

She looked down at the gun. "How can you be dying, yet keep a pistol at hand?"

"It's because I am dying, my dear, that I keep it. The world preys on the infirm. I trust no one, especially not you. The painting stays where it is. Where it *belongs*."

"It belongs to my sister," she protested, but she took her hands from the picture to fold them over her chest. "Just because you stole it doesn't make it yours."

"It was stolen from my family."

"So stealing it back makes it right?" she asked incredulously. "I know things are different here in France, my lord, but not so different that theft of another's property can be considered fair."

"You English and your 'fairness,'" he said scornfully. "You all treat life as if it were a schoolboy's game, with rules to determine the winner."

"It's better than what you have here in France!"

"But you forget, pet, that whether you are English or Hottentot, while you are in France, you obey French laws and customs," he said. So much talking was making him wheeze, the pain in his stomach squeezing the words from him. "And if I say I will shoot you dead if you don't sit like a good girl, then be sure that I will do it."

"What if I don't choose to sit?" she asked, though he could hear the tremor of fear behind her defiance. "What if instead I open this door, and go straight to the magistrate, and tell him that you have robbed property from my sister and kidnapped me?"

"I would kill you first," he said. "Or perhaps I'll simply wound you. This close, even my aim would be good enough to, oh, to shatter your leg. Oh, such agony that would be, wouldn't it, when the surgeon had to cut off your pretty, useless leg? The gentlemen wouldn't crowd about for a dance with you then, would they?"

She stared at him, so long he actually thought she'd dare him to do it, the childish creature. Couldn't she tell he'd done far worse than that?

"I told you, my dear, that I am dying," he said. "All I ask is that you and the picture stay here until I do."

But before she could answer, he heard the pounding on the front door. He heard his servants arguing, other voices raised, and footsteps on his stairs.

Suddenly triumphant, the girl smiled, as if there were more than his unsteady finger between her and death.

"That's my sister," she declared fiercely. "I knew she'd come. For me, and for her angel."

"This is the house of the Comte de Archambault, *monsieur!*" the servant said indignantly. "You cannot enter at will, as if it were some common-house!"

"The comte is expecting us," John said, pushing past the man. Mary swept after him, coming inside as if she'd every right. "There's no need to announce our arrival."

"But you can't go to him now, *monsieur!*" exclaimed the servant, following them as they began up the stairs. "Not at such an hour of the morning! His lordship is a sick man, *monsieur,* a dying man! Have mercy, *monsieur,* have mercy on him!"

"If he's dying as you say, then I shouldn't be wasting my time quarrelling with you," John said, turning at the first landing. "Down here, Mary. Those were the rooms we saw from the street with the curtains drawn, but candles lit behind them."

"*Monsieur,* I'll summon the guard," the servant threatened. "They will arrest you for this trespass!"

"Summon them," Mary said without stopping, "so I can tell them how your master has kidnapped my sister and stolen my painting!"

John pounded on the last door. "Open the door, my lord," he demanded. "Open at once!"

"Diana, are you in there?" Mary called, unable to keep silent. "Diana?"

But John didn't wait for an answer. He drew his pistol from inside his coat and flung the door open.

"Don't, John, please!" cried Diana, standing beside the oversized bed. "He has a gun, John!"

"Listen to her, John," Archambault echoed, his voice a frail croak. He was the same man John had pointed out to her last night, but in that handful of hours he'd deteriorated so much that in another place, Mary wouldn't have recognized him. His face was rigid and gaunt, his gaze strangely unfocused, and his body seemed to have collapsed on itself, dwarfed by the high-backed armchair. But there was no mistaking the long-barreled pistol clutched in his hands, and aimed at her sister.

"Be a good fellow, Master John," he said, "and drop your weapon. There's no need for it here."

"Oh, yes, but *you* can threaten to shoot me!" cried Diana. "You're wicked, my lord, you are!"

"Diana, don't," ordered Mary tersely. She'd no idea what had happened here already, or if her sister realized the man's wickedness, but nothing good could come from baiting him. "Be still."

Archambault smiled, a death-bound grin. "I will shoot her, you know. I've no reason not to, if you don't drop your gun."

"Do it," Mary said softly. "I won't have him put Diana at more peril."

John shook his head. "Mary, I don't think—"

"She's here because of me," Mary said. "I won't put her at any more risk."

John grumbled, but uncocked his pistol and slowly set it on the floor at his feet.

"Thank you." Archambault shifted to brace the weight of the pistol against the arm of the chair, even this small movement making him wince with pain.

"You said you'd let my sister go if John set down his gun, my lord," Mary said. "That's our half of the bargain."

"My bargain was that I wouldn't shoot her," Archambault said with a rattling cough, "and I haven't."

"That's not fair, my lord," Mary said.

"And I say it is," Archambault countered, squinting at Mary. "So you're the one who had my angel. You guarded him well. I'll thank you for that."

"He has your picture, Mary," Diana said quickly, pointing behind them. "He took it when he took me. Look. It's part of a set, just like you suspected."

Mary turned, and caught her breath. It *was* her angel, but in a way she'd never been able to imagine. As he completed the triptych, so he now seemed complete, too, part of a greater composition. The fierceness of the angel's face served as a foil for the Madonna's endearing sweetness, and his gold-bordered raiment and wings gave an innocence to her simple blue robe and cloak.

Though it lacked the impact of the other two, the third panel was as she'd guessed it would be as well: a kneeling family group with three daughters and two sons, all with the same hawkish face of the young woman's portrait that she and John had seen in the Palais du Luxembourg.

"It's the Feroces," she said softly. "The angel was part of their altarpiece."

"My ancestors," Archambault said, his pride turned to a wheezing rasp. "The oldest daughter, there in the front. She's like you, yes? That is Isabella, the only one wily enough to escape the French by coming to France. She married an Archambault; she's even buried among us. A clever little bitch, eh, and fit for my kin."

His laugh collapsed into the rattling cough, yet still he gripped the pistol. "Isabella got the Madonna, and after so many years, so did I. But I was the only one to seek the other pictures, and restore the Blessed Virgin to the glory that is due to the Queen of Heaven."

"And how many died for your unholy quest?" John demanded. "How much blood was shed for the sake of these pictures?"

"And did the Feroces care?" Archambault said. "Do I?"

"Perhaps a man so close to death should consider such things," John said, and Mary agreed. As magical as the angel was for her, it still wasn't worth the price that so many had been asked to pay for it. What would humble Fra Pacifico—

surely a man of peace, with such a name—make of such a grim legacy tied to one of his greatest works?

But Archambault wasn't listening, his gaze shifting from Mary to the painting.

"I've done whatever she asked of me," he said with a fervent croak. "I found her pictures. What more could she demand?"

He was so intent on the painting that he seemed to have forgotten they were there, the heavy pistol beginning to droop in his trembling hands. Slowly John began to bend, determined to retrieve his gun, while Mary held her breath.

"My beautiful Blessed Queen," Archambault said, his voice dropping to a ragged whisper of yearning. Rivulets of sweat trickled down his face, catching in the harsh lines that pain had carved into his cheeks.

"I—I made you whole again," he panted, "with my life's fading breath. I—I would not rest, nor—nor die, until I had. All I—I ask from you in return is forgiveness, and—and release from my pain."

John shoved Diana to one side and grabbed the pistol from the floor at his feet, aiming it at once at Archambault's chest.

"The women will go free now," John said, "and my wife's taking the angel picture with her."

"Not the angel!" Archambault cried frantically, his pistol slipping from his feeble grasp. "The Blessed Lady will never forgive me if you do!"

"Take it, Mary," John said, his gaze never leaving Archambault. "It's your property."

Slowly Mary went to the picture. It was only a painting, beaten egg and pigment brushed on a wooden board. It had no power of its own, no matter what Archambault believed.

So, why, then did the angel appear no longer to look out at her with his old fierce kindness, but only at the Madonna in the center panel? Why could Mary no longer conceive of separating one panel from the other two, for no better reason than property and ownership?

"You can't take it," Archambault whispered, tears now streaming from his eyes. "I won't let you do this to the Blessed Lady, or to me."

And with a last effort, he gathered the fallen pistol back into his unsteady hands and turned it on himself. The gunshot rang through the bedchamber, filling the close room with acrid smoke like brimstone itself.

"Don't look!" called John, but his order came too late for Mary not to see the shattered, bloody remains of what had been the head of the sixth Comte de Archambault. Mary clung to Diana, and John wrapped an arm around each sister. None of them could look away. The *comte*'s chair had been knocked back against the mantel by the force of the gunshot and the lifeless body tumbled with its coverlet to one side like a discarded puppet, while bits of blood and brain dripped and hissed into the fire.

Across the room, in the center of the triptych, the Madonna's smile hadn't changed.

And whether Archambault had found the redemption he'd so desperately wanted would forever be anyone's guess.

Later, much later, that day, Miss Wood dumped the half spoon of sugar into her cup of tea, and stirred it briskly before she poured half the contents into the dish to cool. She sighed softly, and finally looked back to Mary and John.

"I cannot conceive of such a ridiculous notion being true," she said. "How could you be married?"

"It is, Miss Wood." Proudly John took Mary's hand in his,

and set them clasped together on his knee. The new ring caught the afternoon sunlight through the window, the sapphire as much as shouting their announcement. "We were wed last evening."

"But where?" Miss Wood asked sternly. "And by whom? Paris is such a Romish place, I doubt very much you could find a good Anglican minister. And what of the banns? The witnesses? A proper wedding feast? I cannot believe it, my lord, my lady. I *will* not believe it."

"You must, Miss Wood, because it's true." Mary leaned forward, resting her hand on her governess's arm. "You know I'd never lie, especially not about this. I love John, and he loves me, and when he asked me to marry him, I accepted."

Miss Wood's mouth puckered as if she'd put lemon instead of sugar into her tea. "But why was he in such haste?"

"*I* was the one who did not wish to wait, Miss Wood," Mary confessed. "Considering the heat of our passion, I judged it wise not to."

"Your passion, my lady?" Slowly the real meaning of what Mary was saying dawned on Miss Wood, and just as slowly the flush crept up her cheeks. "Then he has—that is to say, you have consummated your marriage?"

Mary nodded, and blushed, too. How glad she was that Miss Wood couldn't read her thoughts just then as she remembered how she and John had passed their shortened wedding night.

"Then you truly *are* wed." Miss Wood pressed her palms to her cheeks and closed her eyes, striving for composure. "Oh, my. What am I to write to His Grace your father?"

"You will write that Lady Mary fell in love with a most excellent gentleman," John suggested, "and that since this gentleman loved Lady Mary more than life itself, you could find no reason to deny the match."

"But His Grace your father wanted you to be a model of restraint and decorum for Lady Diana," Miss Wood said unhappily. "Not—not like this."

"Why not like this?" Mary asked, glancing once again at John. After the horrifying way the day had begun, with Diana's disappearance and Archambault's death, Mary couldn't look to John enough for comfort, and reassurance, and most of all love. "I found a handsome, suitable gentleman whom I could love all my days, and then I wed him with as little fuss as is possible. If Diana can be even half so fortunate in finding a husband as I was with John, then Father will be mightily pleased."

Miss Wood bowed her head over the saucer of tea. "If Diana brings half so much mischief to find a husband as you have, my lady, then my journey to Italy will be a difficult one indeed!"

"Not difficult, Miss Wood," Mary said, and smiled up at her new husband. "Only...adventurous."

Afterword

❦

"You cannot look until I say so," John said, his hands over Mary's eyes as he led her into the room of their lodgings. Though they had stayed in Paris another fortnight after their wedding, and after Miss Wood and Diana had continued on to Italy, this was their last day before they, too, began their wedding-trip south. "I want you to be surprised."

"Of course I'll be surprised," she said, laughing at her own unsteadiness. "How could I be otherwise?"

He felt a flicker of uneasiness. She'd be surprised, yes, but he hoped it would be a pleasant surprise. He was taking a definite risk with such a gift.

"You're almost there." He stopped her, and lifted his hands. "Now open your eyes."

She did, and gasped with shock and, he hoped, delight. Before her, propped on the sideboard, stood the Feroce altarpiece, a gift no one else would know to give.

"I bought the other two panels from Archambault's estate," he explained quickly. "His heirs had no attachment to the pictures, and, like your sister, deemed them unspeakably ugly. They were happy to be rid of them for a price."

She took a step closer to the triptych. "I never thought to see this again."

That was hardly the joyful answer he'd hoped for. "If it brings back unfortunate memories," he said quickly, "or if you believe it's unlucky, then we'll remove your angel, and put the other two panels on the market. But I thought you might—"

"That I might love it." She turned and hugged him, holding him tight. "Oh, John, only you would understand what this means to me! To have them back together again, the way they were meant to be—the only way they *could* be! Only you, my dear, darling husband, would buy me pictures that the rest of the world dismisses as ugly, and know you'd instead given me the most beautiful paintings I've ever seen!"

He let out a sigh of relief. "Then I've pleased you."

"You always do." She kissed him quickly, and turned back to the triptych. "I'm glad the angel's back with the other two paintings. This is where he belongs, John, and no matter that I'd bought him in Calais, it would have been shameful to keep him apart from the others."

Carefully she turned the triptych, looking at the backs of the panels. "The other two still have second panels on the reverse, with the scenes of Florence just like the one we saw in Chantilly. Who knows what became of the one that backed my angel?"

John joined her. "Recall how we'd thought those marks on the back might hold some great mystery? Now I'd wager all they are were some notes from the sawyer who cut the panels."

"Perhaps." She bent closer. "This is odd. Here among the trees, someone added a little message. It's Latin, isn't it, not Italian? I'm afraid Miss Wood neglected both Latin and Greek at Father's request."

"Every Irish schoolboy learns his Latin." He looked to where she was pointing, translating as he read aloud. "'For the wicked there is no'—that's the first panel here—'gold in the kingdom'—that's the second."

"But what of the marks on the back of the angel, John?" she asked excitedly. "Could that be part of the sentence? We tried to make sense of them in Italian or French, but not Latin."

"*Celiae.* Of Heaven." The hastily written marks suddenly became abbreviated letters, and the letters words. "What dunces we've been, Mary, to miss something so obvious! 'For the wicked there is no gold in the kingdom of Heaven.' Considering how deuced wicked the Feroces were, I'd wonder who dared to add that to the back of the painting they'd commissioned."

"Perhaps Fra Pacifico didn't care for his patrons," she suggested, "though I doubt they would have cared to see such a message on the back of their altarpiece."

John snorted. Archambault had been proud of his Feroce blood; if his ancestors had been anything like him, then the world was far better without them. "Likely it would have meant his death, insulting that crew."

"Oh, I know what it means, John!" Mary's eyes widened, sure she'd solved the riddle. "I'd wager it was added by someone who never could find the Feroce gold!"

"And I'd wager you're right, clever wife." He nodded, for it seemed obvious now, a sour comment born of disappointment or frustration. "I told you that gold was gone forever, if it ever existed at all."

"Not even the Feroces could take it with them beyond the grave, though I doubt they went to heaven." She turned the triptych around again, and studied the group of kneeling donors. "Even on their best behavior for the painter, they look like a right band of cutthroats, don't they? How could Archambault say I resembled her?"

John laughed. "They say she was clever, like you," he said, "and you both found husbands in Paris."

"Oh, hush," she said, giving him an affectionate shove. "But I'll tell you what I wish to do today, John. Archambault said Isabella was buried with the rest of his family. Let's find her grave, and pay our respects."

John winced. "Our last day in Paris?"

"Yes," Mary said firmly. "Before we can begin our future together, we should make peace with the past. Making sure these paintings stay together is the first step. We've found Isabella's painting. Now it seems only right to find her."

It took only a few questions to find where the Archambaults were buried. With the last *comte*'s death so recent and his lavish funeral so widely reported in the papers, every person in their inn from the keeper to the scullery maids seemed eager to tell what they'd heard about the wicked habits of the entire Archambault family. That the new *comte,* a cousin from Provence, was reputed to be dull and pious was a serious disappointment to all the Parisian gossips, high and low.

"I suppose I expected something more grand," Mary said as they stood before the ancient church of St. Jacques. Anywhere else its medieval tower would have been a landmark, but in a city full of medieval landmarks, it seemed simply to be another small, old church in a once-fashionable neighborhood in decline. "Considering it's the last resting-place of the Archambaults."

"Considering that," John said, "I'm surprised there aren't devils and demons dancing in the buttresses."

Mary sighed. "You must stop that right now, John. It's disrespectful."

"True," he said as she took his arm. "And besides, I wouldn't want those particular ghosts coming to haunt me."

The church was so small that they soon found the aisle with the Archambault tombs, some sunk into the floor with only brass plaques to mark them, and others more grand, glorified with marble statues and stained glass windows above them. The last *comte*'s was simple and new, his early death coming before there'd been time to commission commemorative art, but it was clear that more suitable statues were expected.

Mary walked by it as quickly as she could. She knew it was disrespectful to think ill of the dead, but she would never forget the circumstances of this particular man's death, nor how close he'd come to claiming her sister as well.

"Are you sure we haven't missed Isabella?" John asked as they neared the end of the aisle. "She might be no more than one of these little markers, or tucked away behind her husband."

"I found her," Mary called softly. "I knew *she'd* never let herself be hidden away."

The tomb was set in a small curved recess, pointedly away from her husband and children. Isabella had had herself carved in marble, lying on her back with her hands folded in prayer over her breasts. Every detail of her elaborate court dress was recorded in stone, every jewel around her throat and curl of her hair. She had lived to seventy-five, yet the imperious stone profile was the same as that of the young woman's portrait in the Palais du Luxembourg; clearly Isabella's desire for truthfulness did not extend to wrinkles.

"Isabella Marie de Archambault, wife of Gerald," read John from the inscription as he joined Mary. "No mention of her being a Feroce, but then she'd lived most of her life in France."

"I suppose her coffin's inside," Mary said, her voice hushed. The statue lay on top of an equally elaborate stone sarcophagus, carved with scenes of Isabella's life: hunting, dancing, sitting with her ladies, listening to musicians. Yet there were none of her family, none of her holding any of her many children, not even any with a pet dog or kitten, nothing at all to show she'd ever let herself love, or be loved. "I should much rather be out-of-doors, in a churchyard beneath the open sky, not alone in here."

"That's you, sweetheart," John said, "not her. I don't think she cared about much beyond being rich and powerful."

"I'd guess that's why she married the man she did," Mary said, rubbing her arms against the church's chill. "All she wanted was to regain the power and wealth that she'd had as a girl, and not for love. There's nothing loving about any of this. How can any woman live without love?"

"I told you, Mary," said John gently, "she wasn't you."

Mary shook her head, linking her hand into his. "I've found such happiness with you, that I cannot imagine my life otherwise."

"Which is most fortunate for me," John said as they walked around the memorial. Suddenly he whistled low. "Mary, look at this. Isn't that the center panel of the triptych?"

Etched into the end of the sarcophagus beneath the statue's head was the same Madonna that Fra Pacifico had painted. Clearly Isabella must have given the original to the stone carver to follow.

"The painting must have meant so much to her that she wanted it with her always," Mary whispered with awe. A cobweb of neglect stretched from the stone Isabella's nose to her hands, and carefully Mary brushed it away with her handkerchief. "If it was, then it was the only thing she seemed to have cared for in her life. Perhaps at the end she worried about her sins just as Archambault did."

"Then explain this, sweetheart," John said, bending lower, beneath the statue's head. Beneath the tasseled stone pillow was a stone strong-box, complete with straps and locks. Carved into one of the locks was a Latin inscription so small that most people would overlook it.

But not Mary, and not John.

"'For the wicked there is no gold in the kingdom of Heaven,'" translated Mary in a shocked whisper. "Oh, John, are you thinking what I think?"

"That she had the Feroce gold buried with her," he said slowly. "That it's in there now, in her coffin."

"Perhaps she thought the gold would give her the peace that heaven wouldn't." Mary took one final look at the woman whose heart had been as cold as the stone that surrounded her now, and squeezed John's fingers. "I've seen enough, John. Let's leave."

By the time they once again stood on the church's worn, sunny steps, Mary was close to tears.

"Oh, sweetheart," John said, taking her into his arms as soon as he noticed. "We shouldn't have come, if it's upset you that much."

"No, no, it's good that we came," she said, gazing up at him as the tears slipped down her cheeks. "Because more than ever, I understand how much I love you, and how that's more important than anything else."

He smiled crookedly. "More important than the paintings? More important than the treasure in gold that's likely moldering away in there?"

She smiled through her tears at him. "More," she said. "Infinitely, impossibly more."

His smile widened. "More than adventure?"

"No," she said, and grinned. "Because loving you *is* my adventure."

He laughed, and kissed her. "Then come with me, my Mary," he said. "The adventure's only begun."

Celebrate 100 years of pure reading pleasure with Mills & Boon®

To mark our centenary, each month we're publishing a special 100th Birthday Edition. These celebratory editions are packed with extra features and include a FREE bonus story.

Plus, starting in February you'll have the chance to enter a fabulous monthly prize draw. See 100th Birthday Edition books for details.

Now that's worth celebrating!

15th February 2008

Raintree: Inferno by Linda Howard
Includes FREE bonus story Loving Evangeline
A double dose of Linda Howard's heady mix of passion and adventure

4th April 2008

The Guardian's Forbidden Mistress by Miranda Lee
Includes FREE bonus story The Magnate's Mistress
Two glamorous and sensual reads from favourite author Miranda Lee!

2nd May 2008

The Last Rake in London by Nicola Cornick
Includes FREE bonus story The Notorious Lord
Lose yourself in two tales of high society and rakish seduction!

Look for Mills & Boon 100th Birthday Editions at your favourite bookseller or visit
www.millsandboon.co.uk

0108/CENTENARY_2-IN-1

2 FREE

BOOKS AND A SURPRISE GIFT!

We would like to take this opportunity to thank you for reading this Mills & Boon® book by offering you the chance to take TWO more specially selected titles from the Historical series absolutely FREE! We're also making this offer to introduce you to the benefits of the Mills & Boon® Reader Service™—

- ★ FREE home delivery
- ★ FREE gifts and competitions
- ★ FREE monthly Newsletter
- ★ Exclusive Reader Service offers
- ★ Books available before they're in the shops

Accepting these FREE books and gift places you under no obligation to buy, you may cancel at any time, even after receiving your free shipment. Simply complete your details below and return the entire page to the address below. You don't even need a stamp!

YES! Please send me 2 free Historical books and a surprise gift. I understand that unless you hear from me, I will receive 4 superb new titles every month for just £3.69 each, postage and packing free. I am under no obligation to purchase any books and may cancel my subscription at any time. The free books and gift will be mine to keep in any case.

H8ZED

Ms/Mrs/Miss/Mr ....Initials ....

BLOCK CAPITALS PLEASE

Surname ....

Address ....

....

....Postcode.............................

Send this whole page to:
UK: FREEPOST CN81, Croydon, CR9 3WZ